THE BARKEEP AND THE BRO

A SINGLE DADS CLUB NOVEL

A.J. TRUMAN

Cover illustration by Sierra Summit Designs

Cover title design by Robin at Wicked by Design

Chapter Character Busts by Michael T Art

Editing by Devon Vesper

❀ Created with Vellum

1

MITCH

Number one rule of owning a bar: the buck always stopped with me.

Except, the buck never actually stopped. It kept going and going.

There was always a fire to be put out, a conflict to resolve. Yesterday, I was without a bartender. He won big betting on a playoff game that ended with a shocking underdog victory and immediately quit. So, in addition to my regular manager duties, I was stuck serving drinks for ten hours. After a lifetime of running Stone's Throw Tavern, I was used to the constant stream of chaos. Some people were married to the loves of their lives. I was married to a bar. I'd been married before, but once was enough for me.

Fortunately, today was Sunday. The bar didn't open until noon, giving me the morning to rest and recuperate. I looked over at the perfectly undisturbed right side of the bed, the sheets and blanket tucked into their hospital corners. Twenty-three years of sleeping alone, and I still hadn't worked up the nerve to sleep in the middle of the bed.

The house I owned was a stone's throw away from my bar, hence the name. It was a small cottage that sat on a dirt road tucked into the woods. It had been a fixer-upper, and back when I had more energy, I was able to rewire all the rooms with ceiling fans, update the kitchen, and build a sun porch. I could hear the gurgling of the Hudson River in the distance.

I enjoyed the silence with coffee and a newspaper, one of the few people left who didn't subscribe to the e-version of *The Sourwood Gazette*. I liked feeling the newspaper in my hands and the accomplishment of reading it cover to cover.

I made a list of what needed to be done. First and foremost, find a damn bartender. Again. Mr. Gambler had only been with me two months.

Afterwards, I went outside to chop wood for the fireplace. Today was a warm day for January—thirty degrees. But the temperature was expected to plummet this week, so I made hay while the sun shined.

While I was chopping wood, Cal and Leo stopped over with a box from Maple Street Donuts. We'd all known each other growing up. Leo and I were friends with Cal's older brother. And by a quirk of fate, we'd all wound up gay single dads–in fact, we called ourselves the Single Dads Club. I didn't have family in the area anymore, so we leaned on each other throughout the years. Watching each other's kids, helping through the latest parenting struggle. Leo had preteen twins, Ari and Lucy. Cal had a quiet ten-year-old boy, Josh, and through his new relationship with Russ, he'd gained another ten-year-old son in Quentin. I had the oldest kid in the group—the benefits of knocking up your high school sweetheart—and so I prepared them over the years for what was to come. From the awkwardness of puberty to the hell of teenagerdom.

"Hey, Lumberjack." Cal walked over and placed the box of donuts on my patio table. "Seriously, were you *trying* to dress like Paul Bunyan this morning?"

I looked down at my red and black checkered flannel shirt. That was not intentional. But with my grizzly beard and broad chest, I definitely looked the part.

Leo grabbed a donut and plopped into one of the patio chairs. Even on a lazy Sunday, he still managed to look sharp with his peacoat and dark slacks. As the mayor of Sourwood, he was always on and probably had some official business to attend to later.

"You know you can buy pre-chopped firewood at the store," Leo said, his tone having a perpetual ring of sarcasm. "They even sell them in neat, tied-together bundles."

"That's for fancy people like you." I placed another log on the chopping block.

"One of the perks of living in a modern society. The only people who chop their own wood are Instagram influencers thirsty for likes."

I didn't know what half of those words meant. A perk of owning a local bar: no need to futz with social media. Down went my ax, two wood halves tumbling off the block.

"Now I'm jealous I don't have a fireplace," Cal said.

"I thought Russ had one." Leo bit off a chunk of his cinnamon donut.

"It's gas. You can turn it on with a remote."

"The joys of suburban living," I said with a smile. Cal's boyfriend Russ lived in one of the fancy new subdivisions in Sourwood, a big step up from Cal's current house on the older side of town. "You excited about the move?"

"I'm too busy packing up and trying to sell my house. My real estate agent says we need to bring in new furniture and stage the house." Cal rolled his eyes. "I feel like my house is entering a beauty pageant."

"Townhomes and Tiaras," Leo joked.

"And you're going to clean it before it goes on the market?" I loved Cal, but the man was a bit of a slob, a habit Russ was admirably trying to break. Fortunately, Josh was more into cleanliness than his dad, but that was an uphill battle I wanted no part of.

"We're tidying up." Cal swirled his finger around the donut box to find the ideal selection and pulled out a Boston cream. "Do you want one, Mitch?"

"Save me an old fashioned." I hurled my ax down and split another log in half, two clean pieces of wood falling to the ground. "Do you need help packing up and preparing the house?"

"You'd help with that?" Cal's eyes opened wide. He was a big kid at heart.

"Of course. Leo and I would be happy to help."

Leo shot me a glare for roping him into this plan, but he didn't object. We had each other's backs. Speaking of backs, I gave mine a strong rub to ease out the tension.

"You okay there, old man?" Leo asked.

"Yep. Fine." I did a quick torso twist and positioned another piece of wood before Leo could dig in. He was a former lawyer. He loved to dig.

"We're planning to put the house on the market this spring during the busy season." Cal paced in a circle, making deep footprints in the snow. "I can't believe I'm moving in with Russ."

"You scared?" I asked.

"I'm scared he's going to follow me around with a dustbuster all the time. But aside from that, I'm excited. I love him.

I love Quentin. The boys get along great. Things are clicking along as they should." Cal grinned ear-to-ear, and the positive vibes radiated off him like he was a helium balloon.

Usually, Leo and I would trade a shared look of mild, good-natured sarcasm. But not this time. Leo radiated similar helium vibes that pushed through his sarcastic smile. It was two against one.

I turned to my former ally. "And how are things with Dusty? Cohabitation also clicking along?"

"It's the best. Morning shower sex for the win."

I snorted. Leo had been staunchly against relationships, but then his straight best friend turned out to be not-so-straight. And now he was apparently having a side of morning shower sex with his coffee.

I raised my ax. My arms paused in the air. My friends stared at me.

"And what about you, Mitch?" I asked in a funny voice. *"You're the only one without a boyfriend."*

"Well..." Cal started. He looked to Leo for backup.

"I'm happy for you both. Really, truly. Seeing you fall in love this year has warmed the cockles of my crusty, middle-aged heart. But it's not for me. I don't have the time to find a boyfriend. First, I need to find a bartender." I threw the ax down a little too hard, and the wood shot off the block. Cal jumped back. "I'm in a long-term relationship with Stone's Throw Tavern."

"But you can't have morning shower sex with a bar," Leo said.

"I barely have the energy to sprout wood in the morning." I rested the ax on the chopping block. "If I were to date someone, they'd always be competing with the bar for my attention."

My attention span for guys didn't go beyond the very occasional one-night stand hookups, which was fine for me.

"Life didn't go the way I expected. For better and worse. I'm grateful every day that I have Ellie for a daughter. But we make the best choices we can in the moment. I'm happy with my bar and my life."

"Point taken," Leo said without enthusiasm. They didn't get it, but falling in love wasn't for everyone. He brushed a splinter of wood off his jacket. "I'll be honest, Mitch. I don't envy you." He picked up the scattered piece of chopped wood and tossed it on the pile. "Running Stone's Throw doesn't seem like it gets easier."

A wave of exhaustion hit me. Not only physical but something deeper. "It's been twenty-five years that I've been running Stone's Throw. I did the math. A quarter century. That wasn't the plan. I didn't want to follow in my dad's footsteps and take over his place. I was going to play hockey for the New York Rangers."

"In your dreams," Leo shot out. But I did have a shot. I was a star player on the high school hockey team and had scouts interested in me.

Cal let out a sigh. "But then Hannah got pregnant."

"That she did. I should've sued the condom company for a product malfunction. I could've made millions."

I chuckled at God's dark sense of humor. The closeted high schooler out to prove his heterosexuality accidentally knocks up his girlfriend. The Lord must've had a good laugh at that. I was eighteen and had no discernible job skills outside of working at my parents' bar, so I kept on doing that to make money to support our fledgling family. Busboy turned to waiting tables turned to shift supervisor turned to assistant manager, then manager. Then once my parents passed, the place was mine.

"I'm glad Ellie didn't want to work with me. She can have a much better life as a lawyer."

"You haven't met many lawyers," said Leo.

"It's better than running a local tavern. She'll work just as hard but make a lot more money."

No more having to be jealous of the popular girls in school with their designer clothes and new cars. No more spending weeks filling out scholarship applications. I did my best to provide for Ellie, but we went through tough times when business was slow.

Now she was engaged to a wonderful guy. Tim was an attorney like her. They met in law school. He adored her, and I couldn't ask for anything more. He was a big step up from her college boyfriend, a loud, cocky fratboy who treated college as a four-year-long party. He was very attractive, but I wouldn't want him as my son-in-law.

"Do you ever think about selling the place?" Cal grabbed a Long John donut.

"I can't. What would I do with my life?" I bit off a piece of donut and tucked the rest into my front pocket. Maybe not the classiest move, but I was amongst friends. "Besides, Stone's Throw is an institution in Sourwood. It's a part of this town."

I took a break from chopping wood and joined my friends at the patio table. It was a cold morning but warm enough that we could eat and drink coffee without freezing our nuts off. I took the spotlight off me and asked how their kids were doing. Leo got me up to speed on the film his daughter was shooting, and then Cal regaled me with the camping trip he and Russ were planning for their wilderness troop. Time flew when we beat our gums.

I carried the wood to the pile behind the house, saving three logs for the fireplace.

We made our way inside. Leo brewed another pot of coffee and poured us each a mug. He was the most addicted to caffeine in the group.

I relaxed in my recliner while the guys took the small, old couch. This was a house designed for one.

My body sunk into the cushy leather. I would have fallen back asleep were they not there.

"Did Ellie and Tim set a date yet?" Cal asked.

"Not yet." Ellie and her fiance were deep into researching ideas and themes for their wedding. It was a step up from my wedding to her mother, which consisted of me shitting bricks and sweating bullets while my parents judged from the back row of the courtroom.

"They really seem in love," Leo said.

"Everyone around me is in love," I said, closing my eyes.

Leo and Cal left a few minutes later. They had families and boyfriends to tend to. I got to enjoy the rest of my lazy Sunday morning. There were perks to being a loner.

2

CHARLIE

"Charlie fucking Porterfield. You are the man."

I gave myself a grin in the mirror.

"You're jacked." I flexed my pecs, still flecked with water from the shower. "You've got a full head of hair." I swished my thick brown hair, wet strands falling in my face. Thanks to the genetic gods, I'd be keeping this hair until I'm eighty.

"According to multiple sources, you're definitely packing heat." I opened my towel, letting my eyes drift down my six-pack to my most prized appendage. Despite being on the shorter side for guys at five-six, mother nature made up for it with a good-sized dick. My former conquests were all pleasantly surprised at its stature. Trimming my bush had a side view mirror effect of making objects appear bigger, too.

"And most importantly, you've got a hot-as-fuck girl-friend and a primo job."

I nodded back at myself, chin up. Whatever tiny doubts and objections swirled in my head at the moment, they were drowned out by the affirmative sound of my voice.

The voice of truth.

I was Charlie Fucking Porterfield. (Actual middle name: Brent.)

And I was the man.

Life was going great, despite what a different voice in my head liked to whisper at inopportune times. I'd read about the importance of saying positive things to yourself every morning, putting these thoughts out into the universe so they became real.

And it worked.

"Charlie, are you almost done in there?" my girlfriend Serena called from the bedroom.

I gave myself one more *you got this* nod and opened my towel to check out my dick again. *We ready to slay today?*

"All yours."

Serena waited on the bed, checking her phone, looking hot as ever. Two years in, and I was still struck by how gorgeous she was. A sexy, ambitious gazelle. Her soft features belied a ferocious animal instinct.

I climbed on top of her.

"Charlie."

"What? The bathroom's all yours," I said while kissing her neck. "Nothing's stopping you."

Like a master football player dodging a tackle, she swerved from my grip and was on her feet in two seconds, phone still in her hand. "No morning sex on weekdays. It takes me twice as long to get ready as you. All the makeup and shaving shit I have to do, whereas guys can just shower, slap on deodorant, and call it a day."

"You don't need any makeup or shaving. You're beautiful just the way you were."

She rolled her eyes while laughing, brushing her soft hair over her shoulders. If she didn't have such an affinity for numbers, Serena could totally be a model. She had the beauty and the untouchability.

"Maybe I should get ready first in the mornings. And you can talk to yourself in the bedroom."

Shit. She could hear me?

"Done. Ladies first."

She leaned down and hovered her lips over mine. "You don't need to give yourself a pep talk. You're already the man, Charlie Porterfield."

———

SERENA and I met as trainees at our investment firm. All the guys in our cohort were attracted to her, but I won out. What I lacked in height, I made up for in charm.

Her competitiveness and ambition fueled me to step up my game at work. I had to constantly prove myself to keep a girl like this. I had fallen into working in finance thanks to a fraternity connection. The job was a lot of numbers and pouring over a computer, not two of my strong suits. But it was a social office, and I made great money, so I was happy. Or at least happy-adjacent.

You have a primo job.

We scrolled on our phones during the subway ride to Wall Street. Serena read stock news while I checked in on sports.

"Demeter is up eight points in pre-market trading." She nudged my elbow and flashed me a smile. "Good job, Porterfield."

Demeter was an agricultural tech startup focused on scalable crop growing. The founder was a few years ahead of me in college, but we met at an alumni event and realized we were both from the same frat. He told me about this new technology he was working on, and I got my firm to invest. Since then, the stock has skyrocketed, and once it goes public, we'll be positively drowning in money.

I opened Instagram and scrolled through before we hit the patch of subway where we lost service. My old college girlfriend, Ellie Dekker, had gotten engaged. We weren't a great fit—I was heavily into my frat, and she was on the bookish side, but she was a really genuine person. I smiled as I looked through her engagement pictures; she and her fiance seemed more on the same wavelength. I loved seeing good things happen to good people.

I laughed to myself when I remembered her dad Mitch. The dude was kinda scary. He was tall, broad-chested, and very bearded. Half lumberjack, half bouncer. I always did my best to engage him in conversation when he visited Ellie at school, really striving for those boyfriend points. I was a social guy, and I could get ninety-nine percent of people to open up. But Mitch was a brick wall. He took one look at my backward hat and flip-flops, and that was that.

Well, hopefully, this fiance fared better with him.

When we pulled into the station, the internet was restored, and all hell broke loose.

Our phones buzzed with a news notification that made my stomach plummet into my shoes. I raced out of the subway and sprinted up the escalator. When I hit the cold January air, on a huge outdoor TV screen were images of the wunderkind Demeter founder with the headline *Report: Demeter technology called into question. Potential evidence of faked test results.*

Oh, holy hell of flaming shitballs.

You got a primo job! You're packing heat! You're not going bald!

People buzzed around me, a dizzy blend of suits and

briefcases scurrying to their offices. I stood in the middle of the traffic, heart officially stopped.

"Charlie, this is bad." Serena's face was glued to her phone. She read from one of the now several articles online. "Internal documents show that the agricultural technology that Demeter stands on, which claims it can cultivate any crop to grow in any environment, is a fiction spun up by enigmatic wunderkind founder Will Watson. The USDA and FDA are now reviewing." Her gorgeous face went white. "Charlie."

"I didn't know! Shit."

"We've invested millions of our clients' dollars in Demeter. Shares are going to plummet."

Maybe this was a big misunderstanding. How could a company completely fake its entire business?

Because finance bros like me fell under the spell of Will Watson. He seemed so cool, his own brand of untouchability, like Steve Jobs without the turtleneck.

"Did anything seem off about them?" Serena began walking to the office. I hurried to catch up. "I knew it seemed too good to be true."

If you knew that, then why didn't you say anything?

"There's no hard evidence yet. It's speculation. Right?"

She spun around. "What kind of vetting did you do with Watson beyond rehashing fratboy memories?"

"I looked over the prospectus and data and test results he showed me." I wasn't completely incompetent. It never occurred to me it was all fiction, that somebody would pull a fake on this level.

She was practically running to get to our office, not waiting for me. I grabbed her arm, out of breath.

"Serena. It's going to be okay."

"How? I invested my clients' money in this, too. Being

one of the few women in our office, I've had to work twice as hard. I don't have the same room for error." Her glare could strip the paint off a car.

"Maybe Will Watson is yanking everyone's chain," I said jokingly.

Her ball-crushing glare reminded me this was not the time for jokes.

"Let's grab a drink. It's early but needed. Bloody Marys for breakfast?"

"Charlie, you need to be serious. You're never serious. Everything is like one big party to you, like you're still in the frat house. This is a big, serious fucking problem."

I tried to smile through the character assault. I tried to bring the light because life was serious enough. I held her arms, holding her in place. She was a little taller than me, which made moments like this a touch awkward.

"We'll figure it out. We'll get through this. It's going to be okay, Serena. There's always a solution." I bore into her with every genuine feeling I could muster and pushed my fear to the side. I took a deep breath and motioned for her to do the same. "It's going to be okay."

It was not okay.

It was very not okay.

An hour later, I was fired. My co-workers all decided to go on a coffee run while I cleaned out my desk with security looking over my shoulder. Serena, too.

I texted her to see about meeting up, but she didn't respond.

An hour later, she dumped me via text.

And because I had given up my apartment to move in with her, an hour later, she texted again to inform me I was now homeless.

Charlie fucking Porterfield, are you the man?

3

CHARLIE

Two weeks later, I was a scoach closer to being the man again. I had a place to live.

After Serena threw me out, I couch surfed at friends' places for a few days, but nobody had any vacancies to let me crash long-term. New York apartments were tiny. But even then, it was kind of surprising that none of my friends would let me stay with them for an extended period of time. My best friends Skeeter and Asa had a studio apartment and live-in girlfriend, respectively. Friends from work weren't returning my calls. My parents were in the process of selling my childhood home, so the timing didn't work.

I couldn't find anyone who had a spare room, but eventually, through pleas on Facebook and Instagram, Amos came through.

Amos and I went to the same summer camp as kids. At camp, we ran in different circles—I played sports, while he focused on arts and crafts. We were friendly in that tangential social media way, where we followed each other and would occasionally like a picture or post, but we'd never make plans to hang out.

He was looking for a roommate for his apartment. And I could get along with anyone. I was voted Most Congenial and Most Likely to Succeed in my high school yearbook. At least one of those was still true.

The only catch was that he lived in Sourwood, a small town about an hour north of Manhattan. It would make commuting to find a job a pain, but as I thought about it, I found myself eager to be away from the city and its bad energy. Sourwood could be a fresh start.

I lay on the twin-size bed I purchased in my own bedroom in my new apartment. Empty cardboard boxes and used Ikea instruction manuals were crinkled on the floor beside a newly constructed dresser. I breathed in the smell of independence and cactus blossom wall scents plugged in the hallway outlet.

Amos knocked at my bedroom door. "Are you decent?"

"Yeah. What do you think I was doing in here?"

"I don't know. That's why I knocked and asked if you were decent."

"I'm actually masturbating," I deadpanned. "Marking my territory."

"Ew."

"Get in here." I waved my hand for him to enter.

Amos spun around the threshold into the room. He surveyed the surroundings, which weren't much. He was one of those people who looked like the adult version of their kid self. Skinny, kind of awkward, curious green eyes, a mop of curly brown hair he kept neatly contained. Even at camp, I remembered him as one of the few kids with a comb.

"Do you have sheets?"

"Shit. I forgot about those."

"We can do a Target run later." Amos sat on the bed, and the springs squeaked for mercy. "They're loud."

"That's probably why I got it for cheap." Amos had insisted I buy a new mattress, not used. *Don't get secondhand furniture a person could've had sex on,* he said. He obviously didn't have that much of an imagination because humans could have sex on anything. "Let me know if the squeaking is too distracting tonight."

"It'll be fine."

I exhaled a breath. I couldn't believe I was here. "Thank you so much."

He held up a hand for me to stop, but like hell was I going to stop.

"No, Amos. For real. Thank you for letting me move in here since I, y'know, don't have a job and have diminishing savings."

When Amos suggested I move in with him, I thought it would never clear with his landlord for the aforementioned reasons about my work situation. Thanks to credit card debt from keeping up with the finance bros, my credit wasn't the best either. But Amos was the landlord. This was his condo that he owned; he took on a roommate to help cover the mortgage. I was shocked when he said that, which was on me for thinking a twenty-six-year-old public school teacher couldn't afford to own. He'd worked throughout college and took on a part-time job delivering pizzas to save up the down payment. He had his shit together more than people I knew making ten times his salary.

I offered to do the bulk of the chores and cleaning to help earn my keep. Amos's place was pretty nice and recently remodeled. He said his decor was a mix of Craigslist and Facebook Marketplace finds mixed in with a few new things.

"I promise I'm a clean roommate. No parties, no loud music."

"You sound boring," he joked.

"Really, man. I know you probably think I'm this crazy partier from what you see on Instagram, but I'm not like that. I'm going to be the best roommate you've had." I rubbed my hand on my thighs.

It kept hitting me how grateful I was to be here, how the forces of fate had brought us back together at just the right time. We hadn't spoken since we were ten, but it was as if we'd been friends this whole time. We were on each other's wavelengths.

More and more, breaking away from my old life seemed like the right call. Score one for good decisions.

"I'm hungry. Are you hungry?"

"Yeah. I've been unpacking all day."

I sat on a stool in the kitchen's breakfast nook while he heated up leftover chicken cacciatore. His kitchen had stainless steel appliances, and the fridge was covered with postcards from different places around the world.

"Where's your favorite place you've been?" I asked.

Amos caught me looking at the postcards. "Those? This is like my vision board. The most exciting place I've been is Delaware. I'm planning a European vacation for my thirtieth birthday."

"In four years?"

"I'm a planner." He shrugged. Fair enough. Last year, a few buddies and I went to London on a last-minute long weekend trip. I didn't remember much from that trip, but Amos most likely saw the pics online.

"So I have a question," he said while watching the microwave tick down. "I'm pumped that you're my new roommate, but Sourwood is kind of far from New York City, and I know that's where a lot of your friends live."

"This is a lot of preamble. What's your question?"

He rested his elbows on the counter of the nook. "Why didn't you move in with them?"

"That was my plan. I was going to couch surf until I found a new job and apartment, but things didn't work out. One of my frat bros lives with his girlfriend in a one-bedroom, and she didn't want people sleeping on her three-thousand dollar Crate & Barrel sofa."

"That's some bullshit right there." Amos took out the chicken and stirred it around before placing it back in the microwave to continue heating. "First of all, Crate & Barrel's stuff sucks. If you paid three grand for furniture, you might as well have flushed that cash down the drain."

I snorted a laugh. I had thought that my frat brothers would hook me up with a place to stay with no problem. After all, they had benefited from all the rounds of drinks and the Ubers I ordered when we went out. I even covered most of our London hotel room bill since a few of them didn't pay me back. It was water under the bridge, favors I thought would be repaid down the road. I was always generous with friends, treating them like kings because friendship was golden in my book. But one by one, as I made my way through my phone contact list, I received different variations of no.

"I thought frat brothers were supposed to have each other's backs. Bonds of brotherhood forged in hazing and late-night circle jerk sessions."

"Why do people think fraternities are filled with clan-destine gay sex?" I shuffled uncomfortably in my seat. I was straight, but I'd much rather put a guy's dick in my mouth than have to do some of the shit they forced on us during initiation.

"A boy can dream," Amos said, pretty much confirming what I'd deduced about his sexuality from his social media feeds.

The microwave beeped. Amos removed the chicken, and the savory aroma filled the air. My stomach growled in anticipation. Moving had built up quite an appetite.

Amos split the chicken onto two plates. He ripped off two sheets of paper towels and got silverware from the drawer. I pulled two beers from the fridge. We met each other back at the stools and shared our first meal as roommates.

I moaned my delight at the food. "This is really freaking good."

"It's from Renaldi's, this chic Italian place on the water."

The chicken practically melted in my mouth. "Did you go there with friends?"

"Nope. On a date," he said with a deflated shrug.

"Props to you for having the balls to get a doggie bag on a first date."

"Well, since I wasn't getting doggie style, a doggie bag would have to suffice."

I choked on my beer.

"Sorry." He pressed his eyes shut. "We probably aren't there yet."

"No, it's all good, dude." I had a good laugh. It was a sign of friendship when people felt comfortable being themselves around you. "I wonder if all teachers talk like this. It would've blown my mind as a student."

"Oh, you have no idea. You'll have to meet my fellow teacher friends at South Rock High. You'd be scandalized."

"Yo, do you think kindergarten teachers talked like this, too?"

"They are human." Amos cut into his meal.

I devoured half my meal before restarting the conversation. "So the date didn't go well?"

Amos heaved out a breath, exhausted. "Another stinker. Literally, he had BO and bad breath."

"Yikes."

"You know, you'd be a catch in the gay community."

"Really?" My ears perked up with sheer curiosity.

"Uh-huh. There's a whole subculture where shorter guys are a hot commodity for big, tall bears."

I didn't know why, and I didn't know what neural desktop folder this memory lived in, but my mind instantly went to Mitch Dekker. He seemed to embody what little knowledge I had about bears, the gay kind. He was a large, strapping man. My pulse jumped at the thought, but I shook it off.

"I'll keep that in mind."

We spent the rest of dinner talking about random nonsense—shows we watched, catching up on more kids from summer camp. I cleared the table and loaded the dishwasher, insisting that Amos relax on the couch. I was earning my keep. He resisted at first but soon sank into the cushions.

"How's the job hunt going?"

"Uuuugh," I groaned, which summed it up nicely. I was persona non grata on Wall Street. My resumes went into black holes. It forced me to do some long-delayed soul searching.

"That good?"

"I was thinking of taking my career in a new direction. Any direction."

I fiddled with fitting bowls into the dishwasher. I would never load these things properly. But I managed to get everything in, toss in a detergent packet, and get this cycle started. At least something in my life had forward motion.

I joined Amos in the living room, plunking down in the adjacent armchair. It wasn't a matching set with the couch, but the colors were a fun enough contrast.

"Can I be honest with you? Ever since this whole thing went down, I've been reevaluating things, and I realized I never liked finance that much. I did it because it was a job I was offered in a cool city, and I made good money." Hearing myself talk brought needed clarity.

Amos pushed himself to sit up from his cushy surroundings. "Well, let's try a different tack. What do you like doing?"

"Drinking," I said with a laugh. "I like being around people, talking with them."

He opened his mouth, but no words came out. He looked deep in thought like he was pulling something from deep in his mind.

"What?" I asked.

"You like interacting with people and not being behind a computer screen. Have you thought about being a bartender?"

"Really? Do they make money?"

"A good bartender at a busy place can make bank. No desk, no cubicle. You're the center of the party, but you're not drunk."

Amos was speaking truth to power, unlocking realizations in my mind. How had I never considered becoming a bartender? It seemed like the perfect job.

"You're a genius."

"I do what I can." Amos pulled up his legs onto the

couch, his body wired with excitement. "And I know someone who needs a bartender."

I tipped my head. "Who?"

"This guy owns a local bar downtown. I actually went to high school with his daughter Ellie."

"Ellie Dekker?"

"Yeah! You guys know each other?"

"She's my ex-girlfriend."

Ellie Dekker was the daughter of Mitch Dekker.

Big, burly Mitch Dekker.

"Small world! So you know Mitch Dekker."

I gulped a lump in my throat. I didn't know why I had that reaction to his name. Was it because I thought about him as a bear a little while ago?

"Stone's Throw is a popular place. They get good crowds, even on weeknights, because there aren't a lot of bars in Sourwood. It could be really good money."

I was liking the idea the more I heard. I could chat with people, hang out, and get paid. I had a personality that could garner tons of tips. But...

"Would Mitch want to hire me?"

"Why not?"

"Well, for one, I don't have any experience."

"You can learn. It's not rocket science."

Question: why was rocket science positioned as the most challenging science? Wouldn't neuroscience—the study of our brains—be more fitting? That was a thought for another day.

"And more importantly, I don't think he was a fan of me. I could barely get two words out of him when he'd visit Ellie at school."

"He's protective of her. She's his only daughter and all. That's sweet and kind of hot." Amos drifted away in thought.

"Have you noticed that you think everything involving a guy is hot?"

"It's a feature of homosexuality, not a bug."

"Fair point."

Amos hopped off the couch and sat on the sofa arm. "Ellie is happily engaged. It's water under the bridge. Stone's Throw is a literal stone's throw from the condo, too." He nodded with certainty. "I think this could be your best opportunity for a job. Hell, not a job, a new career."

Perhaps he was right. My chest filled with hope for the first time all week. I could do this. I would make a great bartender.

Now I just had to convince the big, burly, scary bear of a man, Mitch Dekker, to hire me.

4

MITCH

Monday afternoons were slow for Stone's Throw. Business picked up as the week went on, and people clamored more and more for the weekend. I used the downtime to do some work on the building. Patching up wobbly tables, checking inventory. The usual. The to-do list never ended. One day, I would get around to repainting the bathrooms and cleaning up the storage closet.

Despite being a quaint local bar, the tavern itself was quite large, thanks to expansions over the years. Large windows in the back overlooked a tributary off the Hudson River with what I called junior waterfalls. Snow rested on sleeping tree branches dotted with buds waiting to burst in the spring.

By late morning, I found myself in my usual spot: the upstairs office. There was a spiral staircase by the windows that led up to a loft space my dad had converted to an office in the 1980s. I sat behind a desk with a laptop and extra-large monitor, courtesy of Ellie, going over documents to send to my accountant for taxes.

"Hey, Mitch!" Natasha, my assistant manager, yelled from the bottom of the stairs.

"What?" I yelled back. "Come up here."

"I'm not climbing up those stairs."

Natasha was both a fantastically loyal employee and a headstrong pain in my ass. When you found a quality worker, you held onto them for dear life, so I put up with her attitude at times. She meant well, and her dedication to Stone's Throw was apparent.

With dark roots peeking from her rock star blonde hair and dark eyeliner, she reminded me of the goth and riot grrls from the '90s.

"What is it then?" I called out, not taking my eyes off the monitor.

"We got an applicant for the bartender job down here."

I'd put a sign in the window saying we were doing interviews on the spot to boost applicants; it had brought me exactly one teenager trying to score free booze and a young guy who talked so softly I couldn't understand him.

"Did you screen him?"

I had Natasha do pre-interviews to weed out any obvious no's. I left the questions up to her, but I got the feeling she just stared down the applicant, waiting to see if they'd crack.

"Yeah. That's why I'm yelling up to you. He doesn't suck. Yet."

But when I looked over the balcony, I didn't have the same stoic excitement as my assistant manager. In fact, I was mostly confused.

"Sup, Mr. Dekker." Charlie Porterfield gave me a nod and half-wave.

"Charlie?"

"You know it."

I didn't expect to see him again, not since he and Ellie

broke up in college. Memories of him regaling me with mindless stories of fraternity formals and Cancun spring breaks came roaring back.

"What are you doing here?"

"Funny you should ask." He held out a familiar piece of paper. It was the job application form I used, all filled out. "I was hoping to join your fine team at Stone's Throw Tavern."

"You live in Sourwood?"

"I think this interview would go faster if you two weren't yelling across the room," Natasha said. "Almighty Mitch, can you come down from your perch?"

I shot her a glare, which only elicited a sly smile from her lips. I could do without her zazzing me in front of an applicant—an applicant who used to date my daughter and almost became my son-in-law.

When I descended the stairs, I got a good look at Charlie up close. He still had the clean-cut good looks of a senator, the gleaming smile of a weatherman, and the friendly energy of a morning show host. His big, brown, inquisitive eyes made him as irresistibly charming as a puppy dog. Charlie loved to talk; that I remember. But not in a conceited way. He asked questions and worked to strike up a conversation, which I admit wasn't my strong suit.

He dressed up for the interview with a button-down shirt tucked into khakis, more professional-looking than the other two applicants.

I put on my reading glasses and scanned his application. "You're applying to be a bartender here?"

"Correct."

I read through his job experience, trying to make sense of how he wound up here. "You were working in finance? In Manhattan? And now you're here?"

"Life has a crazy way of working out. I wanted to get out of the city. Needed a change. Wanted to exit the rat race."

I found this was common for people of his generation. Lots of job-hopping masked in the neverending drive to find oneself. I envied people for that. I spent my entire professional career inside this establishment.

"I recently moved in with an old friend of mine who said you were hiring. And faster than you can say Tequila Sunrise, I'm here."

"This is quite a career change."

"Being a bartender, y'know, aligns with my personality better." Nervousness shined through his gregarious demeanor. I liked that he was nervous.

I studied his face. Since I had decades of experience serving people, I'd gotten pretty good at cutting through their bullshit. "It sounds like you were fired from your job, probably for something really bad that blacklisted you in the industry. And then I'm guessing your girlfriend dumped you, which motivated you to leave the city altogether. Is that accurate?"

Panic. Sheer panic crossed his face. It was like something out of a newspaper comic strip. I'd never seen Charlie as anything less than cool and collected. He struggled to regain his confidence.

"Mr. Dekker. You're...wow...you're like a psychic or something."

A twinge of remorse hit me for putting him on the spot. His bright face began to sink. If all that was true, he'd had a rough go of things.

"I'm sorry," I said. "Life can give us a real kick in the ass sometimes."

Like finding out your girlfriend is pregnant right before

high school is over, right as you're on the cusp of starting a new life.

He got quiet, a startling sight from someone as spunky as him. "It's been quite a month."

"You'll get through it."

"With a sweet bartending job, perhaps?" His eyes went wide, and that charming smile crawled back.

I put a hand on his shoulder, and damn if it didn't make a flutter of heat shoot down my arm. I yanked it back as if I'd touched a hot stove. "You don't have the experience, Charlie."

"We all have to start somewhere."

I chuckled at his confidence. "Not here."

"Experience can be gained, but the innate building blocks of what makes a great bartender, well, Mr. Dekker, I have those in spades." He perked up as if he were selling his skills on the Home Shopping Network. "I like talking with people. I'm a night owl. I've seen lots of bartenders in action, so I've pretty much learned this job through osmosis. I was born for this." He flashed me a cocky smirk, despite having no real experience.

"I've been on flights before. Doesn't mean I'm qualified to be a pilot."

"Understood." He put his hands on his hips. "I'm ready to learn."

Charlie strolled over to the bar and admired the rows of alcohol bottles like it was a museum exhibit. "What kind of drinks do people order? Is it mostly beer?"

"Beer, wine, cocktails. It runs the gamut."

"I've drunk all three!" Charlie stepped behind the bar and eyed the tools of the trade. I shuffled after him. He was already breaking a few codes.

"Listen, Charlie, I appreciate you coming in, but I don't think it's the right fit."

"I think he'd fit in great," Natasha said. Traitor.

Whatever heat I felt when I touched his shoulder could not be repeated. Not with an employee. Not with my daughter's former boyfriend.

"I'm a fast learner, and I work hard." He flashed me a confident smile, which made my resolve melt. Charlie leaned on the bar, making his shirt tighten around his arms. Why was I looking there?

"Look, I'm sure other places are hiring for bartenders, ones that are busier than here." I walked down to the edge of the bar. Charlie followed me. He did look like a natural behind there.

"That may be true, but I don't have the experience or connections to work at any of those places. You know me, Mr. Dekker. I was hoping you could take a chance on me."

That was the last thing I wanted to do. Charlie was a fratboy through and through, always down for a good time. Did I want someone like that serving alcohol?

"I know you like to have fun, Charlie."

"I'm very responsible at work."

I scanned his application. "You don't have professional references on here, just friends who will vouch for you."

"You could vouch for me."

I looked at him aghast. Was he being serious?

"You know me. We go way back."

Way back to him meant four years ago.

But he gazed up at me with those big, brown eyes that weakened my disdain for him. He was being serious.

"If I recall, you broke up with Ellie. That already tells me you have poor judgment. Told her you two were on separate paths, from what she shared with me back then. There were a lot of cliches in there." I flashed him the barest smile. It was all water very much under the bridge, but it did irk me that my baby girl was dumped by a guy who wanted to explore greener pastures. I knew how guys operated. "I need someone who can be responsible. Being a bartender isn't about being a master of ceremonies. You have to be in control. You have to juggle multiple orders. You have to know when to cut someone off. I'm sorry, Charlie, but I'm not hiring you for this position. Best of luck with your search."

I grabbed a clipboard off the bar that I'd used for doing inventory this morning. Another responsibility to juggle. Then I left him to go upstairs. Charlie stepped out from behind the bar and followed me.

"Let's back up there a hot minute, Mr. Dekker. Is this about my skill set or Ellie?"

"Both," I said without turning around.

"I was a great boyfriend to Ellie. I treated her well. It didn't work out like most relationships. Was it the most delicate breakup? Could I have handled it better? Could I have done more than Google 'best breakup speeches'? Probably, but that's in the past. Ellie's past it. Why aren't you?"

"If you ever decide to have kids, then you'll realize that when someone hurts them, it hits you ten times as hard." I climbed up the stairs, wincing slightly at the creak in my knees. Twenty-five years going up and down these stairs will have that effect. Charlie bounced up the stairs in my wake like they were nothing.

"I dumped her because I knew she was too good for me."

I stopped at the top, my back to him. I looked over my shoulder, and his expression was nothing but sincere.

"I didn't want to hold her back. She's someone who has her life figured out and goes after what she wants. Law school, partner, up, up, and away. And I'm...still searching. I was in no position to have a serious girlfriend then." He sighed. "Or now."

His forehead creased with thought as if he were coming to this realization on the spot.

"I didn't want to be this stumbling block and mess up her law school years. So I gave her a bullshit breakup excuse, made myself the asshole, and set her free."

I strummed my fingers on the banister, but I couldn't detect any bullshit wafting off him. He was telling the truth, and I could tell it seemed hard. Ellie had been in love with Charlie. Would she have given up law school to follow him?

"And as for the responsible part, I was president of my fraternity. I've had to do inventory, just like you're doing." He pointed at the clipboard in my hand. "I can't tell you the number of kids I had to cut off or outright boot from parties because they were drinking too much. We didn't want to lose our insurance or get kicked off campus."

We studied each other for a moment. He had made solid points, but I didn't want to give him that satisfaction. There was still part of me that wasn't on board. I couldn't risk hiring another dud.

"I want to learn. And I will do a good job. The only thing I love more than partying is proving people wrong." He puffed his chest out and cocked an eyebrow.

I gulped back a troublesome lump.

But then I stuck out my hand for him to shake.

"Welcome aboard. Don't fuck this up." I said, as much to myself as to him.

5

CHARLIE

I woke up with a new feeling—excitement for my job. Today was my first day as a bartender.

Technically, it was the first day of training to be a bartender, but why quibble over details?

I was going to be a bartender. They were like the ultimate party hosts.

Because I didn't have to be at Stone's Throw until eleven, I didn't set an alarm. And I slept. No more having to crawl out of bed at five a.m. to catch a packed train to the office. I wasn't one of those morning people who worked out and meditated before the sun rose. I was a night owl. The midnight oil was where I burned bright.

I thumped into the hall of the empty condo. If my memory of high school served me correctly, Amos was in third period by now; he said he'd stop by on his lunch break at ten-thirty to wish me luck. I forget how early school started. How I ever functioned before nine was beyond me.

"Charlie fucking Porterfield. You are the man." I spoke loud and proud at myself in the bathroom mirror. No more having to speak quietly so Serena didn't hear.

"You're jacked. You've got a full head of hair. And according to multiple sources, you're definitely packing heat." I grabbed my bulge, swollen with morning wood.

There was no more hot-as-fuck girlfriend, and it was TBD if the new job would be primo, but I was staying positive.

I gave myself a grin and fist of solidarity in the mirror.

Another bonus of my new job: no suits! No loafers that scraped my heels! I threw on a button-down flannel, jeans, and my backward baseball hat. Amos had a wide variety of cereal for me to munch on for breakfast, but none of the fun kinds. I poured myself Cheerios and a big glass of orange juice and read articles online about how to succeed as a bartender while cartoons played on the TV. This was the life.

"Yo!" I threw a hand up to wave at Amos when he brushed through the door at ten-forty.

"I can't stay long. I have a student who wants to discuss their latest quiz and why they got a C."

"That's bad? C is average." I coasted through school with C grades. If only kids knew that your grades didn't matter to anyone once you began working.

"This student would implode if they were called average. He and his parents shit their collective pants whenever he gets anything less than an A-minus." Amos raced into his bedroom.

"They sound like a real buzzkill."

"Eh, it's all part of the job." He came back out and handed me a small rectangular gift wrapped in glossy paper.

"Are you serious?" I hopped off the couch, touched by the gesture. I didn't even need to open it. "Amos..."

He held up a hand. "Just a little something to celebrate your new job and to help you out."

I ripped open the paper and found jelly shoe inserts. Um, okay. Not expecting that. "Thanks. Awesome, man."

"I know it seems weird, but as someone who spends his whole day on his feet, those have been a godsend," he said. "Your feet are going to ache. Those will provide generous support so you aren't slumping over the bar."

Damn, he really did think of everything. "Dude, this really *is* awesome. Thank you."

I pulled him into a bro hug with a firm pat on the back.

"Congratulations, Charlie. I hope this works out for you."

"Me, too. I barely got this job. I don't want to fuck it up." I gathered up the wrapping paper and brought it into the kitchen to throw away.

"That bar is like Mitch's second child. He has high expectations."

"He's going to ride me hard."

"Lucky." Amos stopped himself. "Sorry. That comment's for me, not you."

Then why the hell did X-rated images of getting ridden by Mitch flash in my mind for a split second? Sexuality was something we were born with. Amos's gayness couldn't be rubbing off on me. That was scientifically impossible.

I thought.

I wasn't totally sure. I was only a C student in science.

"The wrapping paper goes into the trash," Amos explained to my pensive self as if I were three.

Except three-year-olds don't think about what I just thought about.

Amos studied me for an extra moment. "Is that what you're wearing?"

I pulled at my flannel and jeans. "Yeah?"

"You might get hot, especially if it's busy. I'd just stick to a T-shirt or henley."

I pointed my finger at him. "Amos, you are a next-level genius."

I whipped off my flannel. I had on a black T-shirt underneath. I ran back to my room and threw on a dark green henley. It was a little tight and stretched across my chest. I worked out, and I was proud to put my hard work on display. I didn't know if that'd be appropriate for Stone's Throw. Mitch would have no qualms about letting me know.

I came back out and presented my new wardrobe to Amos. "Better?"

"Oh, yeah. That'll probably help you get better tips, too."

———

IT WAS a weird feeling being in a bar in the middle of the day. Most times, I only went to bars at night, and they were packed with bodies and music pouring out of the speakers.

Natasha unlocked the front door. "Hey there. Welcome to the island of misfit toys."

"Happy to be here." Even though I had on a coat, the winter chill seeped through.

We'd only talked briefly when I applied, but she seemed mad chill. She struck me as one of those girls who didn't take shit from anyone and didn't beat around the bush with what she was thinking.

"How was your weekend?"

"Ugh. Like a punch in the tit."

Girls had told me how much that could hurt, like the female equivalent of a kick in the junk.

"Dang. What happened?"

"Here's a tip for the next girl or guy you date: when she finally gets up the courage to say I love you, don't respond with 'Cool. You wanna get takeout?'"

Guys like those made my whole gender look like trash. That loser better not show his face around here. "Well, if you ever need to talk, I'm a bartender, so I'm great at listening."

"You're not a bartender yet," Mitch said, descending the stairs. Seeing him again, I was struck by how imposing his frame was—his broad chest and height. I thought back to what Amos said, that this bar was his second child, and I better not fuck up.

I gulped back a nervous lump in my throat. "Morning, Mr. Dekker."

"Mr. Dekker." Natasha snorted.

"You can call me Mitch here," he said. He rolled up his sleeves, revealing massive, hairy forearms. I didn't know why my throat went dry for a moment.

"Charlie," he said.

"What?" I shook my head, silently telling my brain to get it the fuck under control.

"I asked if you filled out all the new hire paperwork and brought two forms of ID."

"Right. Yeah." I pulled the required documents and ID from my coat pocket. I wanted to make sure they didn't fall out, so I folded them into a tight square.

"This looks like a note being passed in class." Mitch unfolded the paperwork and looked them over. "Everything seems in order. I'll process these later. Today, we'll be training at the bar."

"Perfecto." I took off my jacket and hung it on the coat rack by the front door.

Natasha whistled like she was a construction worker on

the street.

Mitch's eyes stayed on me for an extra second. Maybe there was a dress code? He and Natasha both wore casual, baggier clothes.

"Is this okay?" I pulled at my henley.

"Uh, yeah." He cleared his throat. "It seems tight. Is that comfortable to work in for an eight-hour shift?"

"We'll find out."

"Do you have a permit for those guns?" Natasha asked, popping her gum.

I looked down at my arms and chest, feeling a bit self-conscious but going with the flow. Women have been objectified throughout history; I suppose I could handle one co-worker noticing. Or was it two?

"I like to be healthy," I said.

"Yeah. Healthy." Her eyebrows jumped in unison to the top of her forehead.

Our conversation came to a halt when Mitch slammed a book against my chest. I took it from his hands.

"*Guide to Mixology*," I read from the cover.

"Read that. Study that. Commit every drink in there to memory," Mitch said.

I flipped through the pages filled with cocktail recipes. "Do customers order shit like this?"

"You never know. You have to be prepared." Mitch walked behind the bar. I followed, thinking I should shadow him.

"Have you made all of these drinks?"

"Probably." He checked the amount left in each liquor bottle and the number of glasses on the shelves above. He left no detail unturned. I started to get nervous. How the hell was I going to replicate this?

"Should I be taking notes?"

"We'll cover this later. There's a checklist for opening up and closing the bar. It's in my head, so I'll get it down on paper."

"Man, you're good at this."

"I've been working here for thirty years, so it'd be odd if I weren't."

Mitch retreated to the supply closet behind the bar. I followed behind, my eyes looking at a wall of flannel. He groaned when he opened the door. "One of these days…"

I glanced around his arms at the mess of a supply closet. Wasn't it law at this point that all supply closets be a mess? Humans were not meant to be so organized. Mitch found his way through and came out with a box of empty colored bottles.

I backed out of his way as he lumbered to the bar. "What are those?"

"Practice for today. It's been a long time since I've had to train a newbie." There was the slightest crack of a smile through his stoic, borderline grumpy veneer, like maybe, on some tiny level, he didn't hate this. "You ready to get started?"

"Hell, yeah, Boss." I stood up tall. I was going to be the best bartender he ever hired.

6

MITCH

I did not want to be spending my morning teaching someone how to bartend. My never-ending to-do list wanted a word. But I couldn't say no to that puppy dog enthusiasm of his. I promised I'd give him a shot; we'd see how he did with following instructions.

I pointed out where everything was behind the bar. Just because people went to bars didn't mean they knew shit about how they operated. I filled the empty bottles with water and stuck them in the well for today's practice.

I took a seat on a stool. Charlie looked good behind the bar. He fit.

"What'll you have?" he asked with that cocky smile that brimmed with unearned confidence.

How hard did I want to be? I wanted this to be fun for me, too.

"Pour me a pint of Sun Crusher."

"You got it." He clapped his hands together, but his confidence slipped as he searched for the glasses. "One Sun Crusher coming up." He searched under the bar. "Sun Crusher is a great brew."

I cleared my throat. "Behind you."

He spun around.

"To the left."

"Thank you, sir." Charlie fumbled a glass in his hands. I held my breath, praying he didn't drop it. Sending my new bartender to the ER on day one would not be an auspicious start.

Charlie ran his finger along the row of draft nozzles, each one with a crazy design for the draft. He found the Sun Crusher. "So, what brings you in today?"

"Uhh..." I laughed a little that he was really trying to play-act with the conversation. "Just traveling through."

"Where you headed?" Charlie pulled the Sun Crusher handle. He angled the glass so it wouldn't catch too much foam, something he probably saw other bartenders do. Or from years of manning a keg.

"Albany."

"I went to college up there. Beautiful city. You should check out the Helderberg-Hudson Rail Trail. It used to be train tracks, and now it's perfect for biking."

He had the schmoozing down. I'd give him that.

Foam came out, but not much else. Charlie pulled the handle again, no dice. "Albany gets a bad rap, especially in the winter, but there are lovely parts to it."

"Where's my drink?" I asked with agitation.

He bit his lip and kept pulling the handle. He looked underneath the bar. "Uh-oh, looks like we're out."

"What do you mean? There's something wrong?"

"Let me go into the back and see if there's another keg to connect to." He maintained his calm smile, my fake frustration rolling off his back.

"Am I right?" he asked, breaking character.

"Correct. We are out of Sun Crusher. I thought that would trip you up."

"I've pumped enough kegs to know when the beer is running low. My fratboy knowledge is paying off. Where do you keep the extras?"

"In the supply closet of hell." I laughed to myself.

"I'll change it."

He didn't wait for me. I stood up and followed him into the closet. With surprising quickness, he found the right keg and rolled it to the bar. He squatted to get eye level to the keg hookups, his henley riding up to expose a golden lower back. And a hint of crack. Not gross plumber's crack.

Smooth.

Golden.

Lickable.

He grunted a little as he positioned the keg, and I needed to get the hell away from there. Since he seemed to know what he was doing, I left him behind the bar.

Charlie hopped back up like his legs were pogo sticks. He swiped a washcloth from the sink and wiped the empty pint glass, then threw the washcloth over his shoulder, Sam Malone-style.

"Well done, fratboy."

Charlie leaned over the bar, his eyes staring into mine with that cocky smirk. "What next, Boss?"

"Make me a rum and coke."

"You got it." He pivoted to the wall of alcohol bottles stacked behind him. He pulled a rum from the top shelf.

"What are you doing?" I folded my arms.

"What?"

"You're giving me top-shelf liquor?"

"You deserve the best."

"I didn't ask for the best. What if I don't want to pay for

the best? Then you just wasted valuable merchandise."

Charlie nodded and cleared his throat. "Sir, what kind of rum did you want in your drink today?"

I shrugged and waved off the question. "Eh, I don't know. Whatever you got."

Charlie turned to the shelf of alcohol, then back to me.

"C'mon, I have a train I need to catch."

"How does Captain Morgan sound?"

"How much is it?" I barked out, giving him no mercy.

"It's ten bucks?"

"Ten bucks for a drink?" I stood up, the bar stool angrily scraping against the floor. "I'll just grab a drink at the train station."

I walked away, then did a U-turn back to Charlie.

"Are all of your customers this cantankerous?" he asked me.

"Some of them, yes. People get crabby when they have to wait for alcohol. Only use the premium alcohol if someone asks for it by name or a drink requires it. Otherwise..."

I pointed at his crotch. Err, the bottles in front of his crotch.

"The well," I sputtered out. "Well drinks."

Charlie snapped his fingers. "Well drinks."

He examined the colored bottles in the trough.

"Whiskey, vodka, gin, rum, tequila, bourbon, triple sec, and vermouth. Those are your well liquors. Most of the drinks you'll be making will include one of those. You can decide which bottle is which alcohol for training, but I'm going to hold you to it."

Charlie named each bottle. I wrote it on my pad so I'd remember, too. He nodded to himself and rubbed his hands together. Since I'd been doing this so long, I was getting to see bartending through a newbie's eyes.

"Let's try it again." I felt my face contorting into a smile. Was I having fun here? The more time I spent with Charlie, the harder it was to find him annoying. "Rum and coke."

Charlie took the pint glass he'd just polished and plunked it on the bar.

"Wrong glass."

"Right. I knew that. I was testing you, Boss." He swiped it back and searched the glass shelf. He held up a short glass. I shook my head no. Then a taller glass, and I gave him the green light head nod. "There's all these little details I haven't thought about. I just wait for drinks, and they appear."

"Isn't it funny how that happens? Ice."

"Yep. And the ice is..." Charlie searched under the bar and found the ice by the well drinks. He scooped cubes into the glass until they overflowed out.

"Not so much ice."

He tossed a few cubes into the sink. He pulled the rum bottle from the well.

"Got my alcohol. Now I need my mixer," he mumbled to himself. It was fun watching him think. He bit his lip again, which sent some kind of rush through me. I found myself on the edge of my stool, wanting him to succeed.

"The soda gun!" Charlie picked it up from its holster. "How the hell do I read this?"

Different buttons had different letters.

"C for Coke," I said.

"Makes sense." He held the rum bottle and soda gun. He exhaled a breath and tipped over the bottle while pressing the gun. The soda missed the glass, spraying across the bar. I jumped off my seat to avoid splatter. "Shit. That thing came out strong."

He moved the soda gun over the glass, while the rum flowed over the ice.

"How much rum are you giving me?"

"I, uh, don't actually know."

"So we have a rum and coke that's mostly rum and half the Coke wound up on the bar."

Charlie wiped his dishtowel in front of my station. It immediately soaked through with Coke. He placed the finished drink on top. "Anything else, sir?"

I quirked an eyebrow. "What garnish goes with a rum and coke?"

"Lemmm...cherr..." He watched me closely to see if I gave away the answer. "Liiii..." I nodded my head. "Lime!"

He pulled a lime from the garnish tray and plopped it in the drink. Droplets spilled out on impact.

I exhaled a breath.

"I'm a fast learner, Boss," he said with pep. "One day in the future, we're going to think back on this moment and laugh." He let out a fake laugh.

"How far in the future are we talking about?" I joined him behind the bar and grabbed two shot glasses. I had visions of customers taking advantage of his cluelessness and getting free top-shelf alcohol.

I picked up the green bottle, which Charlie had designated as vodka. "One shot is a four-count. One, two, three, four."

I counted off as I poured fake booze into the shot glass, and the liquid came right to the top.

"Neat trick."

"You'll obviously want to count in your head when you serve, but that will let you know how much to give someone. When someone orders a mixed drink, that's one shot. If they ask for a double, that's two."

"Got it."

"And flip the bottle over completely. That'll make it

easier and faster to pour." I put the second shot glass right in front of him. "You're up."

Charlie's arm wobbled when he flipped the bottle over. It wasn't natural. Nobody turned a bottle completely upside down to pour. They didn't realize how heavy it was or how fast the fake booze gushed out. Liquid dribbled over the glass.

"Not as easy as it looks?" I had a cloth handy to wipe down the bar.

"I guess not."

"And it gets harder when you're pouring soda and alcohol at the same time. That's why we practice."

"I am officially humbled. Bartending looks much easier from the other side of the bar."

I tossed the shot in the sink and slammed the glass back in front of him. "Do it again."

Charlie took a breath before he tipped over the bottle. I silently cheered him on as, this time, all the booze made it into the glass. I gave a nod of approval.

"That was a great pour!" he said.

"That was one shot."

"I think I'm getting the hang of this." His cocky smirk and glowing eyes were hard to look away from.

"Yeah? Call me when you can do this." I grabbed a tall collins glass. In a flash, I was pouring two bottles with one hand and operating the soda gun with the other. The old man still had it.

"Dang!" Charlie's jaw hung open. I wasn't the type of person who used gobsmacked in casual conversation, but my fratboy bartender was totally fucking gobsmacked.

I wore a gloating grin as I put everything back. "Keep practicing."

7

CHARLIE

We continued to practice pouring throughout my shift. I had my first customers, who fortunately wanted something easy like beer. Mitch moved throughout the tavern—going over schedules with Natasha, checking in with Rudolpho, the cook in the kitchen, greeting customers. I firmly believed he could run this bar by himself with his eyes closed and one hand behind his back. Not exaggerating.

Yet, despite his busyness, he kept coming back to the bar to see how I was doing. "How's it going, fratboy?" he'd ask before throwing new challenges at me. Different drink combinations. Faster speed. Two bottles at the same time. He'd pretend to make small talk with me while I poured to break my concentration. Apparently, customers liked to do that to get the bartender to pour more. It was surprisingly hard work, but I felt challenged and tired in a good way. I wanted to get better at this.

There were times when I managed to complete a complicated task, like making a Tequila Sunrise without spilling, and Mitch's lips would lift into a begrudging smile that lit up the ridges of his face, making all the struggle worth it.

"Soon, I'm going to be a master of the bar," I said. "You're going to be like, 'Did that guy really have no experience when I hired him? Damn, I'm good at my job.'"

I could see Mitch attempt to hold back a smile. "You're a nut, Charlie."

I pointed at him. "But I'm not fired yet."

"True."

Feeling inspired and confident, I picked up a bottle. "Soon, I'll be able to do shit like this."

I spun the bottle in my hand a la Tom Cruise in *Cocktail*. It slipped from my grasp and almost crashed to the floor had my reflexes not been cat-like.

"Hey, I caught it. Right?"

Mitch grumbled.

"You break it; you buy it." Natasha strolled up after putting in a customer's food order. Since it was a slow weekday, she pulled double duty as a server.

"You got any requests?" I asked her, up for the challenge.

A sinister smile crested on her face. I knew she would bring it. "I'm going to pretend to be a customer."

"Awesome. What can I get for you?" I asked, putting on my serving tone of voice.

She waddled onto the stool. "Oof, I had a rough day. It's not easy working when you're seven months pregnant." She puffed out her stomach and massaged her pretend baby bump.

"Congratulations! Do you know what you're having?"

"Vodka soda."

"Funny. I meant boy or a girl."

"We're keeping it a surprise. Vodka soda."

I realized she was being serious. I cocked an eyebrow at her. "Really?"

"Yeah."

"Umm…" I looked to Mitch, who watched on stone-faced, then to Natasha, who drummed her fingers impatiently. This had to be a trick question. I wasn't going to be fooled. "Miss, why don't I just get you the soda today."

"No, I asked for a vodka soda."

"You're seven months pregnant. I can't do that. That would get the bar in trouble legally." I nodded at Mitch like yeah, I got this.

"Stop," he called out.

"Nice try, Natasha." I snickered at her sabotage. "You thought I was going to fall for that?"

"You should have," Mitch said. "You were wrong."

"What?"

Natasha pointed and laughed at me, her cackle strong with victory.

"But she's pregnant!"

"And if you refuse to serve her, that's discrimination, and she could sue."

Natasha hopped off the stool and did a victory dance. "Unfit mothers for the win!"

I tried to process that bonkers piece of information. "So if a visibly pregnant woman comes in here and asks for a Long Island Iced Tea…"

Mitch shrugged. "That's the law."

"That is fuuuucked up."

"That's the Constitution, bitch." Natasha tapped on the bar. "I'm still waiting for my vodka soda, dude."

Before I could serve said vodka soda, her table flagged her down, and she was gone in a flash. A polished man with slicked hair took her place, removing his peacoat.

"Hey, Leo," Mitch said. "What brings you in?"

"I just had a two-hour meeting over new recycling bins. There are people complaining they shouldn't be forced to recycle, that it's somehow an infringement on their rights."

"That's why we re-elected you, Mayor. To put these shit-heads in their place tactfully." Mitch clapped him on the shoulder and shuffled behind the bar. His body smushed against mine to get by, and an unexpected rush of *something* coursed through my body for a millisecond.

Did Mitch's dick brush against me?

I wondered if Mitch felt anything, but he was inscrutable as always, laughing with his friend.

"This is Leo McCaslin, Mayor of Sourwood and my old high school buddy. Leo, Charlie is a new resident, first day on the job."

"Great to meet you." Leo shook my hand and gave me an aggressively pleasant smile. "Don't let Mitch wear you down too much. He's a big old softie at heart."

"I'll take your word for it." I hadn't experienced the softie part yet, so I'd have to go on faith. "Sounds like you've had a rough morning. What can I get you, Mr. Mayor?"

"I'll take a dirty Martini."

Mitch stepped in before I could bullshit my way through. "I'll handle this."

He grabbed a bottle of vermouth from the shelf and spun it in his hand like a master, giving me a wink. Tom Cruise could never. He put together the drink with a grace I could only aspire to.

"You like your Martinis stirred, not shaken?" I asked Leo.

"I do what he tells me." Leo pointed at Mitch.

"James Bond was a weakling. Shaking a Martini melts the ice and waters it down." Mitch dipped a long spoon into the martini shaker and gave it a half-moon stir. He put on the cap, and the clear liquid flowed into the martini glass. "And a dirty Martini means pouring in some of the olive juice."

He tipped the olive juice from the garnish tray, then finished off the drink with two olives perfectly speared. It was as if I watched a maestro conduct a symphony.

"Cheers to your first day," Leo said to me. "Hopefully, the first of many."

"That's up to Mitch."

"You're on your way, Charlie." Mitch laughed heartily and squeezed my shoulder, sending another bolt of heat coursing through my body. And this bolt settled in my balls.

What in the actual fuck?

My shift ended a few hours later, and I left Stone's Throw Tavern excited about my new career but confused about my physical reaction to Mitch, my boss. And my ex-girlfriend's dad. He used to scare me a little in college. Now I was scared for a whole new and confusing reason.

"How was your first day?" Amos asked when I returned home. He was grading papers at the breakfast nook. The red pen was out in full force.

"Dude, it was awesome. I think I'm a born bartender."

"Great. Can you make me a drink? My adult glass of wine isn't cutting it." His face crinkled in a tight ball of stress. I'd probably be the same way if I had to deal with hormonal teens all day.

"My pleasure." I slapped the *Guide of Mixology* book on the kitchen counter. It'd be the perfect opportunity to practice. I really wanted to get good at this. Better tips...and to show Mitch.

We settled on Sex on the Beach. I mixed together the orange and cranberry juices with vodka and peach schnapps while Amos recounted his very long day. Unfortunately, his students did not study for their test, and it turned out teachers did not enjoy failing students.

The glowing amber of the drink reminded me of epic summer sunsets. I decided to make myself one as well.

"So what'd you do today? Did you serve customers?" Amos moaned in pleasure when the drink hit his lips. "That is good. You have a gift, Charlie."

"I served a few. Mostly I trained with Mitch." I also moaned at the sweet, tropical taste. Sex on the Beach was almost as good as the real thing.

"Did he ride you hard?"

My delicious Sex on the Beach shot out of my mouth, and all over the below-average tests Amos was grading. He lurched back to avoid the spray. I coughed and coughed until my throat was clear. My mind was a different story.

"Dang, Amos. Why does everything have to be about sex with you?" Anger tinged my voice.

"That one wasn't. I swear. It's just an expression." He unspooled paper towels to wipe down the student tests.

"How do I know? You're always talking about how hot Mitch is." I could feel my head turning the same shade as my drink.

"My students' tests are going to smell like vodka. As if half of them don't already suspect I'm an alcoholic." Amos patted down the papers.

"Shit. I'm sorry."

We couldn't be angry at each other for too long. I tried to help him out by spritzing cleaning spray on the tests.

"The scent of bleach can overpower anything. Trust me. I've cleaned up enough puke to know this for a fact."

Amos shooed me away, shielding his tests and his cocktail from the nozzle. The tension broke with raucous laughter between us.

"Forget it, forget it," he said. "I'm sorry. There was maybe a kitten whisper of sexual innuendo in my comment. I know you don't see it, but Mitch is a hottie."

"Can we just stop talking about it? He's my boss. I don't want to think about...any of that."

"Deal." He put up his hand and swore on my bartending bible.

I put away the alcohol and juices, giving myself a moment with my back turned to catch myself.

As I asked myself earlier, what in the actual fuck?

I'd *never* had this kind of response to a guy. I was straight but not narrow. If I was going to keep working at Stone's Throw Tavern, I'd have to figure out what the hell my body was thinking—and make it stop.

8

MITCH

C harlie and I had a few more training sessions that week. He liked to joke around, but I could tell he was trying and getting better. Much better than I expected. This morning, I finally took down my help-wanted sign.

Today was his first full shift. I'd be there if he had questions, but I was letting him fly solo. He strolled into the tavern wearing his usual: a henley that bulged against his muscles. Even though it had become a regular occurrence, I still had to tell myself not to stare. Damn, those shirts fit that body well. If Stone's Throw were a gay bar, he'd get enough tips to put himself through law school every night.

"Hey, Boss!" He tossed his coat on the rack.

I descended the stairs from my office after spending all morning dealing with payroll.

"Afternoon," I said gruffly.

Charlie bent over to tie his shoe, giving me a glorious view of something I shouldn't be looking at.

"Are you ready?" I asked him.

He popped up, his cheeks red from the cold. "Heck, yeah!"

I whipped off his backward baseball cap. "No hats when you're behind the bar."

Charlie pushed up his sleeves and headed behind the bar.

My newest waitress, Penny, approached, holding her tray against her chest. She was a friend of Natasha's, but she lacked the matching attitude. Her cheeks were as red as her hair, but not because of the cold outside.

"Hey Charlie," she said before looking down at her feet.

"Penny, what's good? Did you do something different with your hair?"

"I straightened it." She ran a nervous hand through her flat-ironed locks.

"It looks good. You look like Jennifer Lawrence."

"Whatever." She waved her hand at him, and her cheeks went into full blush mode.

"I'm serious! Mitch, doesn't she look like Jennifer Lawrence?"

I wasn't sure who Jennifer Lawrence was, but I nodded my head yes. She wasn't interested in what I thought, though.

"Charlie, come on."

"No, you come on. All of your customers are waiting for you."

"They need their drinks, so they're waiting on you," she said.

She tossed her hair behind her shoulder in a move that brought me back to my straight high school days flirting with my now ex-wife.

"Coming right up." Charlie flashed her his trademark megawatt smile, making her blush and me fume with frustration.

"Penny, two of your customers are out of water." I handed her a pitcher.

"Oh, I guess they were thirsty." She let out a breathy laugh.

"Yeah." I did not laugh back.

"I'll be back for those drinks," she said to Charlie while walking away.

"I'll be back," he responded in a goofy Terminator impression.

The whole cringeworthy scene made me grateful for being proudly single and proudly homosexual.

"Charlie," I said once she was out of earshot.

"What up, Boss?"

I got a fluttery feeling in my stomach when he called me boss, but I ignored it. "Just so you know, there's an unofficial non-fraternization rule at the restaurant. It's frowned upon for staff members to date."

The last thing I needed was romantic entanglements among my staff. I had enough drama to handle.

"That seems like a strict rule." He wiped down his station and began making the drinks for Penny's table. He already knew his way around the bar.

"I've been burned in the past when co-workers began dating. It starts off sweet and romantic, but then they're sneaking off during their shift."

"How many people have you found having sex in the supply closet?"

"More than you'd expect, and I couldn't unsee any of it."

Charlie snorted a laugh.

"But after the highs comes the inevitable breakup, which turns the workplace into a war zone. And this is a small workplace. Tight quarters. I don't need staff members not speaking to each other or crying at the sight of the other. Which again, I've seen more than you'd expect."

After thirty years at this bar, I'd seen pretty much everything.

Charlie opened and closed his mouth and gestured at Penny. "Boss, I—we're just friends. Nothing is happening but friendship there."

I breathed a bigger sigh of relief than was necessary. "It seemed like you two were flirting."

"You call it flirting. I call it being friendly. People like receiving compliments. I thought her hair looked nice." He returned to pouring an Arnold Palmer and vodka cranberry for Penny's table. "I think your hair looks nice, too."

"What hair?" I self-consciously ran my fingers over the prickly black hairs of my buzzed head. I'd stopped trying to grow out and style my hair as soon as Ellie hit her terrible twos. My time was better spent.

"No, I mean it...the buzz looks good on you. You don't have to deal with product."

"I take it you're the opposite?"

"Guilty." Charlie's hair had the artfully tousled style of someone that wanted you to think they just ran their fingers over the top and called it a day. "My dad says putting shit in my hair will make it fall out faster, but I take after my mom's side of the family where the men keep their hair."

"Your hair looks good, too." I stumbled on my tongue, wondering what his hair would feel like under my fingers for a second too long. "I mean, just..."

"No dating co-workers," he said.

"Exactly."

"You don't have to worry about that." He moved her drinks to the waiter station for her to pick up.

"I don't?"

"I'm not looking to date anyone at the moment."

"Oh."

"I need to focus on getting my life in order. Besides, I'm not exactly boyfriend material, as your daughter can attest."

My daughter. Who he used to date. Whatever thoughts were circulating in my head about Charlie, I told them to buzz off.

"I'm glad we understand each other." I wrapped my knuckles on the bar as Penny stopped by to pick up her drinks. Then I headed back upstairs before I could embarrass myself further.

————

WHILE UPSTAIRS, I enjoyed moments of calm. Penny and Charlie hadn't run up to my office with a problem or emergency I needed to help with. This was what it felt like to have competent staff. This was what it also felt like to have few patrons.

I'd hear Charlie schmoozing with a customer while fixing drinks, his affable voice filtering up through the floorboards. I laughed to myself. The kid sure had the gift of gab.

I finished gathering together receipts and numbers for my accountant. It was never fun. It was like a lottery where I usually lost. Margins were slim in the restaurant game. I was proud that I'd been able to keep the lights on and provide a home and education for my daughter.

Later in the day, I ventured back to the main floor and had Charlie pour me a ginger ale. He put down a glass with ice and picked up the soda gun.

"Which one is ginger ale?" he said to himself. He pressed a button, and Diet Coke came out. "Shit."

"It's the one beneath," I said, but he was busy tossing

that drink in the sink and prepping a new glass. He pressed another button, and seltzer filled the glass.

"Now it's a process of elimination," he said with a smile, never flustered. "Only one button left." He quirked his eyebrows and licked his lips, hitting a button inside me.

He prepped a third glass with ice. Ginger ale flowed from the soda gun.

"Thanks." I grabbed the glass and gulped down half my drink. "How's it been?"

"Slow. Good time for practice. I've been studying this in the downtime." He pulled the mixology book from under the bar. It was stained with liquid, and several pages were dog-eared.

"Good work. So tell me, what's in a Greyhound?"

"It is vodka and..." He bit his lip in thought, sending another one of those funny feelings into my stomach.

What the hell, Mitch? It's like you've never seen a twenty-something fratboy before.

"Tomato juice?"

"No."

He pressed his hands into the bar, making his triceps flex. "Give me a hint, Boss."

He was objectively cute, but I could see objectively cute straight guys on any porn site I wanted. No big deal. I pinched my face, willing myself not to be turned on.

"Grapefruit juice!" Charlie said. "Your face gave it away."

Before I could run back upstairs to avoid the awkwardness I felt, the tavern filled with bustling voices charging through the front door. A group of fifteen rowdy guys and girls in matching blue-and-gray flight attendant uniforms beelined to the bar. It was like they were storming Omaha Beach.

"I'm buying the first round!" said a guy with a gut

hanging over his uniform. He slapped down his credit card. "Keep the tab open," he said to Charlie.

"Is there an airport around here?" Charlie asked me.

"There's a flight attendant training school. They must've all just passed their exams." I'd heard of these crowds from other barkeeps. The flight attendant exams happen once a quarter, and when they graduate from their training, they find a bar to blow off steam.

"That's right," said a female flight attendant with side-swept blonde hair. "I'm finally going to fly the friendly skies."

"What's your route?" I asked.

"Buffalo to Cincinnati. Have more beautiful words ever been spoken?"

To my left, the flight attendant with the gut tossed off drink orders haphazardly as he heard them. Charlie nodded along, but I could see in his eyes that he was flustered. I hopped behind the bar.

"So that was two Bud Lights, one Seven-and-Seven, one rum and Coke, one Midori Sour..." I repeated the drink orders back as he said them, which was my way of commit-ting them to memory. Charlie nodded alongside me. Flight attendants crushed against the bar, yelling orders and ques-tions at us, full of jubilation.

"Did you get all that?" I asked him.

"I got most of them." He rattled off the drink orders; I filled in one he was missing.

"You get the beer and wine orders, and I'll handle the mixed drinks."

"Got it," he said with wide-eyed wonder.

I nudged him with my elbow. "Hey. We got this covered." I winked at him. "You're gonna make some amazing tips today."

I got to work lining up glasses, then swiveling my arms between the well and the shelf liquor. I was a marionette puppet controlled by the whims of my customers. Charlie assiduously poured the drafts and plunked off caps of beer bottles. We maneuvered around each other as best we could, but it was tight quarters, and our bodies kept rubbing against each other, similar to his first day. His jeans were tight, the curves of his ass leaving little to the imagination. I pulled all the focus I could muster, but that goddamn friction did a number on my dick. And Charlie's musky body spray mixed with the sweet smell of his shampoo fucked with my nose—and my dick—some more.

I kept my distance as best I could with the mixed drinks.

"You good?" I asked him.

"Great!"

At one point, Charlie bent down to the fridge to pull out a bottle of white wine while I had to reach above him for the Johnny Walker Black. My aching crotch hovered over his ass. I moved carefully to ensure I did not make contact.

That would be bad.

Glorious. But bad.

"Right behind you," I warned. But it was too late.

Charlie inched back to shut the fridge door right into my crotch. His bubble butt was burst by my pointy object.

That was as close to sex as I'd gotten in years, mere hours after laying down the non-fraternization rule.

As soon as our bodies made contact, he popped up like there was a spring in his spine. I'd never seen the human body snap so quickly. He stepped back to the bar, thankfully not witnessing the embarrassment curdling inside me. I went back to my customer, throwing myself back into my job.

The flight attendants drank like their passengers,

gulping down their libations like they were about to expire. People were on their second round before we finished serving the first. At the same time, the lunchtime crowd filled more of Penny's tables, which meant more drink orders. Charlie and I kept repeating drink orders so we didn't forget any. And we kept passing each other in the tight quarters of the bar.

Bodies having no choice but to brush against one another.

More friction.

More of me being grateful I was wearing thick pants.

"Shit," Charlie muttered.

I looked up from pouring a line of celebratory shots to find Charlie reaching his hand above the bar for a tulip beer glass used for one of our draft beers. His fingers grazed the curvy glass. He was too short to make full contact.

"Fuck," he muttered to himself. Frustration and embarrassment darkened his face.

I hadn't even thought about him not being able to reach. I should've had a stepstool on hand.

"Let me help."

"No, I can get it."

"Are you sure?" I reached alongside him.

"Boss, it's all right. I can get it."

But he couldn't. His fingers touched the glass but couldn't grab on. The last thing we needed in this chaos was shattered glass. My arm craned over his. Charlie pushed it away.

"I got it," he said firmly.

"You don't. They're high up." I didn't want him to cause the glass to come toppling down, bringing others with it.

"I. Have. It." Charlie got on his tiptoes and strained every vein in his arm and neck.

I reached over him and grabbed the glass with no problem. Charlie slipped off his toes and fell into me. More heat. More friction. More inhaling his masculine mix of scents. More bubble butt making contact with hardening dick. We stumbled back, two bodies pressed together. I held onto the glass and caught my balance, stopping us from careening into the shelf of liquor.

This time, I was the one with a skeleton made of rubber bands. I snapped away from Charlie, regaining my composure and silently cursing myself for sprouting wood. I slammed the glass on the bar.

"I'll get a footstool for the future. You could've broken a shit ton of glasses," I growled. "Next time, don't try to be the hero."

9

MITCH

From then on, I made sure there was a bar between Charlie and me at all times. For him to get better, he needed to man the bar by himself. True to his word, he was a fast learner and a hard worker, and he enjoyed what he was doing. It was rare to find quality, loyal employees in my industry. Turnover was high. I didn't want to lose Charlie.

And if he felt his boss's erection against his ass one more time, I was certain he'd be out the door. So that meant I needed to keep a fucking bar between us.

"Mitch, go home," Natasha said to me when I descended from my loft office on a gray Tuesday afternoon. It was cold outside but hot and stuffy between my ears.

"I'm fine," I said with a deep sniffle.

"You're sick."

I waved her off. She took a step backward when I reached the main floor like I was radioactive or something. "It's nothing."

"Doesn't sound like nothing." Natasha held her ground, providing a buffer between the staff and me. She was a skinny thing, but I pitied anyone who tried to get in a fight with her. "You've been sneezing and coughing all morning."

"I'm fine." When did we become so fragile about a little head cold?

"Boss." Charlie stepped from behind the bar, looking fucking dreamy as always in a fitted flannel shirt. He approached tentatively. "You're a tank. An ox. A Suburu. You're built strong." He made a fist.

"What's your point?"

"Even tanks can break down every once in a while." He squeezed his lips tight as he continued through his mine-field. "You're sick. Sick happens."

"Thanks for the bumper sticker wisdom." I grabbed a cocktail napkin and wiped my nose, which was sore and sensitive from all the sneezing and sniffling. "I've gotten sick before. It sounds worse than it is. But I'm staying upstairs, not interacting with customers or food and drink."

"Mitch, go home," Natasha said. "Unlike Charlie, I won't resort to similes."

"Actually, it's a metaphor because I didn't use like or as."

She held up a commanding hand to silence him, then whipped her head to me. "Mitch, you look and sound like shit. Take a sick day, go home, and rest."

Under her fierce look and tart language, her eyes brimmed with major mother hen energy.

"Your streaming queue must be miles long at this point," she said.

Ellie shared her password with me, but I never got around to using it. I would rather read or work outside, but the thought of laying on my couch binge-watching anything sounded very nice at the moment.

During my multi-decade tenure managing Stone's Throw Tavern, I'd taken a total of ten sick days, and each time, I was really sick. Like, a step away from the ER, can barely stand up sick. I had a rule: if I was able to come into the office, then I was able to stay.

"I'll take some medicine and stay upstairs."

"Do you want customers to hear you coughing and sneezing above their food?" Natasha cocked her head. She hit me with a business reason. "Charlie already had one customer glance upstairs and hold his drink close."

"Is that true?" I asked him.

"Yeah, Boss." He didn't try to sugarcoat or rationalize it away. He was Team Natasha on this one. "If you're just doing business stuff today, you can do that from home on your laptop."

It was hard to argue against logic when I felt like complete shit. My resolve was slipping as their reasoning made more and more sense in my congested head.

"We won't burn the place down," Natasha assured me, rubbing my shoulder as she shoved me in the direction of the exit. "Though if we do, that'd be a sweet insurance payout for you."

I wasn't too sick to glare at her.

"Kidding," she said.

As soon as I sat down at an empty table, my cold kicked it up a notch. Pounding pain slammed my skull, and my throat burned in agony. Charlie appeared with my coat and laptop bag, a sleek leather number the Single Dads Club got me for my fortieth birthday.

"Do you need help getting home?" he asked.

"I got it." I stood up, refusing to be so helpless in front of my staff. "I'll see you tomorrow. Call me if you need anything. I can be back here in five minutes." I turned to face Natasha and Charlie just before I exited. "Don't make me regret this."

———

I DID NOT REGRET THIS. Not at all. Oh, rest felt nice. Lounging on my couch felt nice. Binge-watching television felt really nice. I drifted in and out of sleep throughout the afternoon, luxuriating in the ability to not do anything. Was this what people in office jobs experienced? They worked from nine to five, but then they relaxed over the weekend without a care in the world. They took a sick day and still got paid.

Lucky pricks.

When I awoke from my naps, I texted Natasha for updates. Stone's Throw Tavern had not burned down. Business was flowing as usual, according to her, with the normal amount of low Tuesday traffic. Which was to say, I picked a good day to get sick. She sent a picture of the main room and one of Charlie at the bar, flashing that confident smile. Crushing it, she said of him.

I'd had enough colds in my life to track their trajectory. My sore throat and stuffed-up head got worse throughout the day, turning me into a disaster zone from the neck up. Somewhere during one of my naps, a knock at the door on TV woke me up.

I opened my eyes, and the screen was black save for a message that asked if I was still watching. Outside, the sky had transitioned to night without warning. Another knock.

Someone was at my actual door.

I pushed off the quilt—handmade by my grandmother —and stumbled off the couch. When I opened the door, I was convinced I was in a cold medicine-induced dream state. Because Charlie Porterfield was standing there looking ridiculously cute, bundled in a coat and hat. His confident smile sent warm sparks through my recuperating body.

"Hey, Boss."

"Fratboy?"

"In the flesh."

And what beautiful flesh it was. The cold had given his skin a soft glow and made his lips extra red.

"What are you doing here? Is the bar okay?" A million horrific scenarios played in my head.

"Everything's copacetic. Relax. I was on my way home, and I wanted to see how you were holding up." He held up a paper bag. "I brought you some chicken noodle soup from this place called Caroline's. Looks like good greasy spoon food."

As soon as the savory, brothy aroma from the bag hit my nose, my stomach cried out for more. Charlie had excellent instincts. Caroline's was perfect diner food, way better than the oversalted canned soup I'd been having.

"Thank you, Charlie." He brought me soup. Maybe the cold had worn down my rough exterior, but I was sincerely touched.

"I'll warm it up for you." He stepped inside, a hand on my chest to create distance, those brown eyes heating me up more than any HVAC system could. "Go lay down."

My dick twitched, thinking about laying down with him. But that wasn't what he meant. He was being nice, and I was responding like a perv.

"The bowls are in the cabinet to the left of the stove." I returned to the couch and sat up straight. I didn't feel comfortable lying down in front of an employee.

The sounds of cabinets opening and closing and bowls and pans clanking echoed from the kitchen. I clicked on the TV and flipped through the channels I got with rabbit ears.

"Natasha said you were crushing it today."

"I made my first Martini. Stirred, not shaken. You would be proud."

I smiled to myself, picturing Charlie behind the bar. He probably kept up a conversation with the customer the whole time he was making the Martini.

"When I'm feeling better, I'll have you make one for me."

"Deal."

Charlie came out of the kitchen with a piping hot bowl of soup and a plate with a roll and cut-up oranges. The presentation was A-plus. He placed it on the TV tray I set up.

"Caroline's sells oranges, too?"

"They do not. I stopped at this bougie supermarket, Market Thyme, to stock you up with vitamin C. Got you oranges, apples, and orange juice."

Charlie folded a paper towel in half and placed the spoon on top. A serving fit for a sick king.

"Thank you. You didn't have to do any of this."

"I know I didn't." He said it with confidence and a layer of something else that added charged energy to the room.

Or that could all be in my stuffed-up head.

"I appreciate it. Let me know how much I owe you."

He shot me an *are you joking* half-grin.

"You owe me a million dollars."

"A million dollars?"

"Yep."

"Caroline's raised their prices."

"Inflation is a bitch." Charlie plopped into the adjacent recliner. "What are you watching?"

"Whatever's on." Caroline's chicken noodle soup was even better than I remembered. Once it hit my mouth, I entered a state of nirvana.

"The Rangers are playing."

"Really?" I flipped through the channels until I stopped at the hockey game currently in progress. The Rangers goalie shoved out his leg to stop a puck. I cheered under my breath in between mouthfuls of soup.

"Nice save."

"Their left winger needs to get better at passing. He keeps letting himself get fouled up charging down the ice," I said.

"They've been having a so-so season."

"That's because their defense sucks. The goaltender is doing all the work."

Charlie studied the TV, then me. "You know your shit, Boss."

"I used to play." The warm soup relaxed my throat, making it easier to talk. "I held the record for most goals scored in a season at my old high school. I think they still have my jersey hanging somewhere."

It felt like a past life. I could still smell the ice and the rank odor of the locker room.

"I didn't know you were a hockey star."

"I wanted to go pro. But...then my girlfriend told me she was pregnant. It was in between fourth and fifth period."

"Holy shit."

"Crazy how little moments like that can change your entire life. You never know when things are going to take a hard left turn, and there's no going back." I tried to remember the guy I was in fourth period, but he seemed like a totally different human. There was a definitive before and after in my life, something I hadn't let myself think about.

"Don't get me wrong. I love Ellie. She is my greatest

accomplishment by a mile, and I can't imagine my life without her. I have no regrets."

"But you would've been a better left winger." Charlie was drowned out by the cheers of a goal on screen.

"Who knows what would've happened? I might never have made the cut. And Stone's Throw would've been sold or gone out of business if I wasn't there to take it over. It's a lot of work running a bar. A lot of fucking work. It's my whole life. But it's worth it."

"Maybe it's good that you didn't have a choice to run Stone's Throw. I remember in my sociology class, we talked about how the more choices we have, the less happy we are. Ever since I was a kid, I was told you can be anything. You can do anything. Well, anything is a lot. In college, I had no idea what I was going to do after graduation. All of my friends had these plans. Med school, law school, investment firms, Hollywood. They had direction. There were a million paths I could've gone down, and I kept thinking about the paths I wouldn't choose. I didn't know what the right one was. I still don't know."

"You'll figure it out. You're a smart guy, Charlie. And the truth is, most people don't know the answer either. Every day I wonder if I should've tried to get a better job, a corporate job, one that would've provided Ellie with a better life. She once came home from the first day of school crying because kids teased her for not having a new backpack. I hated myself for that."

The illness and the soup and the darkness all combined into this weird truth serum because I was not the guy who spilled his feelings like this. These were thoughts that'd been locked away, yet they were tumbling out. Charlie's chattiness was as contagious as my cold.

I shut the hell up. Did I share too much? Charlie didn't

want to hear some old man complain. The light from the TV flickered on his pensive face as he turned to me.

"You're a good man, Mitch."

We quietly focused back on watching the game, which transformed into a nail-biter by the second half. We yelled at the TV, cursed the players, and gave our own running commentary until somewhere in the third period, when I drifted to sleep, my body physically unable to concentrate.

When I woke up sometime later, I found myself lying across the couch. The TV was off, the tray was cleaned off, the quilt was nestled over me, and Charlie was gone.

10

CHARLIE

I made Amos and me Mai Tais on Friday night. He had a rough week at school, and it was eighteen degrees out. A tropical libation was needed.

"I didn't even know I had all the stuff to make one of these," Amos said as he watched me shake the ingredients.

"Yeah, it was a surprise to me, too. You even had the orgeat syrup." That was the key ingredient for a Mai Tai. Otherwise, it was just a sweet drink. "You've got quite a collection of top-shelf liquor."

"It's accumulated from years of Christmas and end-of-year gifts from parents. They love to get teachers nice bottles of alcohol. Do they think we're all lushes?"

"Maybe they know you need it." I followed the mixology instructions and delicately poured the dark rum over the ice cubes. They filled the glass with color. "Ta da."

I put down a paper towel in lieu of a cocktail napkin.

"Do you say 'ta da' for all your customers?"

"Just you."

Amos took a sip. I waited for his reaction.

"Holy fuck, that's good." Amos immediately drank more.

I gave myself a mental pat on the back. "You're really good at this."

"It's my first Mai Tai."

"Are people ordering Mai Tais at the Stone's Throw Tavern?"

"You never know. I want to be prepared." It was mostly beer and basic mixed drinks I served, but one of Natasha's customers ordered a mojito. I liked the challenge of learning complex drinks.

"One of my top students is getting bullied." Amos dipped his straw in his drink. "She was talking to me about it. Kids and parents look to the school to do something about bullying, and sometimes, I want to say violence is the answer, you know?"

"Dude, I've lived my whole life being short. I know about bullies. But I learned to charm them. Make 'em laugh and make 'em like you against their will."

"Not all of us can charm people against their will." Amos sipped more of his drink. "Are you going to drink your Mai Tai?"

"Huh. I don't know." It was pretty watching the dark rum infuse the liquid, like an art exhibit meant to be undisturbed.

"If you're not, then I'm drinking alone, which is sad."

I had gotten so used to making drinks for others and not having them myself that I forgot I was in my home and could imbibe without getting reprimanded by Mitch.

Mitch, the burly bear who looked more like a cuddly cub when he fell asleep, and I tucked him in. He looked... cute? Guys could think other guys were cute in certain circumstances, right?

I kept looking back on that night in his house all week. More than his alleged cuddliness, I thought about how I talked about my aimlessness and anxiety aloud with some-body for the first time. He sacrificed his entire adulthood to keep his bar afloat. I would be nothing less than a five-star employee.

"I think I will join you." I sipped my Mai Tai, and my tongue mentally applauded me for the job well done. Usually, I wasn't one for sweet drinks, but damn, did that taste good.

"Are you working tonight?" Amos asked.

"Mitch doesn't want me working the Friday night shifts yet. I don't know if I'm ready for them yet."

"I think you are."

"In due time." I wiped rum splatter from the counter. My bartending skills extended to keeping the kitchen very clean, which Amos appreciated.

"Then what are you up to? Did you want to go out?"

I spun the rum bottle on the counter. I hadn't been out since I moved to Sourwood. Did that mean I was a worka-holic? "Sure. It's Friday night!"

"I'm meeting up with my group of friends." Amos hesi-tated for a moment, then leaned forward. "We're going to Remix. It's a gay bar."

"Cool."

"Are you cool with going?"

"Yeah." I shrugged my shoulders. "There's a first for everything."

A night out was a night out. It wasn't as if my friends in Manhattan were texting me to come down to the city to party with them anymore or even to see how I'm doing. We used to meet up after work and rage through the night—with me generously picking up the tab.

"It'll be fun. It's always a scene." Amos chuckled to himself. Teenage Charlie would've been shocked to know his teachers went out drinking. "Excellent for people watching."

"Is what I'm wearing okay?" I held out my arms to show off my usual henley and jeans.

"Oh, yeah." Amos sipped his drink. "If you were a bartender there, the guys would happily give you their tips."

I tilted my head, wondering if Amos was talking about money.

———

WERE it not for the rainbow flag waving and the music pulsing from inside, Remix would've been any old building in downtown Sourwood. By day, it was sandwiched between a shoe store and a hardware store. It was squat and brick with a blacked-out front window for privacy. Remix was written in futuristic-looking red letters above the door. A small group of guys smoked cigarettes outside the entrance.

Amos was very correct: what I wore seemed okay with this crowd. I could feel their eyes on me, and I didn't *not* like the attention. They reminded me a little of the way Mitch looked at me when I first came into work.

And that made me think about the busy day Mitch and I had with the flight attendants. All of the unintentional touching of our bodies maneuvering around the bar. Feeling what might've been a boner poke me but was most likely a pen. A very large novelty pen. The warmth of his body on mine when I reached for the beer glass. I kept thinking about that afternoon throughout the week—and getting hard in response. I didn't think Amos would appreciate hearing that I jerked off in his newly remodeled shower.

While thinking about my boss. Aka Ellie's freaking father.

What the hell was up with me? I wasn't interested in dudes. Sure, I was comfortable enough with myself to appreciate when a man was attractive. But this was something different. This wasn't an objective "oh, yeah, he's a good-looking guy." This was a full-body reaction to being near one man in particular and wanting to experience all of his...manliness.

"Charlie." Amos snapped his fingers in my face.

"What?" I focused back on reality. Mitch and his manliness were nowhere to be found.

"I want you to meet my friends." Amos gestured to three guys our age and made introductions. They all worked as teachers at South Rock High School.

"It's a pleasure," I said. "I didn't know teachers liked to party."

"Oh, you ain't seen nothing yet. The chalkboard erasers aren't the only things we like to bang." Amos threw his arm around me and led us all inside.

Appropriately enough, a remix of an Adele song blasted through the speakers. The place was a railroad design— narrow but long. At the back was the main event, a big dance floor with colorful lights flashing around the space. It was empty for now, but I'd been out enough times to know it would be packed later in the night.

Our group congregated in the back bar, behind the dance floor. There was Julian, who taught French and radiated sophistication. Chase taught chemistry, and his thick glasses and shy demeanor reminded me of a NASA scientist landing an astronaut on the moon. And Everett, a tall and birdlike redhead, taught drama and seemed to have a flair for it. I kept using their names so I could remember them better. Everett got the first round. The guys all got Mai Tais on Amos's recommendation while I stuck with beer.

I quickly learned that the four of them had something else in common besides teaching at the same school.

"We have no game," Amos declared over his Mai Tai. He returned to the table after trying to talk to a guy who gave him the brutally icy shoulder.

"Speak for yourself," Chase said.

"I've seen you try and flirt, so I *can* speak for you," Amos snapped back. "I thought that guy was giving me the look."

"What look?" Everett asked.

Amos attempted to demonstrate said look.

"Are you having a seizure or a stroke?" Everett struck me as someone who didn't keep his honest opinion to himself.

"You know the look. They give you the eye, and it's like a tractor beam. I thought he was giving me the tractor beam eye." Amos slumped onto his stool.

I glanced across the room at the guy in question, and he had his back to us—his body language crystal clear. That dog would not hunt.

"Same old story," Chase said.

"Are we not catches?" Amos slapped his hand on the table. "We look good. We have pensions."

"I say this objectively, but you four are good-looking guys." See, I could say that and not feel anything the way I felt when I thought about He Who Must Not Be Named (Or Else I Get Hard).

They were a good-looking quartet.

"Aren't you guys glad I brought him?" Amos said to the group.

Speaking of tractor beam eyes, I felt a guy to my right trying that move with me. He kept looking at me. Even though I was a newbie at a gay bar, I had enough sense not to return the look and give him the wrong idea.

"Hey, maybe you could help us," Chase said, fixing his glasses on his face.

I pointed to myself. "Me?"

Chase walked around me like he was giving a lecture. "So in gay culture, frankly, a guy like you—straight, athletic —is thought of as the ideal. How has your experience been with ladies? You seem like you have no problem in that area."

"I do all right." Before Serena stomped on my heart and left me out in the bitter cold, I had a decent track record with the opposite sex. I charmed them and left them happy.

I had no idea where this conversation was going, though. Amos shot me a look like he was just as confused.

"As the male, you've been the one to pursue the female. You make the first moves."

"Not always, but usually," I admitted. There were women out there who weren't afraid to be forward.

"So you understand inherently and through learned experiences the modern mating rituals that can qualify as a success in the attraction of people to each other." Chase teepeed his fingertips. Was he trying to crack the quadratic equation of sex?

"I am really lost here."

"English, Chase," Everett demanded.

"Teach us how to flirt because we suck monkey balls at it."

I nodded my head, finally getting it. Around the table, the guys all seemed interested to learn.

"Be our heterosexual Henry Higgins," Everett said.

"Wasn't he straight?" I asked. I had watched *My Fair Lady* with my grandma multiple times.

Everett raised his eyebrows. "Was he, though?"

I wasn't going to debate someone who had a degree in

theater and was horny for dick. I hopped off my stool and rubbed my hands together. How did one teach flirting?

"I'm not really sure where to start," I said. "I don't have any moves, per se. I just be myself."

"What if that doesn't work for us?" Amos asked. "I mean, Julian can speak actual French, and it doesn't help."

"Je sui loser." Julian hung his head. "We need your help."

"That's your big problem. Flirting is all about confidence, number one. Nobody wants to hook up with a loser, which you guys are definitely not. But if you feel defeated, you'll look defeated." I went around the table and slapped each guy on the back. I was like a coach giving his team a pep talk. "C'mon, gents. You are four sexy, successful guys. With pensions. Any of these guys tonight would be lucky to hook up with you. Hell, to even talk with you. You are quality fucking specimens. They should be taking a number deli-style to be in your presence."

The soundtracks to all my favorite sports movies swelled in my head. "I've been to countless parties and bars; here's the thing nobody tells you. Everyone here feels the same way you do. They're *dying* for someone to talk to them, but they're too chicken shit to do it themselves. So they sit with their friends and go on their phones. By making the first move, just going up and starting a conversation, you're already braver and cooler than everyone else here. You think I don't get nervous when I go up to a chick at a bar? Of course, I'm nervous. I'm shorter than most guys in most places. But I do it. Doing it separates the men from the boys, if you will. Because what's the worst that happens?"

I look at Chase, and it takes him a second to realize I'm expecting an answer.

"They say no?"

"Exactly! It sucks, but it's just no. We used to have a

saying at my old office. Yes was the best answer you could receive from a prospect, but no was the second best. Hearing that no is better than sitting here and wondering and never knowing. You are in the middle of a sea of dudes. If you get that no, move on."

My words seemed to be getting through to them, judging by how intently they were listening and how they kept nodding their heads.

I clapped my hands twice, and it overpowered the music for a second. "You're going to get out there, and you're going to remember who the fuck you are."

I pounded my fists against each of their backs. "Now, I challenge you to leave this island of introversion and talk to one guy in here. If you get rejected, find another. Don't think about finding your soulmate. Focus on completing the challenge."

"The experiment!" Chase said, eyes wild with ideas.

I pulled my beer from the center of the table and raised it in the air. Their Mai Tais met me in the middle. I had the idea for us to yell Dick at the count of three but smartly decided against it.

The boys wandered off into the club. I hung out at the table and surveyed the scene, but then I decided to do some research. After I finished my beer, I went to the back bar and took a seat. I watched the bartender there do his magic. It was crowded and busy and unrelenting. He didn't take a break. His hands moved at warp speed delivering beer and mixed drinks of all varieties. During one of the brief lulls, I struck up a conversation with him and asked about his background, how long he'd been doing this. He didn't have any magical advice aside from practicing and to keep doing it. I fully intended to keep going. I could feel myself improving, which motivated me to work harder.

The night wore on, and my teacher crew were all indisposed with different gentlemen. Everett danced with a sexy black guy on the dance floor; Chase was engaged in a conversation at the front bar with a burly man; Julian sat at a corner booth with someone who looked very much like him; and Amos was making out by the bathroom with a guy whose face I obviously couldn't see.

Maybe I had a career in being a teacher. I had a proud feeling watching my students. Throughout the night, I had different guys give me the tractor beam eye or try and flirt with me. They were all objectively good-looking, but I had no other feelings for them. My dick had no response.

Later in the night, Amos found me and confirmed I had a key to the house and asked if I'd be okay taking an Uber home.

"Of course, buddy."

His lips were flushed and swollen, his face a bright red.

"Do you have protection?" I asked.

Amos gave me a thumbs up. His gaze followed something behind me.

"Oh Em Gee. Your boss is here," he said, his breath rank with Mai Tais.

I followed his eye line to Mitch, who was there with his mayor friend from the bar and some other guys I didn't recognize.

"He's hot," Amos said, taking the fucking words out of my head. "It's a good thing you're straight."

"He's almost twenty years older than us."

"Doesn't make it not true."

I gave him a hug and watched him go back to his new man. Mitch and his friends walked across the dance floor to the back bar. My heart beat wildly in my chest and a familiar warmth spread through me the whole time I watched them.

Mitch had on a flannel shirt that stretched across his broad chest and arms and tight black jeans that hugged things I shouldn't have been looking at.

And then he found me.

From across the dark, crowded room, his eyes found mine.

The heavy feeling in my gut returned.

Do I wave? Do I hide?

I gave a half-hearted nod. My body could barely move.

His face was stone. He shot me the barest, briefest flint of recognition, but his dark eyes stayed on me. They held me in place, stripping me down and seeing every part of myself.

Holy fuck. My dick got rock hard and pushed against my fly. My groin ached in the tight quarters.

Thoughts flashed in my head like he was serving them to me telepathically. Of our bodies pressed together. Of his calloused hands on my body. Of his beard prickling my face.

And then he was gone. Back with his friends ordering drinks. I could breathe again.

I left the bar and ordered an Uber. When I got home, I headed right for the bathroom and desecrated Amos's newly remodeled shower once more.

11

MITCH

When things were busy at the bar, time didn't exist. The hands on the clock moved like a comet flashing through the sky, six hours passing in seconds.

And then there were days like today when each minute dragged like the clock was soaked in molasses.

Mondays were our slowest nights, but tonight was especially quiet. It allowed me to get some admin work done upstairs, but I could hear a pin drop in the joint. The loudest noise was that of my bank account dwindling. It was pitch black outside, a typical bleak winter night, so I couldn't even enjoy the view.

I ambled downstairs sometime after nine. Natasha played on her phone while sitting at the bar. I couldn't get mad at her because I didn't know what else she could be doing. Charlie diligently cleaned glasses.

My eyes flickered to him for only a second before a pilot light of heat clicked on inside me, the same way it had when we made eye contact at Remix. His lips pouted in focus as he held a glass to the light to check for water spots. I imagined those lips wrapped around my dick and those big brown eyes looking up at me, wondering if his straight mouth was doing this right.

I slapped my hand on the bar. "Nights like this happen. It's good practice since you're still new."

"That's when it pays to have games to play on your phone," Natasha said without looking up.

"Don't be like Natasha," I said playfully. "Slower nights let you take stock of how to prepare for when it does get busy. Making sure the bar is organized. Thinking of ways to be more efficient. Checking inventory for any bottles or kegs that are running low."

"That also means dealing with the stock room," Charlie said with raised eyebrows.

"The stock room's a little messy," I responded in defense.

"Yeah, and it's just a little chilly outside," Natasha said. It was about twelve degrees and windy. Message received.

"I hate going in there. The anal, OCD side of me wants to retch," Charlie said.

My cock twitched in my jeans at the word anal escaping his lips. Damn, was I really this triggered? I needed to get laid.

Not with him.

That was what the internet was for.

"It's fine," I grumble, trying to steer clear of Charlie's anal anything. Though his ass is so perfectly round, it should be studied in geometry textbooks. Every time he bent over, my first thought was how many fingers I could slide in there at once.

"There's no system. Maybe we could reorganize?"

Natasha laughed, still plugged into her phone. "Such a newbie. That's what they all say. New guys and gals come in and think they're going to be the one who can clean up that room. They're like presidential candidates who promise that they're going to be the ones to cut taxes and bring jobs back."

"I don't think it could hurt to have some better organization. Even just labels on the shelves." Charlie shrugged to minimize his suggestion, but I could tell it was getting to him.

"Who knew Charlie was a closet librarian?" Natasha snickered.

"I don't think we should rely on tribal knowledge. You know, if it's busy and a new guy needs to find something in there, he's screwed."

"Okay, Charlie. Go for it." I dared him to take this on. It was one thing to complain about the stock room. Complaining was easy.

"Go for what?"

"Reorganize the stock room."

His face lit up for a second before he realized what he signed up for. Man, this guy was cute. And he knew it, too.

"Let's see what you come up with."

Charlie retreated to the supply room. Natasha would summon him if she ever got any customers. A few minutes later, someone walked through the front door, but it wasn't a customer.

It was my daughter.

"Ellie Bear." I couldn't help turning mushy when I saw her, even though she was an all-grown-up lawyer. She was my little girl forever.

"Hey, Dad." She looked very professional in her fancy coat and purse. No girls ever teased her about not having the latest fashions anymore, that was for damn sure. "I was on my way home, and I wanted to stop in and talk with you about wedding details. Tim and I are reviewing vendor proposals, and since you've catered events, I wanted to get your thoughts on these."

"My pleasure, Ellie Bear."

"I haven't gone by that name since I was eight."

"Doesn't matter to me." She was eight about ten seconds ago in my mind.

Charlie popped his head out from the supply room. "El Dorado!"

He jogged over and gave Ellie a hug. His friendliness and warmth never ceased to impress me. Ellie didn't have the same reaction to seeing him, though.

"Charlie?" She looked utterly confused. "You work here?"

She turned to me, then him, then back to me, then back to him. "I thought you were in the city?"

"It's a long story." Charlie let out a nervous chuckle. He probably had to rehash this story many times over at this point. "I decided on a career and life pivot, and I wound up here. Learning the bartending ropes from your dad."

"Huh." Being my daughter, I knew every emotion on her face, including the undercurrent of frustration laced with her confusion. I worried that I made a mistake in hiring him. It'd seemed like their breakup was amicable, but maybe it wasn't.

"Congrats on the engagement. When's the big day?"

"In a few weeks."

"Coming up!" Charlie's enthusiasm hit new heights to compensate.

"With our work schedules, it was the best time to tie the knot. Good seeing you." She turned back to me and tipped her head at the stairs up to my office.

What if Charlie had sugarcoated what happened between them and Ellie was furious? I couldn't imagine

Charlie as being a bad boyfriend. But I didn't want her to be upset. But I also didn't want to let him go. I weighed my options as I climbed the spiral staircase.

"Charlie Porterfield is working here?" Ellie whispered when we reached my desk. She let out a laugh. Laughter was good.

"He needed a job. He'd gone through a bad experience at his last place, his girlfriend kicked him out."

"I heard through the grapevine. I didn't know he wound up here."

I leaned forward, my heart beating in my chest. "Is this... okay?"

She smiled at the question, that Ellie sunshine coming back. "Of course it is, Dad. I was just surprised. Charlie's a good guy."

I remembered what he said about their breakup, that he didn't want to hold her back. I wonder if she realized that, too.

"How's it working out?" She bit her lip in one of those *eek* gestures. Now I was the confused one.

"It's going well."

"Are you two getting along?"

I gulped down hard. "Yes."

And we would stay that way.

"I remember when the three of us would go out to dinner together, and you seemed to despise every word out of his mouth."

"I was being protective of my daughter. I scared Tim in the beginning, didn't I?"

"This is true." We chuckled at the memory. Her fiance was a straight arrow, and if I really wanted to have fun, I could've made him shit his pants with one eyebrow raise.

She rested her elbows on my desk and peered downstairs to make sure they weren't listening. "Listen, I like Charlie. He's a nice guy. But he's a big goofball. He tanked in his last job. He loves to party. Is he responsible enough to be behind a bar?"

Anger simmered inside me. I tamped it down for my daughter's sake.

"I know you've had trouble with turnover. Did you feel obligated to hire him because of our personal connection?"

"I did not. And Charlie spoke very highly of you."

She blushed slightly, then continued her argument. "I just hope he doesn't take advantage of that and leave you in the lurch. Or have his frat buddies here to drink on the house. You already have so much on your plate. I don't want him adding more stress that you don't need."

Rare were the times when I yelled at my daughter. I thanked the Lord for giving me a respectful, loving child. I'd been warned by other parents about what nightmares girls could be, which I always found sexist bullshit. Yet now, the frustration boiled over in me, and it took every ounce of parental control to reel it in.

"Ellie, I know you mean well, but you don't get to tell me how to run my business," I said in a low, calm voice that instantly wiped the confidence off her face.

"Dad, I was just–"

"You don't get to waltz in here and tell me who to hire. Are we clear?"

"Yes," she said quietly.

"Charlie has been an outstanding employee, one of the best in a long while. I promise you, whatever opinion you have of him is outdated."

She bowed her head and nodded, just as she did when she'd get in trouble as a girl. Some things never changed.

"I'm sorry, Dad. I guess it was a little weird seeing him

here. Like, what are my college ex-boyfriend and Dad doing together, y'know?"

I opened my mouth, about to say we weren't together. But that would only make things more awkward.

"Now, you came over to discuss vendor proposals, right? Let's get started."

She took out her iPad and attachable keyboard and didn't mention Charlie for the rest of her time here.

———

AFTER SHE LEFT, I spent a little more time emailing my own vendors before rejoining everyone downstairs. I enjoyed spending time with my employees. I didn't want to be that boss who barricades himself away and only shows his face to dole out orders.

"How's it coming?" I called into the supply room.

"Great! Y'know, it's gonna be a process. Miracles don't happen overnight."

I admired his hope.

Charlie emerged from the closet, wiping dust off his shirt. His muscles were in fine form.

"So, Mitch, I was shocked to see you out on Friday night."

"What?" Natasha cleaned off a table. "Mitch, you went somewhere and did something?"

I shot her a glare, then gulped back a lump in my throat. I wondered if he was going to bring it up. "Me? You were the one at a gay bar."

"I was there with Amos and his friends." He leaned on the bar. "I gave them all flirting lessons, and I'm pretty sure all of them hooked up that night."

"You should open a charm school for manwhores," Natasha said.

"That's not a bad idea." Charlie laughed, his gleaming, gorgeous set of teeth on display. "But back up. Mitch, I was kind of surprised to see you there."

"We close at one, and Remix is open until four."

"Yes, but you're..." Charlie glanced at Natasha, and I knew what they were thinking.

"Old?"

The young folk bowed their heads in embarrassment.

"I like to go out." Every once in a while, my friends will drag me out to make sure I still have a social life. Even though it's late and we're dog-tired, Leo said it's the most efficient method for finding me a guy to bring home. Standards fall dramatically after two a.m. Not like I ever followed through with that mission. Only on very rare occasions.

"I'm trying to picture you at a bar...having a good time." Natasha cocked her head to the side. "Like, are you looking around judging everything?"

"No."

Yes.

"He looked like he was having fun," Charlie said.

"So did you," I said back. I don't remember anything except staring at Charlie from across the room, remembering how his pink lips and entrancing eyes twinkled in the mood lighting.

"I like being out, around people. Doesn't matter where they stick it." Charlie flipped a dishtowel over his shoulder. He always had one hanging there like it was a prop.

"I think I need that on a bumper sticker," I said.

Charlie was a textbook extrovert. It took me a while to realize that even though I ran a bar, I was not a people person. I needed my solitude.

"So, did you get any?" Natasha asked, raising her eyebrows.

"I'm your boss," I said.

"I care about your health."

I rolled my eyes at her glorious leaps of logic. Charlie got quiet and seemed intent on hearing my answer.

"It's none of your business." I knew I should leave, but I was enjoying the camaraderie with my team.

Natasha studied my face. "I can't tell if that's a hell yes or a hell no."

"Natasha, let the man enjoy his private life," Charlie said, without the usual enthusiasm in his voice.

"I had fun spending time with my friends."

Natasha sighed at my answer.

I glanced at Charlie, whose cheeks flushed with color. He probably didn't want to hear anything about the sex life of his middle-aged gay boss.

"Hey, Mitch, I actually had an idea." Charlie scratched at his chin. "What did you think when everyone at Remix began belting out that song that was on the screen?"

"'Don't Cry for Me Argentina'?" My ears still rang with the offkey pitches of a hundred drunk gay men.

"What if we did something like that here?"

"We do a monthly LGBTQ+ night."

"What if we did it weekly, and if there was a theme of musicals? Not to stereotype but..."

I shrugged. "My people love musicals."

I mean, *I* didn't. But I was in the minority. I couldn't suspend my disbelief enough to follow people breaking into song. I wasn't much of a talker, and I definitely wasn't a singer.

"We could play clips of musicals on all the TVs, and people can sing along. Everyone was really into it. I think it'd be a more fun hook than a generic gay night once a month. Do you want to go with your friends to another LGBTQ+ night, or do you want to go with your friends to belt out musical theater in a crowded bar?"

He had a point. Attendance at our monthly queer night had been dwindling; going to a bar owned by a gay man had become less of a selling point as the country embraced gay rights and marriage equality. The name came to me in an instant.

"Musical Mondays," I whispered.

Natasha sat up straight. Charlie pointed at me. "Heck, yeah. There it is. Musical Mondays, baby!"

"My sister can whip up flyers to put up and post online," Natasha said.

I nodded along, the idea forming in my head. Even if Musical Mondays attracted a few people, that'd be better than the dead zone we were currently experiencing on Mondays. We had nowhere to go but up.

"Good thinking, Charlie," I said.

"Leave it to the straight guy to coin the new queer night," Natasha said with a laugh.

Right, I reminded myself. Charlie was straight, despite what dirty thoughts swirled in my head. The more I thought about him, the more awkward this would be for everyone.

12

MITCH

I had to hand it to the kid. Musical Mondays was a hit right out of the gate. Our deadest night of the week now had a pulse. More than half of the tables were full, and the place was alive. We set up the TVs behind the bar to play YouTube clips of old Broadway performances.

I nearly got my two front teeth knocked out because of some guy throwing his hands out singing along to "Rose's Turn" from *Gypsy*.

Natasha came in to help Penny with the overflow, and Charlie held court at the bar, running that thing like he'd been born there. He made all kinds of drinks while keeping his composure and cocky smile. He was extra-friendly, utilizing his good ole boy charm for maximum effect.

Charlie read the room and made sure to wear his tightest black T-shirt, emphasizing the muscular curves of his chest and arms. It was a good thing I jerked off before coming into work tonight. Though that was becoming a bad habit of mine, the needing to crank it anytime I knew I was going to see Charlie.

He looked so damn sexy behind that bar. His skill level

caught up with his cocksure attitude, making him confident and fun with customers.

I floated around the tavern, making sure all the customers were happy. Unlike game nights or packed heterosexual crowds, there was very little risk of fights breaking out tonight.

On the screens, "Defying Gravity" from *Wicked* came on, and the crowd went wild. I'll admit, while I wasn't a musical theater superfan, there were some tunes I couldn't help but sing under my breath.

Leo's boyfriend, Dusty, swung an arm around me and pulled me to their high top where Cal and Russ sat.

"Mitch, will you do a duet of 'Defying Gravity' with me?" Dusty asked. Even after being a Sourwood resident for almost six months, he still had the sun-kissed skin of his Los Angeles roots. "Leo is being a stick in the mud."

"I think *Wicked* is overrated." Leo shrugged.

"Leo, since you have aspirations of running for governor one day, I suggest you keep that opinion to yourself." Dusty messed up his carefully coiffed hair, which Leo smoothed back into place.

"His favorite is *Rock of Ages*," Cal said.

Dusty played a bit of air guitar. "I can see that."

Leo used to play guitar in a band in college. He brought out his guitar skills last fall during a concert that was a game-changer for his re-election campaign. It became a tradition that the mayor play at all public events. Precedent had been set.

On screen, Idina Menzel burst into the chorus of "Defying Gravity," and the crowd sang right along with her. Dusty and Cal put their fists to their mouths and belted out the words. It was a painful reminder that only Idina should sing this song.

Cal held his fist to my mouth, expecting me to sing. I arched an eyebrow at him.

Girl, please.

He took it back.

"Cal, isn't the point to listen to Idina Menzel sing?" Russ asked.

"No." He pecked his boyfriend on the lips.

I was happy to be a spectator and bask in the glow of paying customers having a blast. Charlie seemed to be enjoying the scenery, too. A sneaky smile danced on his lips as he watched the room blare the lyrics in unison. His dark, transfixing eyes found me. *See*, they seemed to say. *Success.*

"You've been looking over at your bartender an awful lot tonight," Leo said.

Heat flashed on my cheeks. "I like to keep tabs on what's going on at my establishment."

"Sure," Cal said. "Tabs."

"He's still new."

"He seems to be doing a good job. You don't need to keep watching him. I think he's got it." Leo had a devious grin on his thin lips as he sipped his Martini. That was the problem with best friends; they could see through all your bullshit.

"He's cute," Russ said. "I don't think his shirt is tight enough, though."

Now Russ was getting in on giving me shit?

"You bitches can defy gravity on your own."

Penny came by to check on refills. "You should cut them off," I told her. They booed at me. "I'm kidding."

But not by much.

My eyes instinctively found Charlie again, and he was being aggressively hit on by one of his customers. The guy followed him up and down the bar. It looked like he was in trouble.

"Everything all right? You having a good time?" I asked the creepy customer. He was about my age and height, wearing a red t-shirt with a dribble of alcohol down the center.

"I'm doing great, man. Just chatting with your lovely bartender, Charlie."

"About what?"

"Places to check out in New York City." The stench of alcohol was strong with this one, but he could string together sentences and wasn't falling off his seat, so I couldn't cut him off, as much as I wanted to.

"It's all good," Charlie said with a plastered-on smile. He was handling this creep.

"I was telling Charlie about this bathhouse I love going to when I'm in the city. I should take him there one time. He'd really enjoy it."

"I don't know when I'm going back to the city next."

"We'll have an adventure."

The hell you will. My blood boiled. I was ready to throw this guy into the river. Gay or straight, men could be real slimeballs.

"You have such a beautiful smile." Mr. Horndog reached out a greasy hand to caress Charlie's cheek. Charlie stepped back while keeping on his pleasant grin.

Me, not so much.

"Buddy, this isn't a petting zoo. Charlie is here to work." I clapped the guy on the shoulder extra hard, and he winced in pain.

His pissy eyes glared at me. "Can't I have a conversation with the bartender?"

"It's Musical Monday. You should be singing!" Bless Charlie for trying to keep things light. I did not have that tact.

"So sing," I growled at the creep.

"You don't have to be an asshole." He grabbed his drink and sulked off.

Charlie exhaled a breath. "Now I know what it's like to be a girl."

"Are you okay?"

"Yeah, I'm fine." He shrugged off the incident, but remnants of panic flickered across his face. "I guess it's a compliment."

"That went way beyond compliment." I looked down and found my fists balled, ready for action. I shook them out. "It's a busy night. You don't have time to be hit on by customers."

"I guess that guy won't be tipping."

"You'll make it up with this crowd." I gazed at the sea of customers having a blast. "I can't believe how busy we are on a Monday."

"And all we had to do was play YouTube clips of old musicals."

"You're a genius." I put a hand on his shoulder. He clocked it. I clocked it. His hot skin blazed through the thin layer of black.

I pulled my hand back.

Customers hailed Charlie from the other end. A crush of people without drinks in hand pushed up to the bar. It seemed we hadn't hit the busy part of the night until now. Who knew Monday could be the new Friday?

I hopped behind the bar to help out Charlie. Though truth be told, he didn't need much assistance. He took in orders and made drinks like he had two extra hands.

Someone ordered a rum and coke, and he swirled the rum bottle in his hand *Cocktail*-style.

"Have you been practicing?" I asked.

"Maybe."

"Not with my bottles, I hope."

"Amos's empty wine bottles at home."

We weathered the rush of business together. I stayed behind the bar and served customers alongside Charlie. We were like ballet, moving and gliding around each other with ease. We'd learned how to navigate these tight quarters. It was a blast, and I remembered what I enjoyed about bartending. I almost found myself blatantly flirting with Charlie against my better judgment. A hand on his lower back to hear him. Answering his questions by whispering in his ear. His body was a sheet of metal, and I was a helpless magnet. He reciprocated, too. A touch of my arm when he needed to get by, whispering comments about customers in my ear.

I had to get this shit under control. Charlie was my employee. The last thing I wanted was for him to feel he had to flirt with me in order to keep his job. I went back to circulating through the bar, far away from the bartender. Leo shot me a shit-eating grin when I passed him.

That fucker.

———

It was a Monday, and I was exhausted. What a great night.

Natasha, Penny, and I thanked the final customers for coming in and guided them to the exits. The girls sat at a dirty table and counted their tips, gasping at the amounts. Happy staff, happy boss.

"Have I mentioned that I love Musical Mondays?" Natasha put her wad of tips into her apron. "Gay guys tip well and don't hit on me."

"Same with the lesbians. I got so many compliments on my hair, but not in a creepy way," Penny said.

"Mitch, we should turn Stone's Throw into a full-time gay bar," Natasha said, and Penny nodded in agreement. "You're gay, so that gives it extra cred."

"I'll take it under consideration. Have you seen Charlie?" He hadn't come back from taking out the trash.

"You're always wondering about Charlie," Penny said.

"What?"

"You're always bringing him up," Natasha said. "He's your golden boy."

I was *not* going down this path. "Charlie took out the trash a while ago. It doesn't take that long to throw a bag into a dumpster. He still needs to close down his bar."

That sounded responsible, right? I was concerned for my employee.

"He's probably smoking." Natasha shrugged.

"He smokes?"

"No, but it's only a matter of time."

I didn't want that to happen. I didn't want to kiss an ashtray. Err, I mean, smoking kills, and I wanted him alive.

Fuck.

I left the girls and rushed through the kitchen to the dumpster area, where I found creepy Mr. Horndog cornering Charlie against the wall. He had several inches on Charlie and used that height difference to corner his prey.

"Relax," he cooed. "Why are you so nervous? I miss that smile of yours."

"Buddy, I have to close down my station." Charlie tried to maneuver out of his grip, but the creep was big and tall. His hands and feet were like a net that entrapped my bartender.

At that moment, I saw red. Only red. Didn't care if I got

sued and lost my business red. I grabbed the creep by his collar and hurled him against the dumpster, where his worthless body clanged against the metal.

"What the fuck!" the creep yelled. "You again?"

"Yeah, it's me. The owner of this fucking establishment." I stepped forward, this time not self-conscious about my balled-up fists. "We are closed. Go home."

"I was just chatting with Charlie. He's off the clock."

"Go home."

"We're talking about hanging out after this. He's a grown man."

Was that true? Had my jealousy blinded me to what was going on here?

A hand climbed onto my shoulder—familiar hot skin.

"Actually, Kirk, I can't hang with you. I'm taken." Charlie slid his hand down my arm, leaving a trail of goosebumps in its wake and a boner in my pants.

"Fucking the boss? I knew it. Real classy," the creep tossed off. His squinty eyes resembled a rodent the more I looked at him.

I picked up on Charlie's plan. I'd pretended to be the boyfriend of lady friends in public to scare men off.

"Don't fuck with my employee or my boyfriend." I put a protective arm around Charlie. A small round of fireworks went off in my head.

"Jesus, can't a guy have a conversation with his bartender? I was just having some fun."

"Go home, Kirk. This is the last time I'm going to tell you." I was two seconds from throwing him in the dumpster. Only the insane amount of joy bursting through my insides kept me from choosing violence.

He cocked his head. "Are you guys really together?"

I looked down at Charlie, who fit so perfectly in my arm,

for our next move. He got on his toes and put his lips to mine. They were warm, slightly chapped, and flat-out perfection. I turned his body to face me for a better angle. His mouth opened, and I snuck my tongue in there because I lost all sense of reality.

His eyes were glassy and dazed before opening wide. With panic?

The creep glared at us in full stinkface mode. "I think it's very unprofessional for you to fuck your employees."

I stomped up to his face, and he turned so white he was about to wet himself. "Go."

He practically ran to his car, slipping on the ice but not letting that stop him. I couldn't enjoy the scene, not with the sinking feeling pooling in my gut that I'd just crossed a line I swore I wouldn't.

"Let's get back to work. You need to finish cleaning up," I muttered and walked past Charlie into the bar.

13

CHARLIE

"**C**harlie fucking Porterfield. What the fuck did you do?" I asked myself in the mirror when I got home from the first Musical Monday. I couldn't revel in the success of tonight because...

I made out with my boss.

Under false pretenses.

But with very real lips.

Yeah, I wanted to scare off that creep. But I could've found a way out of his clutches. Looking at myself in the harsh light of the bathroom, I knew the truth: I really wanted to kiss my boss.

It had become this craving that kept building and building. And all that shameless flirting I did with him behind the bar...the touching and whispering and big smiling. It was one long row of green lights straight into my pants.

Fuck, Charlie, why don't you just get on your knees and suck his fucking dick?

Ooh, that would be nice.

Stop that!

I had never sucked a dick, but I've had mine sucked so I

could figure it out.

Mitch could help me.

I banged my head against the mirror lightly so as not to damage Amos's bathroom but hard enough to try and knock some sense into me.

I woke up horny the next morning, thinking about Mitch's warm breath and aftershave smell enveloping me. The stubble that scratched my chin. My thoughts traveled to other parts of my body where I wanted him to place his mouth. I cranked it in bed like a horny teenager while Amos made breakfast in the kitchen. What did Mitch's come taste like? I'd tasted mine before. Would it be that kind of salty and bitter?

I made sure my hands were clean and that my pajama pants were firmly on before dashing out of my bedroom. Snow was coming down, blanketing the balcony in a thick white layer.

"Hey, Amos."

He looked up from his coffee maker. He wore khakis and a button-down shirt tucked in—the model of respectability that masked the somewhat raunchy guy I've gotten to know.

"Morning." He poured his pot of coffee into a to-go cup. "How was the inaugural Musical Monday? I was wiped and passed out on the couch when I got home. I promise I'll show up for future nights. I really want to."

He was the kindest, most thoughtful friend I'd had. My frat brothers and Wall Street friends would've flaked or just made up an excuse not to attend...if I still talked to them. Except for comments on social media, I had no contact with them. They didn't text to see how I was doing.

"Amos." I ran my palm over the top of the couch cushion, trying to figure out how to talk about a very new topic for me. "How...how did you know you were gay?"

Amos immediately suspected something was up. He took a gulp of coffee. "It wasn't any one moment. It was a series of realizations." He strummed his fingers against the cup. "And Hutch Hawkins."

"Who?"

"Captain of my high school's soccer team. Our lockers were next to each other, and I checked him out. A lot."

I cocked an eyebrow. "Because there's nothing cliché about that."

"Clichés are clichés for a reason."

"Was he gay, too?"

"It's brutally complicated." His playful demeanor shut down, startling me. "Why are you asking about this?"

"I, uh, no reason. Sorry, didn't mean to pry."

"Is there anything you want to talk about?" Concern washed over his face.

Was I coming out? I'd always liked girls. I'd always had sex with girls. This wasn't like switching from Coke to Pepsi. This was wanting to switch from Coke to...come.

"No reason. I was just curious after bartending last night. It was my first LGBTQ event, and, uh, you know, I was around LGBTQ people. You have to get to school." I took his coat and satchel from the hooks and got him ready for the outside like the world's most awkward manservant. "You're going to be late."

He opened the front door. I ignored the WTF stamped across his eyes.

"There was a time when I was confused," he said. "And you know what helped me?"

"Talking with trusted friends and family?"

He shook his head no. "Watching some gay porn online to see if I was into it."

———

I TOOK his advice and opened the gay porn floodgates. The usual sites I visited had gay collections. There were probably other straight guys who watched gay porn, too.

It was odd to see men in the center of all these thumbnails and not women with big boobs. I watched videos of "fraternity brothers" who had sex with each other while other brothers played beer pong in the background. I rolled my eyes. There were so many code violations in that frat house that I couldn't get invested. I moved to other scenarios and found my dick reacting, mostly to ones about older men.

I came across a guy who reminded me of Mitch. Same buzzed dark hair, same beard. He didn't quite have Mitch's eviscerating stare, but that was a trademark. Instantly, my dick perked up. He plowed into a pizza delivery boy, his hairy chest slick with sweat. I pictured that I was that limber delivery boy on all fours, and Mitch barreled into me with all his might. His calloused, rough hands dug into my shoulders as he stuffed me with his thick cock and grunted above me.

What would that feel like?

I tried a finger inside me, and it was...interesting. New parts of my brain lit up with excitement. My sophomore year, a girl tried to slip a finger up there while giving me a blow job after a homecoming party. That was a hard pass from me. It reminded me of a medical exam.

Curiosity latched onto my brain, though. Wasn't this how anyone figured out what they liked?

Pantless, with my cock hanging free, I walked into the kitchen, opened the fridge, and scoured Amos's produce drawer. I came away with a hearty zucchini. It was green, lean, and mean.

I popped into Amos's room and tried my luck with his nightstand drawer. The dude had *three* bottles of lube. Always the optimist.

My dick hardened in anticipation. I closed my bedroom door.

"It's you and me," I said to the zucchini. "I hope Amos wasn't saving you for a special recipe."

I slicked up my fingers and pressed inside my hole. Once I pressed through the tight ring of muscle, I leaned into the weirdness and had electricity light up my body. The buzz went straight to my cock. Maybe I had to reconsider the finger. I mean, that girl had long nails. I craved more as soon as I pulled out.

But it was time for the main event.

I got on my back. The zucchini was much bigger than my finger, but it was about the size of my dick. Mitch's was probably bigger. My eyes rolled back in my head as it entered my ass. This was...new and exciting, and put my lower half on pins and needles.

I choked out a moan as I slid it in and out of my virgin hole. My hard dick stuck in the air. As soon as my eyes closed, Mitch was on top of me, rutting into my hole, growling as he liked to do. But growling at me. The heat of his chest and thickness of his cock controlling me sent sparks charging through my central nervous system. His dark eyes lasered into me, and I reached up to kiss him, the scorching heat of our bodies making me dizzy.

"Oh, shit. Yeah." I muttered as he hit that spot in me that opened me up. My balls drew up as the orgasm came close. But it was an orgasm times ten, my whole body levitating under these new stimulating sensations.

I tried to hold back. My lips trembled, but I had to say it. "Fuck me, Mitch."

Damn, that sounded good.

"Fuck me, Mitch." His name made my cock stand at attention. I curled my fingers around my rock-hard length and jerked myself until the orgasm was like that Indiana Jones boulder coming to steamroll over me.

I gasped and moaned my way to blowing my load across my stomach.

My eyes flung open.

Holy shit.

I removed the vegetable from my opening and took a moment to catch my breath. My vision remained blurry. I saw my ceiling. I saw Mitch. I saw Mitch and I cuddled together.

My ass felt stretched, like the first workout after a long break.

I sat up and put on my boxers. So that was anal sex...and I liked it. Did I just take my own virginity?

I went to clean myself and the zucchini off in the bathroom. When I stepped into the hall, I came face to face with Amos.

His eyes bolted open, and they locked in on me, then the zucchini.

"Hey," I said.

"Hi," he replied just as awkwardly.

"Wha—what are you doing home?"

"Because of the snow, they called a delayed opening. Is that my organic zucchini?"

"It, uh..." Shit, there was no use lying. This was even more embarrassing than my mom finding my special jerkoff sock in high school. "I was thinking of making a salad?"

"It didn't sound like you were making a salad."

"It was, uh, a very intense salad. A lot of vegetables in it."

"Charlie." He cocked his head. "I can see the lube on it."

"It's salad dressing?"

I clamped my eyes shut, willing myself to wake up from this hella awkward nightmare. Then, by the grace of God, Amos broke out laughing. Hysterical, had-to-catch-your-breath laughing. I thanked all my lucky stars he was cool.

"Do we need to have the birds and bees talk?" he asked.

"Negative," I deadpanned. Then I laughed, too, releasing all the tension in the condo. "I was...experimenting."

"With my produce. I was going to make ratatouille! Wait." He ran into his room. "You used my lube, too?"

"Guilty."

"How did you know I had any?"

"I took a guess. Also, why do you have three bottles of it?"

"I was a Falcon as a kid. They taught us to always be prepared."

"You are literally the horniest person I've ever met."

"Where are you going?" Amos blocked me en route to the kitchen.

"To wash it off?"

"You were going to put that back in the fridge? Charlie! Think of the bacteria! No amount of oven or frying pan heat would sterilize that zucchini. That is going in the trash. Actually, wrap it in this Gap holiday shopping bag, then throw it in the trash."

He pulled a crinkled, durable-looking plastic bag adorned with Santa and snowflakes from under the sink. I did as instructed.

A few minutes later, after I'd showered and thrown on clean clothes, I coyly joined Amos in the living room, where he was grading papers from his armchair. I sat on the far end of the couch.

"So..." I said. "Um, I think I might be bi."

He nodded. "Everything about this morning is clicking now."

Right. I'd asked him about his coming-out experience earlier.

"What's going on, Charlie?" His eyebrows joined together in concern. "I couldn't help but overhear you in your room...asking Mitch to fuck you. I can't unhear that one."

I threw my head back onto the couch. "First of all, thank you for not kicking me out on the street. Dude, I don't know what the fuck is going on with me. I've always been one hundred percent into chicks. I've never thought about being with a guy. Never crossed my mind."

"So you never thought about jerking off with your frat brothers or giving each blow jobs after a frat party?"

"No! And I watched some of those videos this morning. What a totally unorganized frathouse. The guys weren't even playing a regulation beer pong."

He smiled hopefully. "You're bi. That's awesome."

"I never thought about guys, though. Not until..."

"Mitch."

I clamped my hand over my eyes. "My boss."

"And Ellie's dad."

"And Ellie's dad," I repeated, emphasizing the awkwardness. I held a pillow over my face as I said, "And last night, I kissed him."

Amos ripped the pillow off my face. "What?"

I told him about the creep from last night and pretending Mitch was my boyfriend.

"How was the kiss?"

"It was…" That bit of tongue that he slipped in was like a zucchini up the butt. "Awesome."

"This happens. Everyone's coming out story is different. Some people don't realize they're queer until later in life. It's all fluid."

Perhaps Amos had a point. I wasn't scared about coming out as bi. I knew lots of people who were on the rainbow spectrum, and those who weren't were cool. But being bi for Mitch was a whole set of problems.

"Just keep doing what you're doing," he said suggestively.

"Oh, hell no. I'm finally at a job I love. I can't put it in jeopardy by trying to hook up with the boss. I've finally gotten Mitch to tolerate me as an employee." Besides, I doubted Mitch was into me like that. He still saw me as Ellie's fratboy ex. I was the one shamelessly flirting with him, although there were times last night when he gladly reciprocated.

"I guess it's for the best," Amos said. "Mitch may be gay, but he doesn't seem to act on it. I've never heard of him dating anyone. He's demisexual for Stone's Throw Tavern."

Mitch cared deeply about his bar. He'd sacrificed much of his life to keep the lights on. The last thing he needed was an employee trying to cross the line.

Amos retreated to his armchair to grade papers, but a smile never left his face. He was still cracking up over what had happened. So was I.

"I'll go to the store today and pick up a fresh zucchini."

"You better." He looked up again. "May I make a recommendation? If you're going to continue down this path of sexual exploration, go online and invest in an actual dildo. Please don't violate any more of my organic produce. They don't provide the vitamin D you're looking for."

14

CHARLIE

I t was time to set boundaries. I had to keep whatever this was in the pants. For the rest of the week, I used every droplet of willpower to keep things strictly professional with Mitch. No more Chatty Charlie, which was a gateway to Flirty Charlie. No mention of a kiss. Let that water flow directly under a bridge. I came in, made some drinks, punched out, and did not check out my boss once. Even when his chest (and crotch) looked extra beefy in his flannel and jeans.

Mitch seemed to prefer this, too, as he stopped hanging by the bar, making bartending a little less magical.

Friday could not come soon enough. I was going into the city for my friend Asa's birthday bash, the first time back in Manhattan since my downfall. I hadn't heard from anyone and almost wondered if I was completely cut off.

"Have fun this weekend. Don't get blackout drunk," Natasha said with a knowing smirk.

"Be safe," Mitch grumbled out while polishing up pictures around the bar.

I stepped outside into the cold air. I was ready to rage.

A few hours and a train ride later, I found myself in a place that was both familiar and a foreign world: a swanky downtown Manhattan bar filled with young professionals looking to mingle and hook up and use their disposable income to get wasted. I remembered Asa's birthday last year —well, not all of it. But that meant it was a banger. We stayed out all night drinking, then continued through the next day.

My body yawned in protest. A week of being on my feet would do that. I vowed to power through. I could still party like in my days of yore.

My frat brothers Skeeter and Asa yelled in celebration when I arrived, and we all did one massive bear hug.

Asa wore a belt around his waist with a sign hanging over his crotch that said Kiss the Birthday Boy.

Subtle.

"Dude, I haven't seen you in forever," Asa said. We pushed our way through to a corner booth where our other friends hung out with drinks and balloons tied around the coat hook. Birthday balloons never got old. They always elicited joy and wonder.

"Where the fuck have you been living?" Skeeter yelled into my ear. His familiar body spray scent took me back to a million Friday nights just like this, whether at the frat house or prowling the streets of New York. He worked in finance while Asa was in med school.

"I'm up in Sourwood, where Ellie's from. I'm bartend-ing." I waved off his odd look. "It's a long story."

"Nice, man! Smart move slumming it for a while until you come back."

The comment didn't sit well with me. I wasn't slumming anything. I was busting my ass at Stone's Throw. I was going to say just that, but when I opened my mouth, a yawn ripped out of me. My legs and feet also hurt with the week's worth of standing.

Skeeter and Asa shot me skeptical looks. A yawn at a bar on a Friday night was as disrespectful as a fart in church.

"Do you need a nap?" Skeeter asked.

I clamped my lips shut and shook my head no. I was no old man. I could still party like the rest of them. I dug into myself and found my second wind.

"Another round?" I waved my hand around our table. My friends cheered in response. They shouted their drink orders at me, and I remembered each and every one, impressing myself.

"The tab's under Pileggi, Walter, and Stratton," Skeeter said. That was the investment firm where he worked.

"You're putting this on your corporate card?"

"Lilly over there works for one of our clients, so I can technically get this expensed." He seemed full of pride over that loophole. I was reminded of just how flush with cash the finance world was. "Besides, not like you're able to buy rounds anymore on a bartender's salary."

I grumbled at the comment and made my way to the bar. It was three people deep. The bartender was going nonstop. I could only imagine how much he was making tonight. Way more than a busy night at Stone's Throw.

I watched in amazement at his quick hands and feet flitting around the bar, making all of the drinks like a crazy mad scientist. Soon that would be me. The girl next to me ordered a Mai Tai, and I chuckled to myself, thinking of Amos and his friends. That was a fun night, and I'd been totally sober.

"Not sure if you heard, but Serena's dating Rick Shaugnessy," Skeeter informed me when I returned with my hands full of drinks.

Rick and I were on the same team when I started on Wall Street. He loved to play office politics. He was the perfect blend of sociopath and sycophant that got him fast-tracked for promotion.

"Rick's an asshole." Skeeter always elbowed his way to talk to Rick at networking events. "Don't give up, man. You can still win Serena back."

And to that, I...shrugged. I'd never admit this to Skeeter because he'd never believe me, but until he brought her up, I hadn't thought about Serena in a while. That chapter of my life felt a million miles away.

And you were busy obsessing over Mitch.

As the night wore on, drinks turned into shots which turned into more drinks. Skeeter kept putting them in my face, and I didn't want to mellow the party vibe. Despite working around alcohol all the time, my tolerance had plummeted. I was stinking drunk and having a fucking blast. I chatted with people I hadn't seen in months or years and met new people in Asa and Skeeter's expanding social circles who didn't know anything about my former life as a finance bro. I talked and talked, drawing power from social-izing. I chatted about news, TV, and random college shit. I even had an in-depth discussion with Lilly the Loophole about the lasting legacy of Blues Clues. She was hot, too. Blonde, decent rack showed off in a lowcut top, high black heels that showed off her long legs. Somewhere in our discussion, she slipped her hand onto my upper thigh, but my dick had no reaction. Not even a twitch.

Huh. Was I that drunk that I couldn't get it up? That didn't bode well for later.

Sometime after two, we piled into a series of Ubers and wound up at a karaoke bar in the East Village. I belted out "Circle of Life" from *The Lion King*, which devolved into me yelling into my microphone. Skeeter, Asa, and I did the classic "Living on a Prayer" by Bon Jovi, our voices slurring together into warmed-over karaoke soup, but we all thought we were the shit. Lilly dragged me on stage one last time to do a duet of the *Star is Born* song "Shallow." During Lady Gaga's long note, we just yelled into the mic at the top of our lungs, making everyone cover their ears. They still gave us a rousing round of applause. Time dripped by, and we left the bar sometime between night and morning. We frolicked around the city with a kind of childlike glee like it was a factory our dad owned. The city was dark, but people were out, grabbing food and drinking in parks. It wasn't like Sourwood, which was a ghost town after nine, though the peace and quiet of nature had its charms.

Asa, Skeeter, and I lined up against the wall of a post office and took epically long pisses. The girls muttered behind us about how disgusting boys were. Nobody was stopping them from doing the same thing. I was all for equality among the sexes.

"I can't believe you're a fucking bartender." Skeeter chuckled to himself as he scrolled Instagram with his free hand. He sounded like a seal. "Give it a little more time, and I can see about referring you to my company. You may have to start back at entry-level, but it's better than what you're currently doing."

I had a sudden urge to piss all over his designer shoes. The thought of going back to work on Wall Street didn't sound appetizing, nor did leaving Sourwood. As fun as tonight was, I couldn't believe I used to do this all the time. I missed quiet nights hanging with Amos and getting to know regular customers at Stone's Throw.

I pulled up the train schedule to hightail it back to Sourwood, but my head hurt trying to navigate a webpage on my phone. Skeeter slopped his sweaty palm over the screen, the one not holding his dick to pee.

"Nah, man, crash with us."

"Yeah, that makes sense." I rested my head against the wall as a river trailed between my legs. Peeing while drunk was a wonderful feeling.

When I finished, Asa coordinated the Ubers. Lilly swung her arm in mine and leaned into my ear. "I'm on the way to Asa's apartment."

She looked me in the eye, and I knew what she wanted. And she was hot, and I wanted it, too. Only my dick remained dormant. Nothing. What the shit?

She rubbed her soft hand on my arm, and I wanted it to be Mitch's firm grip. I wanted to smell his musky scent, not her flowery perfume.

"Why don't you come back to Skeeter's apartment? He's having some people over," I said. The afterparty continued.

Lilly's lips downturned, and I hung my head as I climbed into the Uber.

———

TEN OF US made it back to Skeeter's apartment, where he poured vodka shots in his tiny kitchen.

"Porterfield, get the fuck in here!"

I was already a drunken mess. Alcohol sloshed in my stomach and danced through the gray matter of my brain. I decided to stay on the couch.

Skeeter poked his head from the kitchen. "Seriously?"

"Unless you want me to puke on your furniture..."

"Man, what's gotten into you? You can do one more shot. For Asa's birthday," he pleaded.

Weren't all the previous shots for Asa's birthday? I

played the good soldier and marched into the kitchen. I didn't want to be accused of being a party pooper. We clinked shot glasses. Fortunately, since I was drunk, the alcohol didn't burn on its way down my throat.

When I stumbled back to the couch, Lilly the Loophole was there to comfort me. She massaged my shoulders.

"You're a lot of fun, Charlie." She nudged her lips up against my ear. "We can have more fun."

A beautiful woman wanting to have sex with me. I'd hit the jackpot.

Right?

"Can we take a raincheck? I'm not feeling so hot." I bolted into the bathroom.

Confession: I wasn't going to hurl.

But I still felt off.

I didn't want the delicate touch of a woman.

I wanted...

The bathroom was especially white, and all the brightness made me dizzy and heightened my drunkenness.

"Porterfield, what the fuck is up with you?" I asked myself in the grimy mirror dotted with dried toothpaste splatter. I wasn't able to give mirror me an answer.

In the haze of liquor, the fog in my head cleared. I came up with a genius, brilliant, foolproof idea.

I dialed Mitch.

15

MITCH

Charlie's name buzzed on my phone. I sat up straight, my body poised and tense.

"Charlie? Is everything okay? Are you all right?"

"Yeah. I'm all right. I'm great! Just hanging out in my friend's bathroom. How are you, Boss?"

"I'm good. I got back from closing up a little bit ago." He sounded like his happy-go-lucky self, allowing me to relax. It was a comfort to hear the lightness in his voice. We'd barely spoken this week, and I knew why.

I had enjoyed our fake kiss a little too much. Fuck, enjoy was too soft a word. It had lit me up inside, and I couldn't find the damn dimmer switch.

"Was it a busy night?"

"Yeah. A bachelorette party came in. Haven't had one of those in a long time." My regulars weren't thrilled about a bunch of squealing girls at first, but they brought a fun energy with them. Soon, they were giving out sashes to random patrons.

"I'm sorry I wasn't there."

"Don't be. Enjoy your weekend with friends. Are you having fun?"

"Totally. It's been a banger. I've had a little too much to drink."

Was it possible to hear someone smile over the phone? Because I did. Charlie's dimpled grin played in my head. I relaxed on my couch, the history show I was watching on mute.

"Did you call just to say hi?" I asked.

"I'm in the bathroom, hiding out." He had the sing-songy, super gregarious tone of a definitely drunk person. "Can I be really honest with you, Boss?"

"Sure." I should've told him to stop. He was trashed and unfiltered, and I was sober and his boss. What honesty would come out? I didn't want him to put himself in an awkward position. "Or maybe it's best that you drink some–"

"It's not the same as it used to be. I kinda miss being at the bar."

Oh. Not what I was expecting. What *was* I expecting?

"You've been through a lot lately. New town, new apartment, new career. You're finding your groove." It made me smile that he loved working at Stone's Throw.

"You always know what to say, Boss."

Hearing him call me Boss made me smile from the inside out every damn time.

"And..." I heard his mouth get closer to his phone. "there's this girl who wants to kiss me, and I don't want to kiss her," he whispered.

"Why not? Is she not pretty?"

"It's because I keep thinking about kissing you."

Shit. My dick jumped in my pants. I readjusted myself but kept my hand there. I'd been unable to think about anything but kissing him.

"Shit. I shouldn't have said that but wait a minute...you kissed me back. You slipped me tongue, Boss. Huh. Why did you kiss me back with your tongue?"

Because I wanted to wrap you in my arms and completely devour *you.*

I couldn't use *that* answer. I knew I had to say something. I couldn't let sleeping dogs lie. "I was trying to protect you from that creepy customer. I'm really sorry, Charlie."

"Why are you sorry?"

"Because I..." I couldn't bring myself to say I didn't mean it, that it was a mistake. It wasn't a mistake, not for me. Fuck. "It wasn't appropriate for me to do. I never wanted to make you feel uncomfortable."

"You didn't. The honest truth is that...I've been thinking about it. A lot." His voice dropped and made my dick throb in my jeans.

"What do you mean 'a lot?'"

Charlie nervously laughed. "I...I can't believe I'm telling you this, and it's only because I'm super duper drunk, but I might've thought about it...while touching..."

My throat went dry. Every cell in my body tensed.

"...Myself."

Holy shit. I was hard as a fucking rock. I wasn't getting to sleep without rubbing one out, that was for sure. My desire for Charlie was now full-blown lust, overpowering all of my good sense.

"Pretend you didn't hear that," he said.

"What if I don't want to pretend?" I chugged the rest of my beer. "How did you touch yourself?"

His breath hitched, as did mine.

"Just regular. Hand on my dick. Good old-fashioned jerking off. I...might be touching myself right now."

Damn. This boy was drunk and horny. I wished he was

here, but I closed my eyes and pictured his warm brown eyes and gorgeous smile.

"Are you touching yourself over your pants?" I kept my voice steady.

"Uh-huh."

We'd already crossed the line by kissing. You couldn't cross the same line again.

"Unbutton your pants, Charlie."

He let out a low chuckle, and at first, I thought he was going to call me out and hang up. But a tiny gasp came over the phone line, and I knew he'd done it.

"Are you hard?" I asked.

"Y—yes."

"Me, too." I stroked myself over my jeans, making out the imprint of my thick shaft.

"Are you touching yourself, too, Boss?"

"I am. Is there a lock on the bathroom door?"

"Yeah."

Seconds later, I heard the lock click. My heart pounded in my ears. I was full of heat and need that had lain dormant for too long.

"What next?" he asked.

"Pull down your pants and underwear." My tongue went thick in my mouth. "I'm going to do the same."

I also made sure my front door was locked and the shades drawn. I lived on a secluded road, but I wasn't taking any chances. I plopped into my armchair, my dick heavy between my legs. I put the phone by my crotch so he could hear my zipper open. I unleashed my cock from my pants. It was fully hard, the head red and engorged.

"Are you touching yourself, Charlie?"

"Yes," he breathed out. "I'm stroking my dick. Are you?"

"Yeah." I grunted as I jerked my stiff dick. I pressed my

eyes shut and imagined Charlie next to me, naked and erect, both of us jacking off. "Fuck, I am so hard."

"Me, too. I'm so hard, Boss." His whispers were pleas.

"Good, fratboy."

"I have an idea," he said. Better than jerking off together over the phone?

Seconds later, he sent two texts. Both pictures.

My eyes and jaw flew open. Fratboy had a nice dick. Bigger than expected. Goddamn he was hard. I made a promise to myself that I would delete these in the morning, but they would live forever in my memory.

"That's so hot. If I were there, I would take you in my mouth."

Was I actually doing this? I couldn't blame alcohol, not the lone beer I had. I was drunk on something else, a hunger I'd ignored for far too long.

"Spit on your hand," I commanded.

He did as instructed.

"Stroke yourself."

"Fuck," he cried out. "This feels so good."

"Charlie..." I licked my hand and stroked my hot dick, the slickness sending fire through my balls.

"Oh, my God. Boss." He had the high-pitched moan of a man on the edge of coming.

"You want to come."

"I'm so hard. Oh, my God." His voice was a desperate whisper. The faint hums of party music sounded in the distance.

"I'm going to come, too. I'm going to think of you as I do."

And then I listened. His voice cracked with a ferocious exhale as he pumped himself dry. It was music to my fucking ears. Holy hell. I would play that sound on repeat until I died.

Not to leave him hanging, I grunted and groaned loudly as I came all over my furry stomach.

We both caught our breaths. Neither of us spoke. Reality slowly seeped onto the line. I took a good look at myself: pants down, dick spent while on the phone with my employee.

"Enjoy your night, fratboy."

16

CHARLIE

I awoke to the sounds of someone throwing up. Bright sunlight streamed through the window of Skeeter's apartment. My feet hung over the arm of his couch, and a small blanket was draped over my fully clothed self. A string of saliva dribbled onto the throw pillows that supported my aching head.

The couch had no back pillows. I lurched up and found Asa sprawled on the floor, using them as a mattress.

The hangover was real. My body ached something fierce, but then I thought back to all the fun times last night.

All of them.

I sat up straight, which sent a pounding into my head. Last night...

Did I...with my boss...

Maybe it was a dream. *Oh, please, Lord, let it be a dream.*

"What the fuck?" Skeeter yelled from the bathroom. "Who jizzed on my shower curtain?"

Shit.

A LITTLE WHILE LATER, after staying quiet and letting one of the other party guests get blamed for Jizzgate, Skeeter, Asa, and I threw on some clothes and headed to the corner diner for a carb-filled breakfast to soak up the booze.

The diner had the comforting smells of coffee, grease, and eggs that made my stomach do flips like an eager puppy. I hadn't been out to breakfast in weeks. I made oatmeal at Amos's condo to save money.

Skeeter ordered a round of coffee before we even sat down. Like all New York diners, the place was packed with a steady stream of customers. My eyes caught the shelf of liquor behind the counter—diners had bars? A wave of nausea hit me. I hadn't drank that much in a long time, and my body was adjusting.

Asa chugged his water, his body crying out for hydration.

"Birthday boyyyyy." I drummed my fists over Asa's back.

"Dude, last night was crazy," Asa said. Fortunately, the waitress swooped in to refill all of our waters and coffees.

"Epic." I let the caffeine fairy save me. Diner coffee had its own distinct taste.

"I can't believe I'm twenty-seven. If I were a rock star, this would be the year I die." Asa referred to the eerie coincidence of famous musicians dying in their twenty-seventh year. Cobain, Winehouse, Hendrix.

"Fortunately, you're a boring med student and not a rock star."

"I play a mean air guitar."

"You suck at air guitar, too," Skeeter said.

We all looked wrecked but in a good way. It reminded me of lazy Saturdays and Sundays around the frat house.

"I'm so hungry. I want to get rolled in a cocoon of pancakes and have to eat my way out." I looked forward to crashing once I got home this afternoon. Hell, I'd probably take a nap on the train.

A weird lull hit our table. Usually, I could find something to talk about, especially with my friends, but my brain couldn't come up with any suitable topics. Discussing the *phone sex* I had with my boss was off the table.

"Lilly was into you last night," Asa said.

Oh, right. There was that.

"She texted me this morning asking for your number." He raised his eyebrows, looking at me for the green light.

Fuck. What was wrong with me? She was beautiful. I would've hit that last night, no question under normal circumstances. And under normal circumstances, I wouldn't have had phone sex with my boss. I cringed at the hazy memories from the bathroom...which then made me hard...which made me cringe more. It was a vicious cycle.

"That's all right," I said about exchanging digits with Lily.

"She's hot," Skeeter said, almost taking offense. He dumped his usual mountain of sugar into his coffee.

"Beauty is in the eye of the beholder." I poured a dash of milk into mine.

"What the fuck does that mean?"

I had no fucking idea. I woke up this morning with a raging boner and thoughts of Mitch on top of me, jerking both of us off in his large hand. What the fuck did *that* mean?

"Do you have someone up in Sour Patch Kids?" Asa shot Skeeter a gossipy look.

"Sourwood," I growled. "And no."

"C'mon. You need a rebound to help you forget about Serena."

"Who?" I shot out before remembering my ex-girlfriend. I should've called her for phone sex last night. Why didn't I?

Asa and Skeeter's eyebrows jumped to the ceiling.

"I guess she's already forgotten," Asa said.

"Yeah, guess so," Skeeter echoed, though there was an odd look of frustration he wore, like how dare I not obsess over my hot ex-girlfriend.

"I want to focus on my job."

"Concentrating on your high-pressure career as a beer wench?" Skeeter snorted as he scanned the menu.

I pulled up train times on my phone.

"There's a train leaving at eleven this morning, so I'm going to head out after breakfast."

"What? This was only part one of the birthday extravaganza. We're going paintballing this afternoon. You want to miss out on that?" Skeeter could be a pain in the ass about plans and people flaking. He took it so personally. "You love paintballing."

That was true. I was pro-gun control but also pro-paintballing. I didn't yet know how to square up those views in my head. We were all full of contradictions, like me being straight yet dying to jack it in person with a guy whose hotness gave me freaking goosebumps.

"We haven't seen you in forever," Asa said, laying on the guilt. "How often do we all get to hang out?"

It wasn't as if they were coming to visit me in Sourwood, even with the lure of a free drink. "I have a shift tonight."

"Workaholic." Skeeter rolled his eyes.

Asa's face scrunched up into a weird look. "I've never known you to bail on a good time."

The waitress came with plates lined up her arm. She plopped a glorious dish of golden pancakes in front of me, and my delirious hunger scrambled my train of thought.

Between my friends and the familiar diner smells, an overwhelming sense of home came over me.

"Just call in sick," Skeeter said as he poured hot sauce on his eggs. "Who hasn't called in sick before? That's what those days are there for."

Did I have sick days at this job? Unlike Skeeter, I didn't work at a big company where my absence wouldn't be noticed.

"My boss called in sick for the first time in a year, and he was on the verge of death," I said, slightly exaggerating.

"What's gotten into you? I never had to pull you back to a party, especially one for a friend." Skeeter's words cut at me like the knives used to cut limes for tequila shots last night. "Did you have some kind of super early mid-life crisis? You lost your job, then all of a sudden left the city and shacked up in that small town serving drinks. The dust has settled on Demeter. Have you even been looking for a new job? Sent your resume to any places?"

I shook my head no.

Skeeter jabbed at his eggs like he wanted them dead. Causing drama was not in my playbook, but I had to stand up for myself, for Stone's Throw, for Sourwood.

"Who are you?" His eyes squinted into a glare.

"We're not in the frat house anymore. Things change."

"That they do. You used to be fun, Charlie."

I came to a conclusion I realized I'd been avoiding all weekend. Did we have anything binding us together besides college memories and getting drunk?

"I guess I used to be." I left my pancakes half-eaten. I threw a twenty on the table, wished Asa a happy birthday, and definitively ended this chapter of my life.

17

MITCH

I spent my Sunday morning being a good friend and helping Cal stage his house for buyers. No longer could a person sell their house because it was a house. Solid foundation, good craftsmanship? Nobody cared. It had to be staged to look pretty on real estate sites. New furniture had to be brought in, and walls had to be repainted to better help buyers imagine themselves in the house.

If I ever sold my house, I would never deal with that shit.

Cal had lived in his parents' old house that he inherited when they passed. Emphasis on the old part, and he wasn't the neatest person. So there was a lot of outdated shit— wallpaper, old light fixtures—which would make the house a tougher sell. At least, this was all according to Cary, his realtor, who had the attention span of a pixie stick. He suggested they bring in new furniture to make the house look "sexier and modern."

But we were in charge of lugging it inside.

"This is going to transform your house. It's going to sell, sell, sell!" Cary buzzed around the house, alternating between texting on his phone and scrolling on his iPad. He was a gay man with a slim waist, pink tie, and espresso pumping through his veins.

Cal and I hauled a taupe couch through the doorway. "And then what happens once it does sell?" I asked. "Who moves all this shit out?"

"Well, all homeowners are responsible for moving their own furniture out, as per the agreement." Cary let out a patronizing chuckle.

"Great," I said with a strained breath. Cal and I lowered the couch against the far wall of the living room. "Hey Cal, am I getting a cut of the sale?"

"Oh, Mitch. You should have your own stand-up set because you are too funny." Cal pushed the couch against the wall. I helped him so he didn't give himself a hernia. "You're doing this out of the goodness of your heart because that's what friends do."

He had me there. Cal had helped me throughout the years, recording ads for the tavern for free, driving Ellie before she had her license. But all that seemed like peanuts compared to all the furniture hauling I was doing.

I hated moving. Absolutely hated it.

The one saving grace was that all of the staged furniture was light (because it was cheaply made!).

Russ carried in an oversized end table, maneuvering so it didn't bang against the door.

"Love that. Love it, love it, love it," Cary said, making another note on his iPad while taking a call on his Bluetooth.

"I'm taking bets on whether Cary sleeps or just takes a series of power naps," Russ said.

I let out a laugh. I liked Russ. He was like me, serious and no-nonsense but perhaps a little more uptight. Somehow, he and Cal made it work.

We moved the rest of the living room and kitchen furniture, then took a break before bringing in the beds and nightstands for the upstairs bedrooms. Between moving Cal and Josh in with Russ, moving his furniture to storage, and moving this staged shit in, I felt like I've been moving furniture in this house for months. Cal was going to put me in an early grave all for the sake of escrow.

Russ ran out for sandwiches and brought them back. Cary said we couldn't sit on the couch, but I gave him a look daring him to fuck with me, and he backed off.

"Thanks again for helping with this, Mitch," Russ said. "Leo had a bunch of city council meetings."

"Leo hates doing manual labor, so I'd take his excuse with a grain of salt. He was the only kid I knew who could consistently get out of gym class." I tore into my sandwich, ravenously hungry.

Cal came in and passed around sodas and waters. "Last Monday was so much fun! I told Russ we should go to Musical Monday tomorrow, too."

"Yeah, the place was packed." I'd never seen that many people in my bar on a non-holiday Monday maybe ever.

"I forgot how much I loved musical theater," Russ said.

"On the car ride home, Russ admitted he loved *Cats*." Cal shook his head.

"I said it didn't deserve all the flack it gets."

Cal stuck his thumb out at Russ and gave me a *can you believe this guy* smirk. Russ smacked it away. They were a cute couple, though a flicker of jealousy lit up in me, wondering if I'd ever have that kind of cutesy shorthand with someone.

My thoughts immediately circuited to a certain someone I should not be thinking about.

"Your bartender also did a great job," Cal said.

Dammit.

Charlie entered my brain, and my jeans tightened as I thought about what we did Friday night. I crossed a line. I crossed a line real bad.

But in my defense, Charlie crossed it first.

Would he even show up at work today? Did he remember what happened? What if he was only joking, and I was the only one who actually jerked off on the phone. I'd spent the past quarter-century practically monk-like, then a cute fratboy smirks at me, and I'm having phone sex.

I looked up and found Cal wearing a satisfied grin, like a kid who got to say ass when talking about donkeys.

"What?" I uttered.

"I said your bartender did a good job. That was all."

"Not this again." I rolled my eyes, steeling myself from thinking about our kiss and my out-of-control tongue. "He's straight. He's my employee."

"Straight is a relative concept," Cal said.

"You say that about everyone," Russ said. "The whole world isn't queer."

"I know, but I'm working on it." Cal took a bite of his sandwich. "I looked over a few times when you both were behind the bar, and it seemed like he was giving you the look."

"What look?" I tried not to sound too curious.

"*The look.*"

"You were drunk, Cal."

"I know what I saw."

I wanted to believe Cal, but I also...didn't. Charlie was flirty with everyone. He was a fun, social guy. He flirted with customers, male and female, gay and straight. I couldn't let his personality trick me into thinking of something that wasn't there.

Even though we kissed. And phone sexed. And it was wonderful. For me.

I hung my head.

"What is it, buddy?" Cal rubbed my back with concern.

I shouldn't be talking about this aloud, but I could trust the guys, and I needed to get this off my chest. "We kissed."

Cal dropped his sandwich, but Russ swooped in and saved it from splattering on the borrowed couch.

Before Cal could freak out, I explained the situation that precipitated our lips meeting. It wasn't born out of passion but rather saving Charlie from a creep.

"How was it?" Cal sat at the edge of his seat.

"It was...good."

Cal didn't ask for more. He could see the real answer written on my face.

"Is that all that happened?"

I couldn't share the phone sex revelation. I was still processing it myself. So I answered his question with a head nod.

"Then that's not so bad," Russ said.

"Was there anything bad about it?" Cal asked his boyfriend. "He got to make out with a hot young stud."

"We didn't make out. It was one kiss," I clarified.

Russ looked at Cal like he was crazy, a normal occurrence for them. "Was there anything bad about it? Uh, yes. Charlie is an employee. You kissed your employee. Your straight employee who might not have pushed back out of fear of losing his job. That might be 'hot' on TV," he said with air quotes. "but in real life, not so much."

"You have no imagination," Cal said. "Which I can understand because there aren't any hot people in your office."

"Yes, there is!"

"Who?"

"There's Jaron the Intern."

"Seriously?" Cal went to respond but had a change of heart. "Yeah, I guess Jaron is attractive."

"Have you seen his TikTok?"

"You're following him on TikTok? Wait, you're on TikTok?" Cal had a weird mix of disgust, horror, and intrigue swirling in his eyes. "We'll get into that later. But back to you, Mitch."

I held up my hand. During this lover's quarrel, I had a moment of realization about what to do about Charlie to ensure this situation didn't blow up in my face.

"I need to get to the bar. Good luck with selling the house."

———

I HOLED up in my office while Charlie came in for his shift. I was nervous about seeing him, but I was the boss. The man in charge. I had to make this right and cut off whatever dangerous path we were on.

"Hey." I descended the stairs.

Charlie gave me a big smile back, but the sheer nervousness behind his eyes was very obvious. "Hey, Boss."

I had a flashback to him calling me boss on the phone.

"How was your time in the city?"

"Good." His voice squeaked.

It wasn't good. His boss took advantage of him while drunk.

"Look, Charlie."

And he did look at me. Those big, brown puppy dog eyes stared at me, giving me their full, undivided attention —and taking my words with them. My mind went blank, and in the place of a practiced speech was the sound of Charlie coming through the phone lines.

"Boss, I am really sorry I kissed you last Monday. Man, that was hella awkward to say." He tossed in a self-effacing laugh, which did nothing to lessen the sting. "Thank you for going with it. I panicked. I remember some sorority girls I knew said they wore wedding rings out at bars because it was the only way to keep guys from hitting on them, which is such a bullshit, sexist thing of our society. Like a woman can't be single just to be single. Such horseshit. But I guess I thought if that creep knew I was dating someone, he'd back off. And you were the closest guy there. You came outside at the perfect time." He shoved his hands in his pockets and balanced on his heels again. He had it all figured out. "I'm really sorry I did that. And I'm sorry for drunk dialing you over the weekend. Can we just forget...all of that?"

His eyes were practically pleading for me to wipe my memory clean. His entire face was a palette of desperation, begging me to never bring up those moments again.

I gave him a tight nod, hiding the fact that inside, my mind and heart deflated.

"It was totally inappropriate. I promise it will not happen again." He sounded definitive and confident, each word a fresh kick in the groin.

"Agreed," I said, the only word I could get out.

"Just please, let's never talk about it again. I really like working here. I don't want to fuck up another job."

"We'll never speak of it again." I wanted to be sick, but I held all that emotion back. I wasn't going to put that shit on him.

Silence hung in the air.

"I guess I'll go back upstairs."

"Cool. Should be decent traffic today with hockey on."

Once I made it upstairs, I let out a huge exhale. My chest clamped tight, and I heaved for breath. Why was I letting this kid mess me up like this? This was why I avoided relationships; they got in the way of more important parts of my life. I had payroll and orders and planning. I didn't have time to have all the feels, as Penny loved to say.

And if I did want a boyfriend, there were plenty of guys out there I could date. Guys with hair on their chests and years of life under their belt. Why did I have to go and get feelings for the overgrown fratboy who had zero interest in men, least of all me?

I overheard him joking around with Penny downstairs, and my heart, against my consent, did a somersault at the lighthearted lilt in his voice.

Charlie promised that this would not happen again. And at that moment, I made a promise to myself, too: this gooey shit clogging up my heart ended *now*.

18

MITCH

Over the next month, I kept my promise to myself. I laid off flirting with Charlie and putting myself in positions where I would be tempted, which wound up being a lot. No more squeezing behind the bar with him. I bought a footstool so he could reach the glasses up top. I made sure we didn't wind up alone at the end of a shift.

I had to be the boss and keep my distance. Back to how we used to be when I had little faith in him.

It was excruciating. The more I distanced myself from Charlie, the more vivid my dreams about him were. But it was for the best. He turned out to be a great employee, and I didn't want to lose him because of my perpetual erection.

Fortunately, I had Ellie's wedding to look forward to. She and Tim had taken the reins of wedding planning and were creating whatever Instagram-ready event they had up their sleeve. At Leo's urging, I treated myself to a new, tailored suit that I wouldn't be busting out of. While I was excited about the wedding, I had a bit of dread, as I'd be attending solo. Guests would see Hannah and her new husband, and the father of the bride would be by himself.

A week before the wedding, Ellie called me in tears. She showed up at the house thirty minutes later, tears streaking her face. I immediately put up a pot of coffee. Seeing my daughter upset was agony, but it gave me a chance to be her hero once again.

"Ellie Bear, what is it?" We sat at the kitchen table overlooking the steady drizzle misting the woods.

"Empire Catering canceled."

"Your caterer canceled on you?" In my three decades of working in the food and service industry, I had heard of a lot of shit. Caterers canceling was extremely rare, and I'd never heard of them canceling a week before an event. "Why?"

"They double booked without realizing."

"Did you book first?"

"I don't know." She wiped her nose on her sleeve despite a tissue box being front and center. "But Tim saw a video they posted on their TikTok celebrating that they booked a last-minute celebrity birthday party."

"And he thinks you guys got bumped so they could kiss celebrity ass?"

Her eyes went cold. "It'll be incredible publicity for them."

She was right. We lived in a famewhore culture where the whiff of a business being connected to a famous person sent sales skyrocketing. Years ago, Daniel Craig stopped in for a drink at Stone's Throw, and when word got out, we had our best month of the year.

"You have a contract, though."

"They're refunding our deposit."

"They should help you find a new vendor."

"They're not going to do that." She rubbed her face, smearing red all over. Sometimes when she cried, she reminded me of that little baby rubbing her eyes for sleep.

"You were right, okay? They were trendy but not dependable. We wanted to have a cool wedding, one of those weddings people share pics about on Pinterest. You should see some of the weddings we've gone to. Everything is so curated and artisan. I can't keep up!"

"You don't have to. Who cares what other people are doing? You're getting married because you love Tim, not to impress random idiots online."

"I know, I know." She didn't need any more salt rubbed in this wound. "I don't know what to do. I have a list of vendors. The ones I've called are booked. Should we postpone?"

"No." I put my hand on hers and made her meet my eye. I was really going to do this, wasn't I? It was best not to think too hard. Being your daughter's hero came with downsides, which I would think about later. "I've got you covered. I can cater it."

"Dad, no. That's so much work and only a week away. I promise that wasn't why I came up here."

But the excitement and relief had already crested in her face. There was no taking it back. My daughter deserved a great wedding.

"I couldn't. We'll find a solution."

"I can do it. I've catered events before." And this way, I could stay busy at the wedding and avoid those pitiful looks.

"I'm paying you, and I won't hear another word about it." She pointed her finger at me, and I sat up straight. She unleashed her courtroom voice. "The same fee I was going to pay Empire."

"Deal. Because of the tight turnaround, you don't have many options with food choices. It'll be what's on our regular menu."

"I love Stone's Throw food. So does Tim." She pulled me

into a hug, her thin arms stretching around my neck. She barreled my cheek with kisses. "Dad, seriously. I can't thank you enough. I know we messed up."

"You didn't. You better write reviews of Empire Catering and plaster the web with them so they don't do this to other people."

She made notes on this development in her phone while I cataloged a growing to-do list in my head. I didn't trust technology to handle all my tasks.

"Who will you have to help?" she asked.

"I can see if Natasha is available to run point. I'd given her the weekend off since I was closing the bar to attend." I pet her hand.

"What about Charlie to bartend?"

Charlie, as in the guy I couldn't stop thinking about despite my active work to avoid him? That guy? Just hearing his name sent a curl up my spine down to my toes.

"What about him?"

"Would he be available to work? You said he's been doing a great job. I'm sure he'd love to be there, shit-talking with everyone behind the bar."

Charlie did enjoy that. He could chitchat with anyone, weaving small talk from thin air. I was not blessed with that gene.

"He's likely busy."

"Could you see if he might want to work the wedding?"

"Are you sure he'd want to? Would it be uncomfortable for him to be there but not as a guest?" I threw out every excuse I could find, but Ellie's suggestion made the most sense.

"You said yourself he was doing great, really stepping up. He could be your right-hand man."

I ran through the mental list of other possible people.

My other bartender was going out of town that weekend. Most of the good for-hire bartenders were already booked by this point. I didn't want strangers working with me on this important event. Everything kept coming back to one answer.

"I'll ask him," I said.

"No need." Ellie typed away on her phone. "I just texted him. He said he'd love to do it."

I internalized the world's biggest sigh. This wedding was going to push me to my limit of restraint. "All right then."

19

CHARLIE

We had one week to pull off a wedding. No problemo! If the big dude in the sky could create the earth in a week, we could throw together dinner and drinks.

Mitch and I met to go over what would be involved. He had drafted an insanely detailed list of all our responsibilities and what we had to do to prepare. My insides were screaming about all this close proximity with him, but on the outside, I stayed cool. I had to. I had two very inappropriate strikes with my boss. One more, I was out on my ass.

I reminded myself, like a morning mantra, that these feelings in my head weren't reciprocated. Ever since the phone sex debacle, Mitch had kept things strictly business. Hell, he pretty much avoided me at the bar. I knew my employment with him was on thin ice if I tried that kind of shenanigans again.

Noted. Unfortunate, but noted.

These days were the busiest of my life. I thought planning a fraternity formal was a lot of work, but it didn't hold a candle. Originally, I was brought on to serve drinks, but my role kept growing. I took on more jobs as he became stretched thinner. I wanted to prove to him and Ellie that I was serious about this job.

Mitch put me in charge of compiling an inventory list and curating a menu of what drinks we'd serve. We weren't able to bring the entire bar to a remote location, so we had to devise a limited drink menu. I came up with a list of beer and wine choices I knew our friends enjoyed, a mix of low cost yet delicious libations that made us feel classy but not broke.

Ellie wanted her event to feel special and curated, and that gave me the idea to look into craft beer. In this area of America, craft breweries were popping up like Starbucks franchises. From talking with craft brewers and distributors, I learned that there was a glut of supply, which we could leverage for good deals. I researched local craft breweries in the area and put together a beer tasting for Ellie and Tim at the bar. Natasha helped me make it all fancy—tablecloths and a pretty sign for the tasting. Ellie posted about it on social media, which earned me lots of points with Mitch.

Mitch nodded tightly and commended my good idea from afar. No back pats or flirty smiles. Which was for the best.

Next was working with the distributors to lock in prices and inventory for the hard alcohol. To save money, Mitch had the idea of buying the non-alcoholic mixers in bulk from Costco. Waters, soda, juices. That could be a better deal, and we'd have an easier time returning what we didn't use. We also found other foods there that we could use in the menu. I couldn't help being a little kid and zooming through the store on the massive cart. Even though Mitch had reverted to his quiet, quasi-grumpy self, we still managed to have a good time together.

He talked through deals and sales with me, the next level of the service industry beyond serving drinks. I watched his business acumen at work as he negotiated prices and asked thoughtful questions. Mitch wasn't a small talker, but when he did talk, he made it count. He didn't bullshit. Care and authenticity layered everything he said. He remembered the names of guys' kids and wives and boats and where they went on vacation. His mind was the NSA, but like in a non-invasive way.

The catering equipment Mitch had in stock couldn't handle the older, smaller kitchen at the venue. The ovens weren't big enough to keep food warm, and there wasn't enough counter space. Mitch said that was the price of choosing the ambiance of an Instagram-friendly stately manor over the function of a banquet hall. We would have to buy special equipment to accommodate; Ellie did not seem to care about the price.

I used my internet sleuthing skills and found a restaurant in Nyack that was having a going out of business firesale. Everything that wasn't nailed to the wall was up for grabs. We managed to get gleaming trays and buffet stations on the cheap. I found a guy online with a portable oven he'd rent us. Why he had one in his backyard was a question not worth asking. It worked. Mitch accompanied me to the pickup, and we gave each other near-constant side-eye. This guy seemed like a hoarder. We made the sale and got the hell out of there as fast as we could, laughing about it all the way home.

I missed his laugh, missed his smile. All these fun moments tugged at my heart. I ran myself ragged on top of bartending, but there was nobody I'd rather do it with than Mitch. I found new facets of him that I tucked away in my memories. The way he said *bullseye* to himself when he found a good deal. The way he lip-synched under his breath to songs on the radio, thinking I couldn't see him. They were each small glimpses into a man who refused to let people in. And I resisted every urge to bang at the door.

After closing down the bar one night, I trudged up to Mitch's office, where he sat on the couch going over the final menu. I'd been up since six in the morning doing wedding coordination, then worked a full shift. I could barely keep my eyes open. Yet Mitch plowed away like the Energizer bunny.

I plopped down on the couch next to him. The soft leather cushions pulled me into a hug.

"I think we did it." Mitch looked up at me over his glasses, which gave him Clark Kent vibes. "I think we actually pulled it off."

"Wedding of the Century?"

"Maybe."

"What was your wedding like?" I leaned my head back on the couch. My whole body exhaled with comfort.

"Let's see. We were crammed into the judge's chambers at the local courthouse. I wore the one suit I saved for church and funerals, and my mom burst out crying during our vows but not out of happiness. I then ran into the bathroom and threw up."

I closed my eyes and smiled. I was too tired to laugh.

"Ellie's wedding will be slightly better."

"Not by much. There'll probably be someone who throws up." I let out another yawn. They rolled out of me like thunder. "When are you coming in tomorrow?"

"Opening at eleven."

"I can't believe you do this all the time. What about during the wedding? What's going to happen to the bar?"

"I'm closing it for the whole weekend. First time in my

life." He had hesitation in his eyes. When the bar wasn't open, he wasn't making money.

"Nervous?"

"Always. That's the life of being an owner." Dark circles rung his eyes. He had a coat of exhaustion to him at all times, the stress of the job compressing him.

"How do you do it?" I couldn't keep a goldfish alive, let alone a business.

He seemed as stumped as I was. "You just take it one day at a time, I guess." He picked at something on his shoe, the wheels in his head turning. He was a constant mystery in that way, one I kept trying to unravel from a safe distance. "I've been thinking about selling."

That jolted me from my exhaustion. "Selling Stone's Throw?"

I couldn't imagine Mitch not here. It was as if he were going to sell his internal organs.

He exhaled a breath. "Maybe it's time. I've been working here for thirty years, twenty-three years at the helm. Twenty-three years of keeping this little place afloat. Twenty-three years of fighting back against big chains and the next hot place. Twenty-three years of keeping up staff and benefits and payroll."

"Hasn't this place been in your family for generations?"

"Two generations. My dad started it because he couldn't think of anything better to do, and it was a slog when he was around. We had tight months, and I see it now that I'm older, how stressed he was and how much he tried to hide it from us kids."

I appreciated how open Mitch was being and that he chose to share this with me. It wasn't often people let others in. So I trod lightly.

"How much have you thought about it?"

"It's something that's always in the back of my mind. But it's been getting louder lately."

"With the wedding?"

"She's a grown woman with her own life." He sat up and groaned, rubbed his back. "Maybe it's time I got one of mine, too."

I didn't know how to respond. This was some real adult shit, the kind that simmered for decades. I was out of my depth, unable to say something meaningful. I didn't want him to sell, but this wasn't about me.

"You're the kind of person who puts a lot of thought into what he does. Whatever you decide, it will be the right choice."

The corners of his lips curved into a relaxed smile as what I said seemed to resonate. I loved talking with people, but these kinds of conversations, the real real shit, was tough for me. In my family, we didn't talk about things. We talked around them and fortressed ourselves in small talk.

It was time to leave, but my body refused to move. It had been fully annexed by exhaustion, slumping deeper into the couch. In what seemed instantaneous, my eyes lost their fight and drooped close. When I woke up sometime later, I had wound up nudged against Mitch's chest, fixed in the crook of his arm, our breaths in sync. It reminded me of lounging on the life-size teddy bear I had in my room growing up, which I totally got rid of before high school.

I wanted to live in this moment forever, enveloped by Mitch's warmth. His beard rustled the top of my forehead. His body felt so good, the ideal mix of hard and soft. How could I ever go back to sleeping on a mattress when Mitch's torso seemed molded for me?

Mitch tipped his head down, his beard prickling down my cheek. I looked up at his half-closed eyes, his pink lips.

I sat up, letting my smooth cheek nuzzle against his beard. Closer to his lips. I told myself I was readjusting to get more comfortable. I told myself lies.

And speaking of readjusting, my pants were getting very tight in the crotch area.

I was being a troublemaker, tiptoeing dangerously close to a line I swore I wouldn't cross. It was the exhaustion that wore me down...and the feeling of being in Mitch's arms.

I "got more comfortable" and turned my cheek slightly, moving my lips a bit closer to his. His broad chest rose and fell with slumbery breaths, whereas my heart was beating like a madman. His exhales sent chills over my skin.

We were so damn close. I shifted a touch closer, closing a touch more of the gap between our lips. We were fully cheek to cheek. *Oh, I fell asleep like this*, I could say the next morning.

I was scared and also desperate to keep going. But Mitch was asleep.

Or was he? Because when I glimpsed down, there was one big part of him fully awake. Pressing against his jeans.

I feasted on the sight. But I was a good boy and kept my arms inside the moving vehicle. Even though I wanted to grab that elephant trunk.

I leaned back and tried to let myself enjoy resting cheek-to-cheek. The feeling didn't last long. Mitch turned his head and pressed his lips to mine.

The kiss was magical. Like Disney magical. His hot breath danced on my tongue. His mouth guided me as he kissed me with more force, lighting off a row of fireworks within my chest. I softly moaned into him.

I grabbed his throbbing dick through his pants. I'd never touched another man's dick before. It was harder and warmer than expected; the heat burned through the denim.

I stroked him over his pants, felt him get rock hard under my touch as he grunted into my mouth. My fingers found his zipper and pulled down.

Our eyes remained closed, our bodies still as if we were both pretending we were still asleep. This kiss was everything, reaching into the deepest part of myself.

And then it was over.

Mitch leaned back and shifted away in his seat. "Charlie...we can't."

It was like someone had turned on the brightest lights in the joint. He stood up and zipped up his fly.

I opened my mouth to say something, but nothing swirling in my chest could be properly translated into words. I gave Mitch the most awkward head nod in history and bolted.

20

MITCH

I had to give credit where due: the estate where Ellie and Tim booked their wedding was beautiful. Breathtaking. One of FDR's old houses, it was situated on a sprawling hill overlooking a valley of blooming trees with glimpses of the sparkling Hudson River in the background. The old Victorian mansion had a wraparound veranda and large windows looking out into the valley. Springtime in New York was risky for an outdoor wedding; the weather report said there was a more than fifty percent chance of rain. We had an outdoor plan but also the main ballroom available if we had to be indoors. The two upstairs floors had been converted to hotel rooms, complete with an old-fashioned check-in desk downstairs that had mail slots for each room with a key. The overflow of guests for the wedding would stay at a small one-story motel across the street.

Ellie flitted about the venue when I arrived. She, Tim, and their friends got to work decorating the space in their faux-bohemian style. The DIY wedding had a charm to it, as each piece meant something. The mismatched globe centerpieces Ellie had found by scouring Goodwill shops and

Facebook Marketplace symbolized their love of travel. Each
guest received a passport holder when they checked in,
complete with itinerary and table seating.

It hadn't hit me yet that my only daughter was getting
married this weekend. I was in catering mode. By the grace
of God, we had pulled off all preparations. I roped in the
Single Dads Club to help with last-minute food prep over
the past two days.

Charlie and I drove up together in the truck holding all
the food and equipment. We didn't talk much during the
drive, mostly going over the logistics of the event. I kept it
business only and avoided the strangeness that hung
between us. Charlie didn't bring it up either, and he seemed
distant, like maybe he regretted it.

I wanted to tell him how much I thought about what
happened on the couch, how his lips and hands brought me
to life and were a drop of water in a desert. But dammit, I
shouldn't have given in, no matter how badly I craved his
body. I was going to hold it together this weekend, and then
we'd have a talk when we returned to Sourwood. Maybe
Stone's Throw wasn't the best place for him.

"I'll start bringing in the kitchen equipment and set it up
so the food can stay warm tomorrow," Charlie said when we
arrived. He was all business. Didn't even end his sentence
with Boss. He hopped out of the truck and immediately
began unloading. His muscles flexed under the weight of
the equipment he hauled out.

"I'm going to check in," I said when he came back for
another haul. "I can check you in, too."

His face dropped. "Oh."

"What?"

"I thought you were booking rooms for the staff." The
way he said "staff" lanced my heart. It was almost clinical.

"I..." Oh shit. As organized as I was, there was always one thing I forgot. One task that slipped through my mental cracks. In all the craziness of preparing, I had only booked a room for myself as the father of the bride. Charlie had evolved into my right-hand man for this operation, so he'd need to stay on the premises, too. "I'm going to check in and figure it out. Keep unloading."

He didn't say anything, just went back to doing his job. He seemed mad at me. Just what I needed this weekend. Being a responsible adult wasn't fun for me, either. I wanted to keep going on the couch. I wanted to twist him into a fucking pretzel.

But we couldn't.

Inside the lobby, a wiry man in a suit manned the check-in desk, which was bookended with fresh cut flowers.

"Mitch Dekker. Checking in."

His face lit up. "Ah, Mr. Dekker. Father of the bride. Welcome, welcome. We have you booked for two nights in a room with a king-size bed and a lovely view of the valley." I was already looking forward to collapsing on the bed at the end of the night. He turned to his cubicles of keys and plucked one from the center. He clacked away on his computer, confirming my reservation and payment. "Excited about this weekend?"

"I'm also working the event, so it's hard to get excited just yet. I have a party to pull off."

"It'll be wonderful. It's going to be a lovely evening, clear skies." He handed over a goody bag of snacks and water that Ellie had put together for guests three nights ago. "For you."

"Uh, listen, I forgot to book a room for my employee who's working the event." It sounded even stupider when I said it aloud. I chuckled so he'd maybe find it funny. "Do you have any extra rooms available?"

He made an exaggerated frown face that veered from customer service to kindergarten teacher. "I'm sorry, Mr. Dekker. We are all booked up for the big event." His eyebrows jumped, but I did not share his excitement about the big event currently.

"You have no rooms? None?"

"It's not a large space."

"What about the motel across the street?"

"Let me check." He called them and relayed the conversation to me in more exaggerated facial reactions. He hung up and frowned.

"They're all booked up, too?"

"For—"

"The big event."

"Precisely."

Shit. I wrapped my knuckles on the desk, wracking my brain for an alternative idea. Perhaps he could stay with a friend or stay with another guest he knew? But I didn't know what their situations were, who they were bringing. He was integral to set up, so I couldn't ask him to drive up and then home two days in a row.

I flicked my eyes at the hotel employee who clacked away at his computer. Was he looking for rooms or avoiding more bad news?

"Do you have an extra key for my room?" I asked, resigned.

"I do." He handed it over.

We could both fit on a king-size bed. Charlie wasn't a huge guy. *Perfect for spooning.*

"You can put him on my reservation. Charlie Porterfield."

"Shacking up with your bartender?" Cal appeared behind me. "Checking in. Last name Hogan."

"We're not shacking up. I forgot to book Charlie a room."
I was going to have to explain myself all weekend, wasn't I?

"Interesting. I wonder why."

I ignored his raised eyebrows.

"You are all set, Mr. Dekker," the front desk manager
said. "I have you and Mr. Porterfield sharing your room."

"What's this now?"

Ugh, of course, Leo and Dusty showed up at this exact
moment.

"Nothing, Leo."

"Mitch and Charlie are shacking up together, but it's *only*
because Mitch forgot to book him his own room." Cal
smothered his words in sarcasm.

"Interesting," Dusty said. "I wonder why."

"And I'm guessing there's just one bed," Leo said, having
way too much fun at my expense.

"Do you have a cot we could put in the room?" I asked
the front desk manager, practically brimming with
desperation.

Another big frown. "We do not. But I have a crib?"

"For a grown man?" I shot back.

"Whatever gets your rocks off," Cal said.

"We'll stick with the king-size bed. I'll sleep in the bath-
tub." I swiped my keys from the desk. "You guys are
assholes," I grumbled as I left.

———

THE ROOM WAS SMALL, and ninety percent of the square
footage was taken up by the bed.

It was comically too big for this room. The TV hung
on the wall, and a pitiful-looking desk cowered in the
corner.

I looked behind me at Charlie, who studied the furnishings with a stone-faced eye.

"I feel like a damn idiot for not remembering to book you your own room. There are no other vacancies here or across the street."

"It's cool." He sauntered past me and hung up his garment bag in the closet. He threw his gym bag with the rest of his stuff at the bottom.

"It's a big bed," I said in a half-hearted attempt to find a silver lining.

"We'll be so exhausted we'll just pass out." He sat on the edge and scrolled on his phone. It was odd watching Charlie be taciturn, like something against nature.

"I don't move much when I sleep." I liked sleeping in the center of the bed, though, so that would be an adjustment.

"Me neither."

I remember. Resting with him on the couch was its own form of heaven. His soft breathing and fresh scent lulled me into a peaceful sleep.

I went into the bathroom and washed up for the rehearsal dinner, throwing ice-cold water on my face. "Are you coming to the dinner?" I called out.

"Am I invited?" he called back.

"Yeah, I think so." Even though he was working the wedding, he was like an unofficial guest. Unlike the hotel, they could squeeze another chair at the table. I didn't want him sitting in the room by himself while we were enjoying our meal.

I stepped out and found Charlie shirtless, standing over the bed. He ruffled through his gym bag. His body looked even better than I'd dreamt about. And I had *very* vivid dreams. I pulled a button-down shirt and slacks from my bag and got changed, too. I avoided sneaking peeks at him and wondered if he did the same for me. My heart rate jumped just knowing we were undressing at the same time, and his half-naked body was mere feet away. My dick swelled up accordingly.

I got dressed in record time and nearly pulled a hamstring getting into my pants.

Charlie went into the bathroom. I sat on the bed to put on my shoes, and the comforter shifted, sending his gym bag toppling to the floor.

Now, I couldn't exactly describe the feeling that surged through me when I noticed a bottle of lube that had tumbled from his bag. Shock and confusion gave way to excitement. It made me jittery with nerves like I was a boy going to my first amusement park, even though I had no idea why he packed the lube. There could be somebody else he was planning to screw at this wedding. I shoved his stuff back in his bag and replaced it on the bed as he re-entered the room.

"Let's go." I clapped once and marched to the door.

"Your shoes aren't tied."

I looked down at straggly laces flowing over my feet. "I'll tie them in the hall. I'll meet you outside. I don't want us to be late."

My circuits were scrambled like Charlie had poured a bucket of water over them. Make that a bucket of water-based lubricant.

I can make it through this weekend, I told myself. *I can do it.*

21

MITCH

Ellie and Tim booked one of the restaurants at the Culinary Institute, whose main campus was in the Hudson Valley. Students worked at the restaurants on the main grounds perfecting their techniques. The bride and groom made their way around to each table to greet out-of-town guests, a primer for tomorrow. Charlie and I kept our distance. He hung out with his college friends, and I spent time with family members I hadn't seen in a while (and who all asked me if I was dating. Ugh). Tim's parents and I had a pleasant-enough conversation about local politics and summer plans. I averted my eyes from looking over at Charlie lest Cal or Leo catch me in the act. Charlie's voice carried through the room as he regaled friends with tales of bartending.

Dinner was delicious. I had a chicken parm that melted in my mouth. I enjoyed the meal because it'd be the only relaxing one I'd have this weekend. Ellie and Tim canoodled and shared food on each other's plates. My ex-wife, Hannah, cuddled against her husband as they shared a slice of cheesecake for dessert. I was happy she'd found someone, but watching them turned a crank of longing inside me.

I wanted to get a good night's sleep before the big day tomorrow, so I planned to leave shortly after dessert. I interrupted Charlie holding court at his table.

"I'm going back to the room to go to sleep."

"Okay," he said over his shoulder.

"Don't stay out too late. We have a busy day tomorrow."

"Yeah, I know."

Message received. I said my goodbyes to Ellie, Tim, and family members. When I got outside, I found Charlie leaning against the truck. I gulped back my attraction and desire to tear off his clothes. My cock stirred in my pants, thinking about sharing a bed with him.

Calm the fuck down, dick. Nothing is happening.

"You didn't want to stay?" I asked.

"You're probably right. I should get some sleep, be ready for tomorrow."

I nodded because I liked being right, and we piled into the truck.

Back at the estate, my heart beat wildly in my chest as we made our way down the hall to the room. I unlocked the door, and once inside, we got ready for bed in silence. We took turns using the bathroom. I was used to sleeping in only boxers, but I put on a t-shirt for obvious reasons.

Charlie didn't get the memo, though. He wore pajama pants and nothing else. It took all my willpower not to run my tongue all over his bare chest.

We stood on opposite sides of the bed, playing our own game of chicken. "Which side do you like to sleep on?"

"I don't sleep on a side. I just sleep in the center," he said.

"Me, too," I lied.

"I'll take this side then."

But neither of us moved to get in bed. The game of chicken continued.

"I'm sorry." The words gusted out of him. He knelt on the bed. "I said it wasn't going to happen again, and it happened again."

"What happened?"

He tipped his head. "You know."

Oh, right. That. My dick stirred in my shorts thinking about that night.

"I'm sorry I kissed you again. I'm starting to think I'm not totally straight. But that doesn't mean you need to be an asshole."

"Wait. What?"

"You've been avoiding me like I'm the guy at the gym with b.o. You barely talk to me at work."

He wasn't wrong, but I didn't want him to be right. Keeping my distance had been torture. "I'm busy handling a million things. Running a tavern and now planning a wedding."

"You act like the bar is radioactive. You can't come near it."

"I'm running around like a chicken with its head cut off every damn day," I said over him.

"I crossed a line, I know that, but you liked it."

"I liked it?" I huffed out, anger building inside me. "You think I like not being able to concentrate at work? You think I like having to keep my distance from you while also thinking about you *all* the time?"

Charlie's face turned as furiously red as that balloon from the scary clown movie. He inched closer to me, his cologne doing even more dangerous things to my mind. "You think I like working for a guy I can't stop thinking about who won't say more than three words to me? Do you know what it's like working for the world's sexiest brick wall?"

I stepped closer, too, my legs against the bed. No way was I losing this fight. "And what about you? Looking at that cocky smile all day and watching you walk around in those tight-as-fuck henleys makes me dizzy! It's goddamn torture."

"I hate working for you!"

"And I hate having you around!"

A second later, I pulled his body against mine. My lips crashed onto his like a boat willingly getting shipwrecked. His warm body and hot breath made me fucking dizzy all over again. I cupped a firm hand around the back of his neck. We kissed until we ran out of breath and then kissed some more. His hands scoured through my beard.

"I can't believe I like kissing someone with stubble so much."

"It's not stubble. It's a beard, fucker. Now I didn't say you could stop kissing." I pulled him to me again and shoved my tongue into his mouth. He scratched down my back, a moan gushing from his lips. With my free hand, I squeezed his firm ass cheek and let out a groan. His rock-hard dick pulsed against my thigh.

I picked him up, and he wrapped his legs around my waist. I pushed him against the wall kissing the life out of him until my lips went numb. I hadn't made out like this since I was a teenager, and it sent jolts of electricity through my chest.

Charlie shot me that cocky grin on those swollen, pink lips. "How long have you been wanting to do that?"

"Too fucking long."

"I've destroyed Amos's plumbing with all the times I've jerked off in the shower thinking of you."

"Baby, I want to destroy your plumbing." I jammed a

hand into his pants, down the crack of his ass until I reached Valhalla. I tapped a finger against his tight hole, and he shuddered against me. "Shit, am I going too fast?"

He's straight, I remembered. Or at least he was until a minute ago.

"No," he said, biting his lip. "I've been, uh, experimenting down there. Just a little sore."

I arched an eyebrow, my imagination spiraling. "What've you been putting up there?"

"I'll take you to the supermarket one day and show you." His face split in half with a smile, and my whole body quivered in delight. There was no other place on this earth I wanted to be at this moment.

I massaged his back, felt the muscles under his taut, tanned skin ripple in reaction. I wanted to explore his whole body with my hands and then my tongue.

"Why the fuck are we still wearing clothes?" he growled as he dragged his teeth down my neck.

"Beats me." I spun us around and dropped him onto the bed. We shed our clothes in two seconds flat. I didn't care if I tore the fabric. My dick stuck straight out, like a compass pointing me to salvation.

I took a second to rake my eyes over his body, which had a creamy softness to his skin. A light dusting of hair sprinkled his chest. His abs charted a path to his thick cock.

"Do you shave down there?" It did make him look bigger. "Are straight guys doing that nowadays?"

"I like to keep a clean workspace. Ladies appreciate it."

"Well, I'm no lady." I leaned over him and growled. "No more trimming."

"Whatever you say, Boss." He shot me a wink.

This guy was going to destroy me, wasn't he?

I tipped my head to kiss him, our bare chests meeting in

golden heat. He groaned into my mouth as our cocks touched. He opened his legs to let me come closer, and what I wouldn't give to fuck that hole. Not yet, though. Not tonight.

I rutted against his dick, his pre-come sliding against my shaft.

"You really like doing that," I said as his hands found their way into my beard again.

"I love this beard. It's so weird getting scratched while kissing."

"Weird?"

"Good weird," he corrected, his pupils like saucers. "Very good weird."

"One of the many benefits of fooling around with a guy. There's also this." I threw his legs over his head and rubbed my beard against his taint, then around his hole.

His guttural moans filled the hotel room. Music to my ears. It was so loud I thought he'd shot his load already. I swirled my bearded chin on his pucker, then up to his balls. His legs shook under my grip. I had the fratboy in the palm of my hand—or rather, in between the hairs of my beard.

"Holy fucking shit," he muttered through breaths.

I wanted to stretch his pink hole with my cock so badly. It was there for the taking. But I also wanted to take things slow.

He pulled me into a kiss when I returned from down below. His cocky grin vanished, replaced with a desperate, serious hunger that flushed his cheeks. I steadied myself above him, our eyes tethering us. I wrapped my hand around both our cocks and stroked, using our combined pre-come as lube.

"Holy shit, Boss." He threw his head back.

It was hot when he called me Boss on a normal day. Tonight, it was sexy as hell.

He leaned up to kiss me, our lips hovering over each other as he shut his eyes and moaned. He fucked into my hand and filled it with his hot seed, his whole body shaking as he came. I used his come to slick up my dick and continued stroking us in unison. Ropes of come covered his chest. I swiped a thumb through it and pressed it to his lips.

"I want to taste yours next," he said with a devilish smile that sent me over the edge.

I released across his chest and shot up to his neck. Spent in every way possible, I collapsed next to him. My dick went hard again at the sight of him tasting me. I knew that we'd go again before we called it a night.

One of the busiest days of my life was tomorrow, but fuck it. I wasn't getting any sleep.

22

MITCH

I woke up the next morning smelling Charlie on my sheets, his taste still on my tongue, but no Charlie beside me. I ruffled the comforter, which was so thick I thought it would suffocate us, yet found no sign of his compact body.

"Hey, Boss." Charlie emerged from the bathroom wearing a towel wrapped around his waist. His chest and arms were slicked with moisture. His wet hair gave him a shaggy dog look that I found irresistible. I wished he were still in bed with me, but I didn't mind this view either.

"I'm not sure 'Boss' is still appropriate." I wiped sleep from my eyes.

"That's why I like it." He shot me a wink, which was basically a blow job in eye form. It made my dick stand at attention. Fortunately, this heavy whipping cream of a comforter hid it.

He ran his fingers through my beard. Pleasure sparked on his face as if he were the one being pet. "We should get up. We have a wedding to prepare for."

My eyes bulged at the clock. "Holy shit."

A mile-long to-do list popped up in my head.

"We're good on time. You have a few minutes to take a shower."

Dried come pulled at my chest hair when I turned to face him. "We need to start setting up and preparing food."

"First, you should shower." He looked down at me with those brown eyes I wanted to drown in.

"How is it?"

"It's big enough for two."

We put that theory to the test minutes later when Charlie took the second shower of the day, this time with me. I picked him up, and he wrapped his legs around my waist. He fit perfectly there, tucked against my body. I got flashes of him folded in my arms as we slept, the world's perfect little spoon. With him pressed against the shower wall, I wrapped my hand around our cocks and gave a repeat performance of last night. This time, though, I came first. His moans echoing off the shower kicked me over the edge.

"So you think you're bi?" I asked him as we got dressed. "You'd said that last night."

Before I jammed my mouth against you.

"Yeah. I think this proves it, doesn't it?" Charlie stood in his boxers, ironing his white shirt. He told me he had become an expert ironer thanks to his years working a desk job. And damn if I didn't want to devour his body for a third time in twelve hours. "I'd never been into guys before you. But everyone's journeys are different, y'know? It's like Jason Bourne."

I cocked my head, not making the connection, although Matt Damon was always fun to think about. "Are you a spy?"

"You know how Bourne had amnesia, but he still had all

this spy knowledge and skills inside him, and it suddenly got released when he had to fight?"

I'd only caught the Bourne movies on cable over the years, but this did not sound like the plot. Charlie was so earnest that I didn't have the heart to correct him. "Sure."

"That's like here."

"I've activated the killer inside you."

"Yeah." He put on a sleeveless T, then his crisp white shirt. I wanted him only to wear the undershirt. Damn, this guy was drowning me in sexy. "Well, swap giving hand jobs for shooting guns."

I let out a laugh. I couldn't get enough of him.

"But yeah, I'm pretty sure I'm bi. And horny for you." He said it with a surety and confidence that honestly blew me away. As someone who struggled with his sexuality for years, to the point of marrying and fathering a child with a woman, I admired how well he knew himself.

And I was definitely horny for him. Jesus, I'd have to duct tape my dick to my thigh to make it through this weekend and every shift at Stone's Throw.

"I'm happy you've discovered this new side of yourself. But this can't happen again, though. For a whole host of reasons." I had to be the adult here, which sucked. Supremely sucked. But it was the only responsible avenue. I hated this more than people who used the word adulting. "I'm your boss, Charlie. This would be a really bad look for us to continue. Really bad. Borderline unethical."

He nodded blankly, as if he understood the words but they weren't calculating in his head.

"We'll just leave it here. Tonight, we'll be so tired from the wedding that we'll crash. Then we'll wake up and go back to Sourwood and continue on with our lives. There are lots of guys out there, a whole world out there for you to explore with your bisexuality."

The thought of him experimenting with other guys flipped every jealous, possessive switch in my head. But again, the whole maturity thing.

He answered with another blank nod. I could tell he was holding back a smile. What the hell was so funny?

"Do you understand?"

"I mean, I do." He buttoned up his shirt. There was that cocky grin again. "But I also want more."

I gulped back a horny lump in my throat. "More?"

"I'll stop if you want to stop. But I would like to do more. A lot more."

My mind spiraled with possibilities of more. *Keep it together, Mitch.* I blinked back to reality, and Charlie was fully dressed.

"I'll see you down there." He left me alone in my underwear with my thoughts of more.

"We're not doing this again!" I called out, but the door had already clicked shut.

———

I MET Charlie downstairs to start setting up. We moved supplies from the truck to the kitchen area. We took the food out of the fridge and plugged in the portable heaters. The kitchen space was small but still workable. There was a deep sink and some counter space along a window. Charlie moved food into the fridge and beer into the coolers we'd brought. Heavy gray clouds blanketed the sky, ready to burst. They were water balloons floating into a needle.

We maneuvered around each other in the kitchen, too

busy to focus on any lingering sexual tension. What did Charlie mean by more?

"Alanis said rain on your wedding day is good luck," Charlie said.

"How do you know Alanis Morrisette?" I laughed to myself. "You were born after that song came out."

"I know the classics."

Jagged Little Pill was considered the classics? I just died inside.

"Although, are any of the things in that song actually ironic or just shitty luck?" he asked.

I hummed the song to myself before Charlie cued up the whole album on Spotify.

"This album was the first cassette I bought when I got my license. I thought I was so cool because I had a tape deck in my car. Hannah and I blasted it every morning when we drove to school." It was funny how time flew. Listening to "Ironic," I could feel the blast of the heating vent on my face as I drove to school on those cold mornings, condensation streaming down my car. The heat in my first car had two modes, off or scorching.

"We played it at '90s parties in college and sung along."

'90s party. I died inside again.

Charlie danced in place as he put more trays into the heating station. His butt swayed to the beat, and I found its round shape through the loose slacks. I watched for longer than I should have. A roll of thunder rumbled outside and in my belly.

Ellie burst through the kitchen, eyes welling with tears. I pulled my glance away from Charlie.

"Ellie Bear, what is it?" A ripple of shame flared in me, thinking of what I did with her ex-boyfriend. Did she find out somehow?

"It's raining!" She pointed outside to the heavy drizzle. "The forecast said it's supposed to rain all day. The estate owner said we should plan for an indoor wedding."

I wrapped a soothing arm around her. "We knew this was a possibility. That's why we have an indoor contingency plan. It'll be okay."

Charlie watched from his corner but stayed quiet. I wondered what he was thinking, if he felt any awkwardness. Or if he still wanted more.

"I had this whole vision." She wiped her eyes. "We had this spot picked out for pictures, and we were going to get married overlooking the valley."

"The ballroom has those same views. And you can get lovely shots inside."

"It's not the same."

I shrugged. I couldn't argue with the weather. Maybe it was the lack of sleep, but I found myself getting annoyed with her crying.

"Ellie, you and Tim decided to have a wedding in April, the month with the most rain and inconsistent weather. You knew this was a possibility."

She sniffled, pulling out all the stops. "I know, but the forecast was looking hopeful leading up to today."

"What do you want me to do? I can't change the weather. I'm not that powerful."

I felt bad for being short with her, but I had a lot of work to do today because she and Tim couldn't pick a more reliable caterer. I was out of sympathy.

Charlie came over and sat down next to her, slumped his shoulder against hers. "Ellie, what is going to happen tonight?"

She cocked her head as if that were a trick question. "A wedding?"

"And what's going to happen at this wedding?" He looked at her with full intent. He was listening, and he made you feel like what you said mattered.

"Tim and I are going to get married?"

He nodded at the correct answer. "You two are getting married. Rain or shine. No matter how the pics come out on the 'gram, you two are getting married and are going to spend the rest of your lives together. This," he waved his hand at the rain, "is nothing. A speed bump on the way to happily ever after."

He pulled a cloth napkin from the stack behind them and used it to dry her eyes. I wonder if this was what he was like as a boyfriend, bringing calm to their relationship.

"Thanks for the pep talk, Charlie," she said.

"Anything for you." He shot her a wink, and a flash of red tore through me. Right. They used to date. He probably winked at her all the time. It wasn't reserved just for me.

Charlie hopped off the table. "I'm going into the truck to grab the glasses. Boss, I might need a hand."

The smile that climbed his lips sent a spark of need fissuring in my stomach. I might've checked out his ass as he strutted away.

Ellie wiped lingering tears from her eyes.

"I'm sorry for freaking out, Dad," she said with her typical level-headedness.

I couldn't be mad at her. I kissed the top of her head. "It's a big day. Weddings make everyone crazy."

Crazy enough to have shower sex with an employee.

"I got my bridezilla moment out of the way early."

We shared a laugh. The red in her eyes began to clear. The same could not be said for the rain.

My phone buzzed with a text.

I could use a hand in the truck, Charlie texted with three eggplant emojis.

That fucker. I wasn't too old to know that wasn't a reference to produce.

"Is everything okay?" Ellie asked as she read my face.

I shoved my phone as deep into my pants pocket as it would go. "Yeah."

I knew exactly what kind of hand he wanted.

And it wasn't going to happen.

Nope.

My phone buzzed with another text. It was a picture of Charlie grabbing his package through his pants.

"I'm gonna go to the bridal suite and start getting ready!" Ellie kissed my cheek and bounced away. "You seem very stressed."

That I was.

But I was not going out to that truck.

Nope.

"I'll see you later, Ellie Bear. I need to help Charlie get something out of the truck."

23

CHARLIE

F ive minutes later, I climbed Mitch like a tree.
    When I was little, I hated broccoli. Typical kid. I battled my parents when they served it at dinner. I had no interest. But then I went away to college, and it was in the dining hall, and I started eating it. And I thought, hey, this is pretty good. Now I love broccoli. I imagined that hooking up with Mitch was a lot like broccoli. I wasn't sure if this metaphor made much sense. But the TL;DR of it all was that I really really liked fooling around with Mitch.

I was bi as fuck.

"We can't be doing this," he growled into my lips as he pushed me against a stack of crates. Glasses rattled on impact. The sounds of people buzzing outside wafting into the truck.

"I didn't make you come to the truck," I said between kisses. I wished I could talk and kiss him at the same time because removing my lips from his for even a second was its own kind of torture.

"You said you needed a hand." He bit at my lip, and I moaned into his mouth in a greedy response.

Speaking of hands, mine slipped under his shirt and roamed his body, running up his broad, hairy chest and down the rippling muscles of his back. The feel of his rough skin and thick chest hair under my fingers sent sparks shooting through my body. The erection in my pants was a given. Could dicks be hard enough to bust through denim? I was putting that hypothesis to the test.

"I do need help bringing in the glasses." I grazed my hand over the crotch of his jeans and grabbed his thick cock.

Mitch shoved me harder against the crates in response.

"You're going to break all of them if you keep doing that," I said.

"Good," he whispered in my ear.

I opened my legs so he could get closer to me, consume me. I wanted to be consumed by a guy?

Apparently so!

I was very bi as fuck.

Mitch licked a stripe up my neck, leaving shivers in his wake. I ground my raging boner against his crotch. I wanted to recreate last night. Mitch on top of me. Our cocks mashing together in heat. His beard teasing my ass. I couldn't think of anything else. My mind was a one-screen movie theater.

His calloused hands slid under my shirt and teased my nipples. I couldn't catch my breath. Waves of pleasure hit me.

"Your beard," I muttered out, unable to form coherent sentences.

"You like this beard," he let out a gravelly laugh. His eyes sparkled with their own dark magic.

"I do."

"'Cause you've been messing around with all these hairless chicks."

Which I had enjoyed, but my sexual experiences couldn't hold a freaking candle compared to Mitch. He made my body vibrate in ways I didn't know possible—and we'd only done hand jobs.

Mitch brushed his chin against my left nipple, then my right, unleashing chills that spiraled down to my toes.

My throat cracked with a stifled moan, which made the fucker laugh.

"You know, you can grow your own beard," he said.

"It won't look like yours." I grew facial hair in patches that didn't connect. I was born to be clean-shaven.

Mitch kissed down my chest and stomach, his beard scratching at my tight skin. He looked up at me as he unbuckled my belt, a rare smile lighting up his face. It was a devious smile, but a smile nonetheless.

My body quaked with excitement at what I was sure was going to be the best blow job of my life. We had a busy day ahead of us, so he didn't drag out the teasing. He yanked my pants to my knees and disappeared my cock into his mouth.

Holy fucking guacamole.

My entire being turned to jelly. His tongue knew its way around a dick, licking up the underside of my shaft and swirling around the head. Ecstasy flooded my veins. He grabbed my balls in his large hand and gave a light squeeze. I wanted to scream his name but bit down on my lower lip as more stifled moans slipped through my teeth.

Sweat clouded my vision. We were in a small, cramped space in the back of the van, my muscles tensing to keep me standing.

His hands and tongue worked my dick, filling my body with heat. I held onto the crates behind me for balance. He moaned as my dick hit the back of his hot mouth, and that did it for me.

I opened my mouth to give warning, but my body clenched with orgasm—including my vocal chords. I flooded his mouth with my come, but he didn't seem to mind. He sucked me dry. A few drops dotted his beard, only adding to this pinnacle of sexiness.

He stopped me from having my bare ass collapsing onto the crates. They held glasses people would be drinking out of tonight.

He stood up and wiped his mouth with his shirt, revealing a sliver of his sexy belly and putting me back on the path to hardness. He picked up a stack of crates and carried them out of the truck.

———

A LITTLE WHILE LATER, guests began to check in. The estate filled up with people, bringing a buzz to the festivities. I was exhausted from setting up this morning, which was difficult while carrying around a boner the whole time. But the busy time was coming. During a brief break, I caught a cat nap in the room, which gave me a second wind.

My phone woke me up with a buzz.

*I have arrived!*Amos texted.

I was incredibly grateful that he'd remained good enough friends with Ellie to secure an invitation.

I bolted up and asked him to meet me in the courtyard just outside the kitchen. The rain had subsided to a drizzle. We huddled under the awning.

"How's everything going?" he asked. He had shaved and gotten a haircut but hadn't put on his suit yet. "Has today been crazy?"

In ways you wouldn't believe, bro.

"Yeah. It has." My voice jumped an octave like I'd been kicked in the nuts. "It's been busy."

"I'm sure it'll be great. But promise not to cut me off tonight at the bar."

"Don't make me." I was mostly kidding. Amos could sometimes be a sad drunk, not the vibe we needed at a wedding. "But yeah, it's been good."

"It sucks that it's raining, but what can you do?" Amos clocked my jittery hands. "Did you want to talk about something?"

"What?"

"You said you wanted to talk." He read my face and body language and seemed to instantly size up the situation. And then he started laughing. "Holy shit."

I shushed him.

"What did you do?"

I told him about last night and today in the truck, making sure nobody was around us. Amos's jaw comically dropped to the ground.

"Holy shit," he said again. "How was it?"

I wanted to collapse against the wall like some fucking heroine in a repressed Victorian society. Mitch had that kind of effect on me. The dude played me like a violin.

"That good, huh?" Amos quirked an eyebrow.

"Really good."

"Better than my organic produce?"

I turned red. "We didn't do that, though we got close." I shared the things he did with his beard. Amos's eyes lit up in vicarious pleasure.

"I knew he had a wild side. Mitch is a prime DILF."

Jealousy flared in me at the thought of Amos or other guys having their turn with Mitch. Like a bout of dizziness, it came and went but felt weird.

"I...well, I'm definitely bi."

"Oh, you definitely fulfilled that criteria."

"But even though I have lots of sexual experience, it's all with women." I kneaded my hands together. "I want to reciprocate with Mitch, but I'm afraid I'll suck at it."

Amos opened his mouth to retort, but I stopped him.

"The wrong kind of suck. He's been leading with everything so far, but I want to show I'm no slouch in the same-sex sex department." I scratched my head, thinking of how best to put it. "How do I blow job?"

Amos gave me prayer hands and bowed. "The teacher has become the student."

"Do you have any tips?" I shoved my hands in my pockets. Over the years, I had built up a repertoire of moves that drove ladies wild. I could find G-spots so easily, it was as if they were hidden objects in a *Highlights* magazine puzzle. But with guys, I was at square one.

"Do I have tips?" Amos asked with amazing confidence before drumming his fingers on the table. "Do I? I have a few. Don't worry about trying to fit the whole thing in your mouth right off the bat. Work your way up to that. Guys like it when you stroke and suck at the same time."

"Mitch did that. It was incredible."

"Charlie, leverage the benefit of doing it with another guy. You have a dick. What've you liked in blow jobs? What you like, chances are, he'll like, too."

He had a good point. I was a simple man with simple pleasure. It didn't take much to get me off. Please, Mitch could growl at me with that rough twinkle in his eye, and that'd be enough to make me cream my pants.

"I liked when he played with my nuts," I offered.

"Good! Do that. The things he does to you are the things he wants guys to do to him."

Huh. That was another good point. "You're good at this. Why are you not teaching sex ed?"

He rolled his eyes. "I don't think blow job lessons are part of the sex ed curriculum."

I shared the things Mitch did with his tongue on my head and shaft, a new wave of heat coursing through me. Thank God Amos was the type of friend without boundaries.

"That's hot," Amos said. "He'll give you cues. Just follow the yellow brick road of his moans, Dorothy."

"I just hope I'm not rusty like the Tin Man or scared like the Cowardly Lion."

"There are people stupider than the Scarecrow who still manage to give good head. It's not rocket science. Oh, there's this video of a guy who I think gives good head."

Before I could wonder if this was a YouTube tutorial, he pulled up a porn clip on his phone. It was a POV shot of a guy receiving a blow job from a hungry and willing participant. Moans and slurping sounds boomed from his phone's speakers.

"Now, do you see how he's using his hands as much as his mouth? How they complement each other." Amos had his droning teacher's voice on. He pointed out the example, and I imagined this was how he talked about feudal European society in his classes.

The guy on screen was a smaller dude dealing with a thick cock. I wondered if Mitch was that large. From what I felt through jeans and what I glimpsed last night, my guess was a hard yes.

Very hard.

"He is going and going," I commented.

"I'm sure he's built up stamina doing this lots of times. As will you."

"Hey, Amos!" Ellie walked up to us. "I didn't know you were here already."

Amos fumbled with the phone in his hands to shut it off, but his hands were too jittery to catch it.

"Hey, Ellie!" I said and jumped up to distract her. She had on make-up. "You been having fun in the suite with your bridesmaids?"

"We've been drinking mimosas."

"Not too many, I hope."

The phone crashed to the ground right as the guy on the screen alerted us all that he was coming, first verbally, then through a loud howling moan that I was certain could be heard down in New Jersey.

Ellie looked to the phone, then Amos, then me.

"What was that?" she asked.

"It was…" Amos started, then looked at me for the magic answer.

"That's a good question because that was…a video."

"Of a guy coming?" Her brows mashed together in confusion.

"Amos was showing me…" Telling her I was receiving blow job lessons would open a can of worms that needed to stay firmly sealed. "A video. Of one of his former students. Who is now doing porn."

Amos threw his hands up in the air. "He wasn't very good at remembering historical dates."

"It's always the quiet ones," I added.

Ellie shrugged. "Huh. Well, good for him. I'm sure he's getting paid well."

"I hope so," Amos said with a nervous laugh.

"There's a guy in my office who does OnlyFans, makes a nice side income from it. He used it to take a trip to Tokyo."

"Really? Hmm..." Amos slipped his phone back into his pocket.

"Charlie, have you seen my dad?"

I gulped back a nervous lump. "Why would you ask me something like that?"

"Because you're working with him..."

Oh, right. "Sorry. He had to run into town to get lighters for the buffet heaters."

"Okay, I'll catch him later." She leaned down and kissed both of us on the cheek. "See you later, boys."

I exhaled a breath once she left. Amos seemed deep in thought.

"She doesn't know," I told him. "We've been extremely discreet."

"No, I wasn't thinking about you and Mitch. I'm thinking maybe I should do an OnlyFans so I can go on a nice vacation."

"Lord knows you have the supplies in your nightstand for ample content."

I thanked him for his help and squared my shoulders. The next time I saw Mitch, I would be ready.

Ready to suck.

24

MITCH

C al looked at me the whole time I drove into town. Studied practically.

"What?" I asked, finally having to break the silence.

He scratched at his beard like he was unraveling a mystery. "You're smiling."

I waited for more. "And?"

"And you never smile."

I rolled my eyes at the accusation. "That's not true."

"There've only been five official smiles on record."

"You've been keeping track?"

"Me and Leo."

This was premium horseshit. Cal spent too much time in his recording studio. It was draining badly-needed oxygen from his brain. To hear it from them, I was some dour sourpuss.

"I smile. You're never around for it because you never say anything funny." I turn into the main drag of this small town. Small businesses hanging on by a thread dotted the street.

"You think you're smiling when you're around us, but it's

not a real smile." He put his thumb to his chest. "We can tell."

Cal wasn't going to distract me from parallel parking. My dad drilled this skill into my head when I got my learner's permit; it made me the king of downtown Sourwood before they built a separate parking lot. I could always find a spot.

"Cal, if recording jingles doesn't pan out for you, you should look into being a private detective."

I put the truck in park and hightailed it into the Walgreens. Sadly, more storefronts were being taken over by chains here. Fortunately, Leo had put an ordinance in place that prohibited national chains from setting up shop in our downtown. It kept a small-town vibe that made Sourwood such a wonderful place to live.

I was on the hunt for lighters, but I needed duct tape to shut up Cal.

"Why are you so concerned with my smiles?" I asked him once he caught up to me.

He touched random things on the shelves. He was a big kid at heart. "Because I want to know what's making you smile that big, gushy smile."

"Uh, it's my daughter's wedding? The moment every parent dreams of. She's marrying a wonderful man."

"Yeah, that's not it."

I plucked a box of matches off the shelf and pushed past Cal, hoping he didn't see my cheeks heat up.

"I can't be happy for my daughter?" I tossed over my shoulder.

Cal met me at the cash register, once again examining my face for clues. This time, he'd only see stone. I couldn't let it get out what I'd done with Charlie, even if my face had other plans.

He finally gave up and shrugged with disappointment.

"I'm sorry, man. You're right. You seem really happy about Ellie. We all are."

I clapped him on the shoulder. "It's okay."

"You really seem happy. Glowing. Almost giddy."

"I went from never smiling to giddy?" I kept my head down, thanked the cashier, and took my purchase.

"I mean it. You just have this light. Well, for you. I saw you in the kitchen earlier prepping the food and mouthing along to some song in your head. It's a scientific fact that sad, grumpy people don't sing."

Thanks to Charlie, "Ironic" had been playing in a loop in my head all day. It was annoyingly catchy, and the thought of him singing along to it made my damn heart lift.

Apparently, it made me borderline giddy.

Back in the car, I managed to change the subject to Josh, and Cal went on a rant about standardized testing and the uptight PTA moms at the school. The muscles in my face strained while keeping a lid on any smiles.

When we returned to the estate, I bumped into Hannah in the lobby. Her hair and makeup were done, an odd match against her casual sweater and jeans. She snaked her arms around me, ignoring the shopping bag in my hand.

"Hey, what's wrong? Is everything okay?"

"Vince said he wanted to talk to you."

What did her husband want to talk to me about? We got along fine, mostly talked about hockey. More extended conversations proved challenging.

"Did he say what it's about?"

She shook her head no against my chest. She looked at me with watery eyes. "Our little girl..."

"I know. They grow up so fast."

Hannah got emotional at big life events. She once told me that she saw her life as an ongoing TV show, and momentous occasions made her think of clip show episodes where you flashed back through the years, remembering all the good times with the characters. She indulged her love of the rearview mirror, while I preferred to keep looking forward.

"It feels like only yesterday I was teaching her how to put on makeup, how to tie her shoes." She wiped away a tear with her blue-colored nails.

My leg buzzed with a text. I checked my phone to make sure it wasn't anything urgent, and my eyes nearly shot out of my head cartoon style.

Charlie texted me a selfie from the staff bathroom shirtless with his jeans around his ankles, his glorious cock framed by tight white boxer briefs.

Wanna meet me in the bathroom?

Jesus, another sext? While I was comforting my ex-wife? I forgot how irrepressibly horny twentysomethings could be.

I tried to pull away, but Hannah wasn't letting go. She hugged me like the armoire Rose clung to in *Titanic*, one of the last movies we saw together before she got pregnant.

"Do you remember when we took her to her first day of kindergarten?"

"Uh, yeah, I do." I rubbed her back with one hand and slipped my phone into my pocket with the other. I willed my cock not to get hard with Hannah pressed against me.

"She just walked right in. She didn't cry like the other kids. And remember when she stopped at the door and blew us a kiss."

"From day one, she was a badass." My eyes crinkled with a nostalgic smile.

"It feels like yesterday."

"It does." My damn phone buzzed again, and blood instantly rushed to my groin.

I made sure her head was against my chest as I checked the new message.

I'm waiting for you, boss... he texted with a pic of his rock-hard dick outlined in his underwear. That dick felt stupendous in my mouth.

I leaned my hips away from Hannah like I was some middle schooler at his first slow dance. This guy was going to be the death of me, wasn't he?

"Ellie's turned out wonderful, thanks to you," I said, smoothing a now sweaty hand over her hair. "You've been a great mother and a great role model."

"Mitch, I know life didn't go the way we planned. We had to make big sacrifices. Were it not for a broken condom, you might be in the NHL." She glanced up at me with those eyes that still had the same shimmer as in high school. "But we raised an incredible young woman. I'm grateful we were able to both be there for her. I've seen so many divorced couples where they can't even be in the same room as each other."

Zzz. zzz.

Charlie, stop fucking texting me!

His message was the telltale heart beating in my pocket.

"We made it work. Because we both love her. And now she's...shit, I didn't know I could cry this much." Her tears formed a puddle on my shirt.

Zzz.

Dammit.

"It's an emotional day," I started as I slyly took out my phone. "She's, uh, always been our little girl. Now she's going to be a wife and eventually a mother. Circle of life."

A little taste for you... He texted me a video, which I should not have hit play on. It was so not the time. I turned my phone on mute.

But my mind and my dick had other plans.

"Our little girl," Hannah cooed into my chest.

On my phone screen, Charlie whipped out his dick and jerked himself off.

"Who's texting you?" she whipped her head up.

I hit stop and activated my phone's lock screen.

"Uh, it's...there's an emergency in the kitchen." I kissed the top of her head. "We raised an all-timer, Hannah."

I backed away, and my walk morphed into a sprint to the kitchen. I barreled through the swinging doors and charged to the bathroom off to the side for staff. I practically ripped the door off its hinges, then did the same to the stall door. Charlie leaned against the wall, flashing me that cocky smirk.

"You fucker. What the hell do you think—"

He cut me off with a ferocious kiss that sucked the air out of my lungs and replaced them with fireworks. His tongue pressed through my teeth and explored the farthest reaches of my mouth, turning my muscles to putty.

"You can't just—"

But he cut me off with another kiss. He stood on his tiptoes, which I found hot, knowing how much I towered over him, yet he could still control me in this way. He unbuckled my belt and shoved a hot hand into my underwear. He stroked my dick, which was already hard as a spear. He traveled south to play with my balls. I groaned into his lips, a deep well of need pooling in my gut.

He glanced up at me with heavy-lidded eyes that brewed with lust. He licked his kiss-drunk lips. "I need to repay your generosity from the truck."

"You don't—I—" It was useless. I couldn't form a coherent sentence. I couldn't catch my breath.

Charlie got on his knees and unleashed my dick from its

constraints. It flopped in the air, and the excitement lighting up Charlie's face was unbearably sexy. He disappeared my rod into his mouth. I cried out as he took me to the base, which was no easy feat as I'd been told by past hookups.

I collapsed against the bathroom wall, jutting my hips out for him. His slick, wet mouth sucked my cock, sending bolts of pleasure up my spine. I didn't know what I liked better—the feel of his tongue or the way he looked up at me the entire time. Charlie licked a stripe up the underside of my shaft, then stroked me as he tongued my balls.

"Suck me, Charlie."

"You taste so good."

Was this the first blow job he'd ever given? If so, he was a fucking natural. He made me levitate.

I lightly pulled him by the hair away from my balls. "Go back to my dick, fratboy. Suck it dry."

I worked my fingers through his hair and pulled him closer to my cock. He stroked and sucked, pleasuring me with his nimble fingers and tongue.

"Fuck, Charlie. I'm going to bust and make you drink every last fucking drop."

"Whatever you say, Boss." He smiled at me with swollen lips, which stretched with my cock shoved in between.

Hearing him call me boss lit me up inside. I fisted handfuls of his hair and fucked into his mouth.

"Suck that dick, fratboy. Just you fucking wait." The dirty talk flew out of me. "Tonight, I'm going to fuck you senseless, fill that tight ass of yours with a good dicking."

Shit. Was I? Dirty fantasies possessed my mind, but I had to remind myself that Charlie was a virgin in that department. Twenty-four hours ago, he'd never been with a man. We were going fast, but maybe it was too fast for him.

"I want that so bad, Boss."

Or maybe not fast enough?

"Stand up," I said. He was strong but compact, his head only coming up to my chest. I motioned for him to drop his pants again, revealing his hard cock pressed against his boxer briefs.

"Remove the underwear, too."

And then there he was, completely naked in front of me, all mine for the taking. I whipped off my shirt. His few wisps of chest hair paled next to my furry chest. My mouth watered in response. The head of his dick was engorged and slick with precome.

Without thinking, I pulled him into a kiss, a kiss that reached down my throat and clamped its greedy hand around my heart. I caressed his cheeks as our tongues slowly danced around each other. A tender flame amidst burning heat. It was a kiss that could move mountains and cause tidal waves.

Not a kiss for lusty bathroom hookups.

He seemed dazed, his eyes signaling his coming back to earth. Before I could let any awkwardness simmer, I picked him up and flipped him upside down. I held him by the hips, his cock jutting into my face. He instantly resumed giving me the best blow job in the history of man-on-mankind. This new angle let him go deeper and faster, nuzzling his nose into my sac.

Precome dripped into my mouth. I licked around his head and down his shaft. He rested his legs on my shoulders, revealing his pink, virginal hole. I dipped my thumb into his opening, and his whole body shook against me in response.

"Yes. Oh, fuck." His voice echoed against the walls. "Gonna come. So hard."

His body tensed as his hot, bitter load flooded my

mouth. I held myself back from coming until he was finished.

"You ready for me, fratboy?" My balls tightened as my orgasm pushed me to the edge.

"Give it to me."

And so I did. Waves of it down his throat in one of the greatest releases of pleasure I'd ever experienced.

I put him down gently, his body sweaty and spent. He sat on his pants and looked up at me, his eyes asking me if that was good.

"That was mindblowing," I said, my cock heavy between my legs.

"I should sext you more often."

"No, you shouldn't." I tossed him his shirt. My mind flashed to the kiss we had, and it sent a bolt of terror up my spine that maybe this wasn't just combustible sex.

I didn't want him to get the wrong idea.

But maybe I already had it myself.

"Get dressed. We have a wedding to work."

25

CHARLIE

I took an extra-long shower. My body was coated in sweat, come, and feelings for Mitch that went well beyond flirting and blow jobs. That kiss we shared blew the roof and doors off my mind, but it was done in the name of lust.

I could do lust. I could do flirting. But I was no good at what came next. I wasn't the guy you went to for anything deep.

Mitch saw this as fun, a forbidden fling.

We got dressed in the room in silence. Mitch entrusted me to keep track of all the food and the catering staff we hired while he did his duty as father of the bride. Natasha was arriving tonight to be his number two, and I was thankful to have the assistance. I wanted him to have nothing to worry about tonight.

I ironed my white button-down shirt that went with black pants. A traditional waitstaff ensemble. Mitch wore a charcoal suit that fit his solid body perfectly and made my mouth water. There would be no more sexytimes today. We were showered and dressed and had a wedding to attend. It didn't matter that I discovered how much I loved giving head and desperately wanted to do it again.

"It looks fine. Why do you keep undoing it?" I asked.

Mitch watched himself in the mirror and tied his tie for the millionth time. "It's not how it should be."

"It's a tie."

"The knot isn't big enough. It's not falling down to the appropriate length." The baby blue fabric shook in his hands.

It all clicked.

"Nervous?"

"Me? I'm not the one getting married."

"It's a big day." I took the tie from his hands. I put it around my neck and tied a plump knot. "Ellie's getting married."

"Everyone is having emotional reactions around me today. Everyone is waiting to share with me how momentous today is. Yeah, I know," he said with a nervous laugh. "I'm nervous because I don't want to fuck up the food and spoil the beauty of this wedding."

That was his way of showing he cared. He wanted everything to be perfect for this momentous night.

"The wedding is going to be awesome. You pulled it off." I loosened the tie just enough and slipped it over Mitch's head. I tightened it to fit his neck, then put down his collar.

"Weddings always get me thinking about..."

I brushed lint off his shoulders and stepped back to check my tie-work. "About what?"

He said nothing and shrugged. I pulled him by the tie.

"About what?"

He pushed me back and rolled his shoulders. "Relationships. Love."

The serious stuff. The stuff I had no clue about. My relationships went the distance of a paper airplane. He might've been stoic, but there was a heart beating underneath that wall of stone.

"How does it look?" I nudged my chin at his tie.

He checked himself in the mirror. "You do good work. How do you know how to tie such a good tie?"

"Years of desk jobs and fraternity formals."

"Interesting mix."

I shrug my shoulders. "I'm an interesting guy."

His dark eyes lingered on me, sending my heart into my shoes. "I'll see you out there."

———

I WAS SO excited when Natasha arrived. I needed a heavy dose of fun and levity to forget about the jumble of emotions fluttering inside me. Did weddings bring out this shit in everyone?

Together, we corralled the waiters who would be passing out food and cleaning up dishes during the cocktail hour. We did the final prep of the food, putting it in ovens and keeping it warm. Then we organized the food on trays. My fingers got cramped from organizing mini dishes on mini doilies on the trays. We checked all the lighters for the buffet table trays to make sure they worked. We set everything out. All we needed were guests.

Because of this, I wasn't able to attend the ceremony properly, but I caught glimpses here and there. The wedding party lined up outside the doors, whispering fun things to each other. I gave air hi-fives to everyone I recognized from college. I had no weirdness about working tonight. I was part of the fun!

The piano music started, a simple melody of a song that

sounded familiar. It put a lump in my throat. Chalk it up to wedding fever. Natasha and I prepped more food in the kitchen, doing it in shifts to compensate for limited oven space.

Ellie and her parents waited outside the doors. She looked stunning in her wedding dress, which flowed out like she walked on clouds. Hannah and Mitch held it together as best they could.

I peeked my head in later in the ceremony. My heart hurt watching Mitch sitting alone while his ex-wife had her husband and his best friends had their boyfriends.

"Did Mitch start crying?" Natasha asked me back in the kitchen. Nothing would make her happier.

He did, barely. His eyes watered up as the minister talked about Ellie and Tim. He didn't let any tears fall, but the emotions clogged his face. It was sweet and tender, and those funky feelings I felt for him only amplified.

"Nope. He kept it together," I answered. "Mitch doesn't cry."

"Only when one of us breaks a glass." She took a bite of her Chipotle burrito. She had gotten us dinner to eat before the main event. I appreciated that she refused to let us eat the food we were serving. We could have leftovers, but we wouldn't be the first people to dig into this food.

I wandered back to the ceremony, unable to help myself. Ellie and Tim said their vows to each other. Tears streamed down Tim's cheeks as he read from a piece of paper in his shaky hands.

"Ellie, you are the love of my life. I didn't know I could feel this way about anyone. I see our love in the small moments. The way you pretend to laugh at my jokes. The care you put into our plans. Love isn't a series of big moments. It's the small things, the day-to-day. I won't forget them. I won't take them for granted. My love for you has made me a stronger person."

"Psst," Natasha whispered behind me. "They're about to say I Do, and then we're up. Let's get ready."

Fortunately, she couldn't see my face. She couldn't see the wallop of emotion that put a lump in my throat. She couldn't read me and ask what was going on. Because I didn't want to say it out loud.

My relationships with women had been fun and light. We never scratched below the surface of things. Even with Serena, my longest relationship, things never got deep. We talked about work and the industry and our goals for the future, but there was an undercurrent of competition between us. We were colleagues first, a couple second.

But I wanted what Tim and Ellie had. I wanted those small moments of love. I didn't want only flings. I watched this whole night and wondered if I was built for love.

Real love.

And there was only one person I wanted it with. Unfortunately, he only saw me as the fun guy. The fratboy.

In the rows of guests, my eyes kept finding Mitch sitting there by himself. What was he thinking? The urge came over me to sit with him and hold his hand—the total opposite of the urges I felt for him all through today.

"Charlie," Natasha whispered to me. "It's go time."

IT WAS my turn to be boss, and it felt strange. A good strange, like having Mitch's dick in my mouth earlier. I lined up the three waiters we had on staff for the night; Natasha and I gave them instructions on how to proceed. Which trays to bring out, how to circulate through the crowd. We pointed out all the important people in the wedding party so the waiters would know to keep giving them food and drinks.

I took my position behind the bar. The bar was the only piece of furniture or equipment that wasn't moving tonight. The cocktail hour was held in the lobby, which had been strung with paper lanterns, old photographs of foreign lands, and other cute touches Ellie and her friends had sourced from the never-ending well that was Pinterest. Guests crowded around high tables dotting the floor. The bar station held court outside the main ballroom doors, which were busy being flipped from ceremony to reception by the other two staff members.

"Well, well, well. Look who the fuck it is." Skeeter sidled up to the bar, his tie already loose. He leaned over to check out the goods. "Whatcha got back there?"

"Easy there, buddy." I gently pushed him back. We hadn't spoken since the birthday bash, aka the time I splunked in his bathroom. "What can I get you?"

Asa joined us, with their dates holding back on their phones. I recognized the girls from Asa's weekend birthday extravaganza. Lilly the Loophole was Skeeter's date.

"What do you have?" Skeeter asked.

I rattled off the types of beer and wine we were serving.

"Got anything a little bit harder?"

"There is a small assortment of liquor and mixers. Soda and juice."

"Oh, we won't need the mixers. This is a wedding. It calls for shots." Skeeter seemed pleased with himself. Asa nodded in agreement.

We were ten minutes into the cocktail hour. Perhaps it was too soon to start doing shots? Maybe I would've been all-in on the plan were I on the other side of the bar. But seeing how fast people got drunk, it was best to delay.

"Are you sure about that? We have an excellent selection of craft beer. I know you like yourself some craft beer, Skeet. Remember those brewery tours you dragged me on during that weekend in Boston?"

"This is true."

"You like IPAs. You should check this one out." I yanked a tall bottle of craft beer from the trough filled with ice. I gave Asa the same because for as long as I've known him, he's followed in lockstep with Skeeter ninety percent of the time.

Skeeter had a cool look in his eyes, warning me that beer would suffice for now, but he'd be back for shots. "Cheers?" He and Asa held up their bottles.

I held up my bottle of water. "No drinking on the job."

"True. You're such an adult, Charlie." He clinked his bottle against mine. "My firm is hiring again. I can put in a good word for you."

"You just want that referral bonus."

He smiled into his bottle. "That's a part of it. But come on, man, how much longer are you going to keep up with this?" He waved his hand around my station.

"I like being a bartender."

He squinted his eyes at me. The *c'mon man* was implied. "Everyone likes being a bartender. It's a fun job. Free alcohol and plenty of tips."

"It's actually a really challenging job." An older man came up with two empty wine glasses. I was grateful for the distraction. "You were having the riesling, and your wife was cabernet, yes?"

"Good memory!"

I refilled the glasses. He took out cash and looked around for the tip jar.

"There's no tipping needed." Mitch was adamant that we didn't keep a tip jar out. Wedding guests already had to pay to travel up here, book rooms, and give a gift. They didn't need to worry about shelling out more. They were our guests, Mitch had said.

The older man air-clinked his full glasses at me. Skeeter and Asa remained at the bar.

"This is good," Asa said of his beer.

"You can't do this forever." Skeeter craned his neck to scour every inch of my workspace, making me want to shove him back hard. There were no boundaries when it came to alcohol, apparently.

"What are you doing, man?" I asked while keeping my frustration at bay—just barely. "I appreciate your concern for my career aspirations, but I'm happy where I am."

"You can make so much more money if you come back to finance," Skeeter said. "Aren't you renting a room in some guy's apartment?"

"Condo." I grit my teeth. "I'm saving up for my own place." I would've had more money, but I chose to be the generous friend, picking up the tab for all those happy hours and wild nights out.

"Up here?" Skeeter's forehead creased in confusion. "Don't you miss the city?"

I considered his question. "No."

"You're just going to pour drinks the rest of your life?"

"You sound like my parents."

To my surprise, Skeeter was getting worked up. "You can't spend your life renting rooms from strangers and pouring drafts at some hole in the wall. Yeah, our jobs aren't fun all the time, but no job is."

I took out a six-pack of craft beer bottles and mashed them into the ice bucket. "That explains why you have to get completely shitfaced every single weekend."

"Fuck you, bro. Get serious." Skeeter chugged his beer and slammed the empty bottle on the bar. "We'll have those shots now."

"Dude, it's early."

His eyes narrowed at me. "I said we'll have them now, bartender. They're for the actual guests at this wedding."

He dared me to play this game of chicken. Each word dripped with condescension and malice.

I poured the round of shots, avoiding his stares that made me feel small.

"Good," he said. He took a twenty-dollar bill from his wallet.

"No tipping," I said.

"Trust me, you need it." He left the bill in a puddle of alcohol. Asa and he gathered up the shots and left.

26

MITCH

Forget the bride and groom; the father of the bride was the star of the wedding. I couldn't walk three steps without someone coming up and congratulating me, telling me how beautiful Ellie looked, what a fine lady she'd turned into, and asking how I felt about her being married.

I appreciated all the well wishes, but having these same conversations was its own kind of torture. I should have prepared canned responses had I known I'd be having the same interactions over and over. I preferred to cede the spotlight to others.

The cocktail hour was in full swing. I stood in the corner of the room, watching things unfold. The party went off without a hitch so far. Waiters served delicious food on trays, coordinated under the watchful eye of Natasha. The room was set up beautifully. Ellie shimmered in her dress and glowed with pure happiness. I chose to take this all in from the edges. Being in the center of things wasn't my place.

"You doing all right?" Charlie asked from his station at the bar.

His sleeves were rolled up, and his white shirt hugged all the right places. I could look at him all day.

"Just taking a breather."

"Want anything to drink?"

"Water." He had served me beer earlier. I'd caught glimpses of him throughout the night, and he handled the crowd with aplomb. Tonight was nothing compared to a Musical Monday.

Our fingers touched when he handed me the water, sending a spark of electricity up my spine.

"Anything else you want?" he asked.

Yeah, to experience this night with you at my side, holding my hand.

"Nope." He had driven me crazy today with his sex drive, but it was all I could think about. My back hurt as I walked down the aisle thanks to holding him in a sixty-nine.

Sadness briefly clouded over his face. "What's wrong?" I asked.

Charlie wiped down the bar. "Just realizing my friends are assholes."

"They're rich and young and male. That's par for the course." It must've been tough to be serving your friends rather than partying with them. And partying they were, judging by how rowdy some of them were getting.

"When you were my age, did people tell you to stop working at Stone's Throw and get a real job?"

"All the time."

He looked up at me, surprised.

"Oh, yeah," I said. "I had a kid. I needed a real job, they told me. It didn't matter that Stone's Throw was a family business. I could make tons more money doing literally anything else." Their snarky voices echoed in my head, of people who said they were only thinking about my family but who bailed.

"But you stayed."

"There was no other place for me. At some point, you just have to say Fuck 'em. This is your life."

Charlie crinkled his eyes in a sweet smile. "You're a wise man, Boss."

At least he didn't say, wise old man.

Speaking of rich assholes, Hannah's husband, Vince, came up to the bar and ordered a beer. He then turned my way.

"Mitch, congrats."

I raised my water to him, steeling myself for another round of small talk.

"Got a minute?"

Or maybe not. "Uh, sure."

Vince led us outside. The rain had stopped, but it brought a chill into the air. We manned up and ignored the weather. His suit was sharp and screamed expensive. Leo probably knew where he bought it.

Vince cleared his throat. "I wanted to run something by you, an incredible opportunity."

I appreciated that he avoided platitudes about tonight and Ellie and cut to the chase, but a queasy feeling immediately hit my stomach.

"Shoot."

"I've been working with investors looking for riverfront property. Stone's Throw is in an ideal location. You've done a great job with the space. It's larger than most bars in the area." He slipped one hand into his pocket and leaned against the wall, looking like a model in a cologne ad. I wondered if he'd had any plastic surgery. It wouldn't surprise me. "Have you given any thought to selling?"

I shook my head, trying to make sense of his offer. "Your big real estate investment firm and pool of investors are interested in my little bar?"

"We see great potential there."

"Revenue-wise, we're not blowing the doors off or anything, and it seems like people associated with you like to make money."

"Hannah told me about your struggles."

I cringed at just how my ex-wife described my business. I could be self-deprecating about my bar, but only me. Anyone else, and that was hurtful.

"I wouldn't call it struggles. Running a small business is challenging for everyone."

"What if you didn't have to deal with the challenge anymore?" He asked smoothly. He was pitching me. "What if you sold Stone's Throw and made a nice chunk of change? What else could you do with your life? Travel, invest, start something new, or just take a load off for the first time since the '90s."

What could I do if I wasn't managing the tavern? My mind went blank. It couldn't even dream up possibilities. I'd only known one place for my entire adult life.

"Your guys want to buy it outright?"

"You own the property, yes?"

I nodded affirmatively. "My parents had the opportunity to buy it decades ago."

"They were smart."

"Sourwood was a rustic, nothing town back then. The highway didn't have an exit for us all those years ago."

"They saw the future. The land is getting more valuable by the day. More people are leaving Manhattan and moving there."

Leo had filled me in on population changes. His hard

work as Mayor had helped make Sourwood desirable. I benefited from a steady trickle of business.

But to sell? To give up what was essentially my birthright?

"I appreciate the offer, Vince."

"Mitch, Mitch, Mitch. Don't say no right away." I hated hearing my name on his slick tongue, talking to me like I was some rube. "This is a surprise. I ambushed you at your daughter's wedding. She looked beautiful, by the way. Congratulations."

There it was.

"This is an incredible offer."

"Your investors want a bar?" Something wasn't clicking.

He see-sawed his head. That meant another shoe was about to drop. "It's not the bar they're buying. It's the property."

My body went cold. "They're going to tear Stone's Throw down?"

"That's one possibility. They were actually thinking of building it out, making it bigger."

"How big?"

"Mitch." He put a hand on my shoulder, sending chills down my back. "You work incredibly hard. Keeping the lights on is a seven-day-a-week job. You can't keep doing it alone." He inhaled a breath. I wondered how much of this was practiced, and how much he brainstormed with Hannah to hit the right pain points. "I respect your hustle; I truly do. How much longer do you want to keep it up? You're still a young guy. What else could you do with your life?" He clapped me twice on the shoulder. "Think about it."

27

CHARLIE

I had to admit, it was hard being at a party like this and not being able to dance. The wedding band was playing all the hits, from old school to even attempting a rap song. Amos said they were the same cover band that used to play Applefest, which was apparently a really big deal around here.

I quietly tapped my foot to each song and mouthed the words when nobody was looking. I loved watching other people have fun, though. The dance floor was packed with guests. Younger folk danced in groups while older couples filled out the periphery. But not Mitch, though. He wasn't a dancer. I smiled to myself, imagining him busting a move on the floor.

People gave me compliments throughout the night. There weren't so many people that I couldn't remember what everyone was drinking. I plastered on a smile every time Skeeter and Asa returned for more. Our interactions became less and less friendly and more and more businesslike. Skeeter didn't even look at me when he ordered his last drink. He had graduated from beer to mixed drinks. He slid his glass over. "Double vodka soda," he said with slurred words while checking his phone.

So much for friendship. This was my life, and I was tired of people telling me how to live it. If I wanted to bartend, I would bartend. If I wanted to have sex with a guy, I would have sex with a guy. And if that guy were my boss and ex-girlfriend's father and a good deal older than me, then so be it.

He was hot.

He was more than hot. He stirred my damn soul.

The crowd went wild. During the next song, the mayor of Sourwood himself got on stage for a guitar solo for "Let's Go Crazy" by Prince. The guy had moves. His boyfriend screamed in support at the foot of the stage, and it made me smile.

"Alright, alright," said the lead singer, one alright short of a full McConaughey. "Our next song is a special one. It's the father-daughter dance, as requested by our bride. Even though she knows her father hates to dance."

Guests circled the perimeter of the dance floor, leaving Ellie radiant in the center.

"Where's Mitch?" Skeeter yelled at the top of his lungs. He was wasted and was now in his yelling phase.

The crowd parted, and Mitch came onto the dance floor. His eyes lit up upon seeing Ellie, and his usual stone face was working overtime to contain all the emotion wanting to spill out. I had seen beyond the stone facade. His vulnerable, lusty look when he kissed me filled my head.

I swooned at him, a full-on swoon. Who was I?

The band played a classic—"I Will Always Love You" by Dolly Parton, but I only knew the Whitney Houston version because my old grocery store played it all the time. The song filled the space, and Mitch and Ellie began dancing, swaying in the center of the floor with a spotlight on them. Mitch gazed at his daughter with love pouring out of him. It tugged at my heart.

The sweet moment was cut short for me by Skeeter slamming his glass on the bar. "Fill her up, bartender." The words stumbled out of his mouth as he held onto the bar for balance. His eyes were glassy.

I picked up the vodka bottle, then put it back down. "Actually, buddy, I think you've had enough tonight."

His face dropped in disbelief. "You fucking with me?"

"Have some of this." I handed over a water bottle, which he looked at like I was holding a dead cat.

"The fuck is that?"

"H2O. You've had a lot tonight."

"So? I'm not driving."

That was most likely true, but from my training, I knew I couldn't accept that as fact. I had to make smart decisions. He might've been one of the few who weren't staying over. Or he might've decided to find another bar for an afterparty.

This was not an act of pettiness for what he said to me earlier. This was about making sure we didn't get sued.

"Have some water. You've been drinking a lot."

Skeeter drank a lot whenever we went out. I began realizing it was a recurring problem, and he could down more than any of us.

He became more enraged, the alcohol and anger coming together to turn him a terrifying shade of red. "What the fuck? You can't cut me off. We're at a fucking wedding."

"I can. Dude, cool off for a little while. You've been pounding them back." I kept my voice down since the father-daughter dance was still happening.

"That's what you're supposed to do at a wedding!"

"You're supposed to have fun at a wedding, not get carried out on a stretcher."

"What? I'm not...I'm fine. I can handle my fucking alcohol." His face stretched and expanded in fury. "This is bullshit! You can't do this."

"Skeeter. Bro." My eyes pleaded with him to calm down, but he had fallen over the edge. "Have some water."

"I don't want fucking water!" He spiked the bottle on the ground, and by the grace of BPA-friendly plastic, it didn't burst open. Guests peeled away from the dance to check out the commotion. "Are you on some kind of fucking power trip? Making up for the fact that your life sucks? I am a *guest* at this wedding. Treat me with some respect."

Skeeter went to reach over the bar for the vodka when a hand caught his arm and yanked him back. Mitch squeezed it tight, making Skeeter wince.

"The bartender said you were cut off." Each word was soft and steady but with an undercurrent of barely contained fury. Mitch squeezed harder, his teeth clenched like a growling pit bull, and I could've sworn he was ready to break Skeeter's arm.

"I'm sorry, I'm sorry," Skeeter yelped.

Mitch didn't let go. I'd never seen him so angry.

"My bartender made the right call. We have to be responsible. Are you staying here tonight?"

Skeeter's head jiggled with a nod.

"I think you should go back to your room and sleep it off. You're lucky this is my daughter's wedding and not my bar, or else I wouldn't be this nice."

He released Skeeter, who stumbled back, visibly shaken. He hung his head and skulked out. Like a record that had been briefly paused, my lungs refilled with air.

Mitch stared at me, his eyes loaded with concern.

"Thanks," I said.

"Are you okay?"

"Yeah." I shook out my arm from where Skeeter tried to grab me.

"Did he hurt you?" Mitch asked.

"No. Just a little shook up, to be honest."

Mitch massaged my forearm, his warmth seeping through my skin. "You did the right thing, Charlie. You made the right call. I know it couldn't have been easy since he's your friend."

"I'm not sure if we're still friends." I didn't want someone like Skeeter in my life. He might've had a quote-unquote real job that made him seem quote-unquote responsible, but he was very immature. He was essentially a little kid with his own personal trust fund.

I liked my life. I had a great job, new friends.

Amazing boss.

"It wouldn't be a wedding without drama," the singer said into her mic. "Let's keep the slow dances going. Bring that special person onto the dance floor."

Couples congregated on the dance floor. The tables thinned out with people as they made their way to dance.

Nerves pooled in my stomach because Mitch hadn't let go of my arm, and he hadn't stopped staring at me with those concerned, determined, brooding eyes.

His hand drifted down to mine.

Most people were on the dance floor, but if they wanted to, they could look our way and see what was going on at the bar. Every muscle in my face asked him, *What are you doing?*

"May I have this dance?"

Instead of questioning it, I let my heart lead the way. I stepped from behind the bar and walked with Mitch onto the dance floor. We occupied a corner.

I was dancing with a guy. This wasn't a secret hookup or primal urges begging to get out. Mitch clasped my hand, settled his other comfortably on my hip, and I melted into his touch. The dance floor and the gawking eyes encircling us drifted away. We could've been in the clouds, together in our own universe. The sparkle in his eye was my North Star.

He was warm and protective, and everything about this moment felt right. There was nobody else I was meant to dance with.

I put my head on his shoulder and listened to the melodic rhythm of his heart beating. His beard brushed against the tip of my ear.

"Charlie," he whispered like a refrain.

The lead singer's lilting voice wafted across the room, setting the mood. I didn't want this moment to end.

I wanted more than sex.

I wanted Mitch. All of him.

And I wanted to give him my heart.

28

MITCH

All good things had to come to an end. Including this slow song. I held Charlie close to me, inhaling his cologne and natural clean scent. This was perfection.

The world had melted away, leaving us in a special pocket of the universe unmoored from time and reality. I kept my eyes closed as I held him tight, soaking in this moment, this moment when my body craved him.

When the song ended, the band made a harsh transition into "Uptown Funk." The first thing I noticed was the stares. From Ellie. From Hannah. From my friends. From random guests who I didn't know and who didn't know me but probably found it utterly strange that the father of the bride was dancing with the bartender.

But most of all was the look Charlie gave me. He seemed perplexed, almost scared.

What the hell was going on? He probably wondered. Why was my secret fuckbuddy dragging me out to the middle of the dance floor for everyone to see?

Oh shit, did I accidentally out him?

"Thank you," I said to Charlie and pulled away, giving him the space he keenly desired.

Charlie stammered and let go. His cheeks reddened with embarrassment.

"Hey, there." Cal and Russ approached, still holding hands from their dance. They wore matching ties and matching awkward smiles. "You two looked good out there."

Before I could answer, Charlie interjected.

"I was just doing Mitch a solid so he didn't feel left out," he said with a jocular laugh that needled my heart. "It was weird not being the one leading, but anything to help the boss out." He clapped me on the shoulder.

"You get used to it," Cal said. "I grew up dancing with girls."

"Did you have rhythm then?" Russ asked, raising an eyebrow.

"You really think I'm the one with two left feet here?" Cal crossed his arms at his boyfriend, and to the outside world, this probably looked like a fight. But I knew it was all foreplay for later.

"I gotta get back to the bar. People are thirsty." Charlie gave me another hetero, downright clinical pat on the back. "Enjoy the rest of your night, Boss."

Boss didn't have the same ring. It sounded empty.

But for the rest of the night, I did try and enjoy myself. Ellie and Tim fed each other wedding cake as tradition. The red velvet artisan cake they picked up was delicious and had it been bigger, I would've gotten a second slice.

I hung out with my friends, none of whom asked me about the dance with Charlie. They likely saw the confusion and tension on my face and just wanted me to have a good time. I talked with Cal and Russ about how the move was going. I mused with Leo about his fights with the city council and laying the groundwork for his gubernatorial campaign in a few years. Dusty shared with me his progress on expanding his construction business in town.

Ellie and her friends had a blast on the dance floor. They kept going and going, no matter the song. They had so much energy. I didn't have that kind of stamina at their age, but I was also in a much different place.

Yet through it all, my gaze returned to Charlie again and again. He played the part of social bartender, just as he did at Stone's Throw, but he never met my eyes. I had Russ get me another beer because I felt awkward going up myself. Even after our dance together where time seemed to stop.

Why did I let myself get unglued by this guy? This was why I stayed far away from relationships. They defied all sense of logic.

The wedding flew by. For the last song, the band played "Don't Stop Believing." By that point, most of my friends and other adults had left. Ellie and her friends stayed till the end, belting out every word at the top of their lungs. I got swept up in it and joined them for the final refrain.

The old man still had it.

The night wasn't over for Ellie and her friends. They made plans to go to a nearby bar for more celebrating. Tim's shirt was half unbuttoned, and he wore his tie around his head. He wasn't as uptight as suspected.

"Charlie, you coming to the afterparty?" she asked.

He looked at me as if for permission. His brown eyes pleaded for direction.

"I should hang back here and help clean–"

"You should go. You've worked hard tonight. Enjoy the rest of the night."

"Oh. Cool. Are you sure?" His eyes squinted for clarification. He didn't want to be seen as a bad employee.

"I can handle the rest. Go," I said firmly.

My heart sank as he joined Ellie's group. That was where he belonged. With twentysomethings looking to party, not a fortysomething who wanted to lay down. I shouldn't have let my heart get involved in a romp with a guy who just wanted fun.

"Have fun," I said to Ellie. "Don't stay out too late."

Charlie probably had had too much gay shit happen today, and he'd probably be on the prowl for a girl. It was best not to think about what he'd do, even though a spike of jealousy surged through me.

"What are you still doing here? You joining them for the afterparty?" Natasha asked me once the final guests left.

I snorted a laugh. "Oh, yeah. Party til the break of dawn."

"I think you have a wild side, Mitch."

Heat crept up my neck. Apparently, thanks to Charlie, I did.

"I can help clean up," I said.

"Negative. You are a guest tonight. My team and I have it."

"What about the bar?"

"Charlie got things in order before he left. He'd never leave us in the lurch," she said.

I smiled weakly. He was a wonderful guy.

"Go back to your room, watch some TV, and get some sleep." Natasha proved her bonafides. I was lucky to have her on my team.

"Thanks for everything."

"You don't have to thank me. That's what the money is for." Ever since she binged *Mad Men* a year ago, that had become her go-to line. But I would always thank her. Good people were hard to find. "Also, what's the deal with you and Charlie?"

"There is no deal. I needed a dance buddy."

A dance buddy? That was officially the worst term and would here on in be banished from my vocabulary.

"Okay, then." Natasha nodded along with skepticism flashing across her face. "Well, the wedding is over, so all guests need to leave."

She raised her eyebrow. That included me.

I gave her a salute, then went to my room. Alone.

I SHOWERED and watched a cooking show in my boxers. The cumulative work and stress from the weekend caught up with me, and exhaustion seeped into my bones and muscles. Yet I couldn't fall asleep.

I checked my phone, not sure what I was looking for. A message from Charlie?

I wanted to make sure he got back all right. He was probably just as exhausted as I was. Did he really have the energy to party?

My questions were answered ten minutes later when the door unlocked, and he sat on the far side of the bed.

"That was a short afterparty," I said.

"I didn't go." He had his back to me as he took off his shoes. "I'm tired."

"You turned down a party? I'm in shock."

He whipped around. "Is that what you think of me? I'm just some party animal?"

"No," I said, taken aback by the dark edge in his voice. "I thought you were going."

He tossed his shoes onto the floor. "Well, I didn't. It's been a long day."

A long day that you regretted?

"You should probably get some sleep."

"That's the plan." He whipped off his shirt and threw it on a chair. He stormed into the bathroom, leaving a trail of ice in his wake.

How the hell were we supposed to share a bed when it was obvious he wanted nothing to do with me? Twenty-four hours ago, we'd slept in each other's arms.

Now we were here.

I called the front desk to double-check if they had any extra rooms or spare cots. It was a big no on both fronts.

Charlie exited the bathroom with brushed teeth and the same serious look stamped on his face. He stripped down to his boxers, which would've given me a hard-on had the room not been filled with uncomfortable tension.

"Thanks again for helping this weekend."

He threw his pants on the floor. "Stop thanking me, Mitch!"

Mitch. It was weird to hear my name on my tongue.

"What the hell is your problem? What did I do?"

"Nothing. I mean, it's just..." He paced in the small space the room allowed. "You don't have to thank me. I'm your employee. It's part of the job."

"You went above and beyond."

"Doing what?" His words dared me to tell the truth, to get into the things we did today. "Dancing with you?"

"I appreciated that you did."

"Why did you ask me to dance?"

He waited for an answer, but I couldn't give him the truth. He had just dipped his toe into the bisexual waters. The truth would freak him out. The truth was freaking me out.

The truth was I was falling for him, developing feelings I promised myself I wouldn't get.

I shrugged my shoulders. I'd rather him stay pissed off.

"Just needed someone to dance with, huh?"

"Yeah," I grumbled.

Charlie gave me a cold, hard look. Hurt flashed across his face, softening his eyes, making his bottom lip tremble. I could tell he was working up the nerve to say something, the words building in his chest. Preparing to tell me off and curse me out for crossing every conceivable line with him.

"I'm glad you asked me to dance." He heaved in short breaths and clenched his fists. "I *wanted* to dance with you."

He slumped his shoulders, his body deflating. It was alarming to watch someone usually so alive and extroverted fold into himself. He shuffled into the bathroom and turned on the shower.

I was an idiot. I was a damn idiot.

He *wanted* to dance with me.

It took me a good, long moment to get my behind out of bed, march into the bathroom, and yank back the shower curtain. "I wanted to dance with you, too."

29

CHARLIE

Mitch stared into my eyes with an intensity and vulnerability that would've stripped me naked had I not been naked already. I tuned out the water hitting my body.

"I wanted to dance with you," he said again.

I gulped back a nervous, boulder-sized lump in my throat. It seemed like Mitch had one of those, too.

"I like you, Charlie. I really like you." Mitch's eyes crinkled at the sides. "I feel like I'm a teenager again."

I turned off the water. "I like you, too. It's not just physical with me. Though that part is...really good."

"You don't have to tell me. You have the heart of an angel and the mouth of a hoover." Mitch knocked his fist twice against the wall. "But...dammit, this is wrong. You work for me. And if Ellie ever found out..."

I had the same concerns, but they seemed the size of jellybeans at this moment. "We'll figure it out. We can try, can't we? I can always get a new job, and you can get a new daughter."

Thankfully, Mitch laughed, his sense of humor still intact.

"Is that what you want? To get a new job?"

"No. But I can sign a waiver?"

"A waiver? For what?"

"I'm not sure. I don't actually know what those are, but they sound official."

Mitch let out a deep chortle that made his ridiculously sexy body rumble and let me know things would be all right. Like dinosaur life at Jurassic Park, somehow, we would find a way.

Right?

Mitch broke up my train of thought when he dragged a hand down my chest and pinched my wet nipple. "I didn't mean to interrupt your shower."

"It's big enough in here for two, as we previously discovered." I raked my eyes over his chest and the chubby poking from his boxers.

Mitch's eyes traveled down to my out-in-the-open boner. His finger drifted over my pubic hair, sending glorious shivers rippling in me. "Why don't you turn that shower back on?"

He stripped out of his boxers, unleashing his thick cock. The shower jets sprayed hot water across my chest, but that heat was nothing compared to when Mitch pushed me against the wall and devoured me in a kiss.

My moan echoed at the perfect pitch in the shower. His wet body slicked against mine as he made like Jesus and took the wheel. His large frame towered over me, making me feel delicate and precious, not small. His hands brushed my lips, then traveled down my body, pinching my nipples and tumbling down my stomach. I clenched with need. I could've come right then and there, but I wanted to stretch this out.

Our cocks swordfought, each touch another bolt of lightning. Mitch looked down at me with a protective, lust-filled gaze. He was going to tear me apart in the most thoughtful way.

"I saw the bottle of lube inside your bag," he said between kisses.

"Were you going through my stuff?"

"It was accidental."

"Sure it was." I dragged my teeth down his neck, eliciting a deep groan from his chest.

"Since you have it, we might as well use it." A snarky smile lit up his face. But I wiped it away when I grabbed both of our dicks and gave them a good pump.

"I guess we should."

He did a double-take. Water streamed into his beard and flecked his dark eyelashes. "Do you want to?"

Did I? I hadn't consulted with my gay sherpa Amos. But in my heart, I knew I was ready. I knew a moment like this was not one to be wasted. I wanted Mitch to have full control over my body. I trusted him to make it special.

"Yeah, Boss." I licked my lips. "I want you to fuck my virgin hole. The only part of me left that's a virgin."

"You don't want to be the only guy at the frat house without a sore asshole."

"For the last time, a fraternity is not a gay orgy!" Inside, my body sizzled at the thought of him making me sore. Yes, please and thank you.

"Fratboy." He cradled my chin. "I'm going to apologize in advance because I'm going to fuck you so good you're going to be in agony packing up tomorrow, but I won't make you regret a second of it."

Dang, that sounded like the greatest thing on earth. "Bring it the fuck on."

Mitch pressed me against the shower tiles as he got to his knees and took my cock in his mouth. He fluttered his nose against my patch of hair. I gripped the soap holder, but with the way his mouth was maneuvering around my cock, I was bound to rip it off the wall.

"Fuck, Boss. Feels so good," I muttered out as he rubbed my cock against his lush beard. He slipped a ball into his mouth and sucked, then the other one. Lust fogged my brain and put every muscle on pins and needles. Want burned in my core.

"I'm gonna come," I squeaked out. He pulled my cock from his mouth.

"Not yet." With his large, commanding hands, he spun me around. My ribcage crushed into the tiles. My ass was exposed and for the taking.

"Are you getting the lube?" I asked.

"We're not there yet. Haven't you frat boys ever heard of foreplay?" Mitch spread my cheeks and licked a stripe down my crack. He chased it with his beard. Prickly hairs danced on my sensitive skin, pouring gallons of gasoline on my raging fire.

He spread my cheeks wider, and hot water and cold air hit my tight hole and trickled down my taint. It was a position I'd never found myself in as a once-straight guy, but I had full trust Mitch would take care of me. He wasn't here to pump and dump.

He took turns rubbing his tongue and his chin over my opening. I cried out as he pressed his tongue in me, past the tight ring of muscle.

"More," I begged. He lit up nerves I didn't know existed.

And more he gave. He pushed two fingers inside me,

stretching me wide. But it would be nothing compared to what his cock would do. I leaned into this new sensation, feeling the discomfort, oddness, and pleasure just on the other side. Mitch was as dextrous with my ass as he was behind a bar. His fingers, tongue, and beard combined into the Long Island Iced Tea of salad tossing. Somehow, together they all were absolutely delicious, and I couldn't get enough.

"Fuck, I love when you eat my hole."

"This is only the beginning." He spat on it and gave my cheek a hard slap.

I hope his hand left a mark.

He swirled his thumb around my hole, teasing me. I was going to explode if he didn't stick something larger inside there.

His body overpowered me as he pressed his cock on my hole. I stuck out my ass to give him better leverage, but he didn't enter. He hovered. The anticipation destroyed me.

"Stop teasing me," I huffed out, oxygen barely able to stay in my lungs.

"What do you want?"

"I want your dick inside me, and I want you to fuck me senseless, Dude." I scooted my ass back, but he wouldn't shove inside. His plump head rested on the surface.

He was fucking waterboarding my ass. What was this *Zero Dark Thirty* bullshit?

Mitch chuckled into my ear, making all the hairs on my neck stand at attention like my cock. He grabbed my hair and kissed the point where my neck met my shoulder. His tongue traced a line up to my ear, and he nibbled on my ear lobe. His erection rested in my crack.

"If this is gay sex, I want a refund," I said.

"Fratboy, I know the second I slip inside you, I'm going

to blow. So I'm trying to hold on as best I can. You make it really fucking hard."

"Just do it. Please." My body fucking quaked with such need I could've ripped the tiles out of the grout. The torture choked me. A deep guttural grunt tore from my throat. "Please, Boss."

"You want some of this?" He dry humped my ass in slow, steady thrusts. Every time I thought his cock was finally going to give up and enter my hole, it slid up my crack. "You ready to get fucked?"

"That's what I've been saying, Boss. Get with the program!"

He slapped my ass hard, shutting me up.

I reached behind me to lead his cock to the promised land, but I was blocked. He held my arm behind me and frotted the fuck out of me. Hard thrusts that slapped my sensitive skin, and even though he wasn't technically fucking me, he was still hitting the right spots.

He grunted into my ear, sending me dangling over the edge. Precome leaked from my cock, and I moaned with abandon. Even with the shower running, my voice could probably be heard in the hallway.

Fuck the hallway. Fuck the hotel. Everything was getting fucked except me.

"I'm gonna come, Boss."

And like a light switch, he was off. He stepped back. Cold water and air hit my skin.

No.

That fucking sex demon.

"Dude!" I punched the wall. My body crumbled without the feel of his hot skin. He was trying to kill me, wasn't me?

Mitch spun me around, a fucking slaphappy grin that I

couldn't not find adorable. He wasn't edging me. He was leaving me to dangle off the side of a cliff.

He kissed me tenderly, his lips soft on mine. "Are you ready to get fucked?"

I gave him a *very* exaggerated nod.

30

MITCH

How the hell had I not shot my load already? I was dying to paint his insides white. I wasn't going to last long buried inside that tight, virgin ass, so I needed to stretch this out as long as possible.

Like how I wanted to stretch his hole.

Fuck. This was the best kind of torture. The very few random hookups that had sustained me over the years were pump-and-dumps. We'd get naked, get our rocks off as fast as possible, and then go our separate ways.

But Charlie. This fucking bro had captured my heart, and I wanted to savor every second we had together. I could stare into his eyes until I went blind.

First, though, I needed him ass-up on the bed.

He shut off the water. I picked him up, and he wrapped his legs around my waist. We made out as I carried him to the bed. His compact, muscular frame fit me like a glove.

"Get on all fours," I growled.

"You got it, Boss." He immediately got on his hands and knees and nodded his head. There was something puppy-like about Charlie. He was happy, loyal, and full of boundless energy. Doggie style seemed like a good fit.

I cared for him deeply, but right now, I needed to have him rough.

I spread his cheeks and spat on his hole. Damn, it was beautiful. I kissed and bit both cheeks, eliciting a hiss of pleasure from him. Searching through his bag, I pulled out the bottle of lube.

"Did you really bring this?"

"Amos slipped it in without telling me."

"Funny thing to say about lube."

Rolling on one of the condoms Amos also included, I gazed at the beautiful man I was about to wreck. A part of me wondered if we'd be able to survive outside this hotel room, if the real world would catch up to us. But that would have to wait until morning.

I held the bottle over his ass and dripped lube down his crack. Charlie gasped at the cold. His muscles clenched. I rubbed the slickness on his hole, then pressed two fingers inside. He was already warmed up from the shower, so he didn't fight me.

Each knuckle disappeared into his ass. He pushed against them to take even more.

This boy was ready.

I coated my sheathed, ragingly hard cock in lube.

"You ready, fratboy?"

"Actually, I don't want to do this."

My face dropped to the floor. "Oh."

Charlie looked back at me, his face split in two with his cocky grin.

"You fucker."

"That's what you get for teasing me," he said.

"Well, the teasing ends now." I thrust into him, pushing past his tightness.

Charlie cried out in a mix of pleasure and pain.

"You okay?" I didn't want to hurt him, but goddamn, was it beautiful watching my dick sink into his hole.

His chest filled with oxygen. I smoothed my hand over his tense back.

"Yeah. I can feel you stretching me."

He clenched around my cock, but didn't try to fight me. I thrust in again, his heat and tightness pushing me right to the edge.

"Don't stop."

That was the green light I needed. I grabbed both ass cheeks and fucked him in deep, steady strokes. I didn't want his first time to be with a guy who came in two seconds flat. But damn, this was going to be difficult. His ass was a goldmine.

"Fratboy, you feel so fucking good. How are you feeling?"

"Good, Boss," he said, the side of his face resting on the comforter. "It hurts good like I reached a new max weight on the bench."

"This feels fucking amazing." I sped up. The only way my body could communicate with his was through deep, full thrusts that blazed with passion. He fisted the comforter and arched his back to give me more of himself.

"Want it so bad," he moaned.

"Stroke yourself."

And so he did. He clenched tighter on my dick, and I pounded harder into his tight little ass. Skin slapped skin. Beads of sweat pricked on his back and my chest. Dizzy breaths heaved into the silence. Want created a thick haze in the air.

He let out short groans with each hump, and I couldn't

hold on any longer. By the way he shook under me, neither could he.

I pulled him up straight so his back was flush against me. I had never felt closer to another person. I fucked his hole in hard, short bursts and joined his hand in jerking his leaking, engorged cock.

His head rolled back onto my shoulder, sweaty hair slicking my skin.

"Yes," he whimpered over and over as he shot waves of come onto the bed, hitting our pillows. I kept him from collapsing. I hugged him tight as I filled my rubber.

He gasped when I pulled out. I licked a trickle of sweat off his neck.

"How was that?" I let go of him. He immediately fell to the bed in a puddle of his come. "That good?"

"Yes," he said into the blanket.

I spanked his ass and felt him wince underneath. The soreness was kicking in. It filled me with a sense of pride, knowing I was the one who did that.

I still had it.

"Let's shower and get into bed." With careful fingers, I slowly removed the pillow from under his head. "And let's turn this case inside out."

31

CHARLIE

I woke up the next morning sore everywhere for a litany of different reasons. All of the work for prepping and serving at the wedding coalesced in my aching muscles and bones. And then my ass was sore, which was a new kind of feeling. A great kind of feeling. When Mitch said he was going to stretch my hole, that was not an exaggeration.

We made out in bed, morning breath and all. The thing was, when you woke up cradled in the strong arms of the guy you were crazy about, it was impossible not to put your morning wood to good use. Mitch's spear poked my ass, which despite the glorious discomfort, was not opposed to a round two.

I arched my back so I could meet his erection, uh, head on.

"This isn't helping my dick go down." His raspy voice sent shivers across my chest. My ass seemed to have a mind of its own. It was ready for more.

"We might as well make hay while the sun shines."

"What does that mean?"

"It means I'm still horny." I thrust against his cock for good measure.

"Fucking fratboy." I could feel his smile against my smile, the hairs of his beard bristling on my skin. He pulled his arms tighter around me, putting me in a protective cage.

"I haven't been in a frat in four years."

"Come here." With a sure hand, he tipped my chin up to him, and I gazed into those stormy eyes, my heart lifting, before we melted into a kiss.

This time, after getting situated with the lube and condoms, I straddled him and sank onto his fat cock. It hit me from a new angle, stimulating new parts of me. The exquisite pleasure of last night came rushing back. My hands traversed his hairy, muscular chest as I bounced on top of him.

"Charlie, just like that," he said. "Who knew you were so hungry for dick?"

"Just yours," I breathed out. My cock leaked precome onto his stomach. I imagined him doing the same inside me, and waves of ecstasy flashed through my core.

He reached up and caressed my chest for a moment. "God, you're beautiful."

I fucked him faster, want and need colliding in my system, my balls drawing up. Mitch rested his hands behind his head like he was lying on the beach, something I could never imagine him doing.

"Don't work too hard," I joked.

"I'm liking the view."

"Me, too, Boss." I supposed it was only fair since he did most of the work last night. I stroked my cock and rubbed it through his furry belly. I was so damn close. The days of being able to last a long time to ensure my female partners got off were over.

My body quaked like an oil derrick, ready to burst.

Mitch sensed this, too, since he took my hands away from my dick, all set to torture me again.

"I'm going to make you come hands-free," he said.

"I've never done that."

"That's because you haven't been with me."

He shot me a cocky smirk that threatened to make me blow. I bit down on my lip, wanting to prove him wrong.

Mitch sat up and rested my hands on his shoulders. Then he took over fucking duties. He raised his ass and jack-hammered into my hole in hard jabs. My cock flopped on his stomach, and I couldn't catch my breath. My body coiled and tightened as he rammed the orgasm out of me.

Spurts of come shot onto his chest and stomach, and he grinned from ear to ear before rolling his head back and filling me with his seed.

He won.

Hell, I won, too.

Our eyes connected through the haze of afterglow. Mitch was rugged and handsome and also beautiful in his own sweet way. He filled my heart. I'd been in relationships before, but I never had this. This feeling of the deepest parts of ourselves intertwining, of comfort and safety and...

Love?

Whoa, Charlie.

"What is it?" he asked.

"What? Uh, nothing." I hopped out of bed and went into the shower. I had to cool myself down.

I wasn't the kind of guy who could handle love. My relationships never breached the emotional surface. They were like kids' toys: light and fun and never lasting more than a few weeks. Now I was thinking I was in love? Perhaps Mitch had fucked so deep inside me that he caused brain damage.

Mitch liked me and liked to fuck me, but as I stepped into the hot water, I wondered if this was just light and fun for him. We had good times fooling around this weekend, but did he feel anything serious for me?

Or was I doomed to be the fun bro?

———

ELLIE AND TIM reserved a bunch of tables at a diner in town for all the guests who'd stayed over. I offered for us to go there separately. He could get there early to be with Ellie and other family members, and I could grab a ride with Amos. And we could avoid any whispers of us walking in together, like a couple.

But Mitch refused. He shook off the suggestion with a shoulder shrug, no qualms or fucks to give.

Mitch tried to clean up the hotel room as best he could before we left, but it still had the aura of a sex disaster zone. He made the bed, but it smelled of sex. The garbage cans were filled with condoms and tissues. We left a nice tip in an envelope for the maid.

As soon as we stepped into the diner, conversations came to a halt for a split second. Eyes upon eyes checked us out. What did they know? Was our room bugged?

Skeeter shot me a cold look, but that was one I could easily ignore. Fuck him and his drinking problem. Amos waved me over while Mitch went to sit with his friends.

He reached for my hand, but our fingers missed each other as we went in separate directions.

I kept my head down, but when I looked up for a moment, Ellie and I made brutal eye contact. I didn't need a weatherman to tell me about the cold front coming in.

"Hey," I said quietly to Amos while I put my napkin on my lap. "What are we eating?"

"I ordered blueberry pancakes."

None of the food had arrived yet, but Mitch and I were still late. And was Ellie still looking at me? I was too scared to find out.

"The waitress should be over," he said.

"Can you pass the coffee?"

"Yeah. Sure." Amos flipped over my mug and poured me a steaming hot cup. I drank it black. The caffeine was a much-needed jolt to my system.

Amos leaned in. "So, how was your night?"

"What's that supposed to mean?"

His eyebrows jumped up to his hairline. "Okay, then."

"Sorry." I shut my eyes. I gulped down the coffee and let it burn my throat. "Just...it was..."

"You're in a glass cage of emotions?"

"Pretty much, yeah."

Amos knew me well. We'd only reconnected a few months ago, but I considered him my closest friend, more of a friend than my frat brothers a few tables away.

"What happened last night in your room? Do I need to get a banana and doughnut so you can act it out?"

"What? Huh? What are you talking about?" I held up the menu so it blocked my face.

"Charlie, I saw you wince when you sat down just now. It was the my-butt-hurts-from-a-good-dicking wince."

I put the menu down. It was no use.

He patted me on the back. "I'm glad I snuck the lube and condoms into your bag."

I motioned for him to keep his voice down, though he was being quiet. It was only loud in my head. And what if Ellie had supersonic hearing?

"How was it?"

My heart wasn't ready to turn last night into grist for the gossip mill. I was falling in love with Mitch. Hell, I think I was already there. I hesitated to admit how he made me feel because I was scared it was one-sided.

"It was good. Really good," I said without enthusiasm.

Amos studied my face. Well, at least he wasn't studying my sore ass. His giddy nature subdued as if he were downloading my thoughts.

"You like him," he said.

I didn't answer.

"He likes you, too."

"He likes flirting with me and fucking me. That's all I was good for with girls. It's the same with guys, too. I'm not the best when it comes to actual, real relationships."

"I saw the way he looked at you during the slow dance."

I took it so did others, which is why we got stares when we entered.

"Amos, just drop it." My eyes flicked up, and two tables away, Mitch gave me a clandestine wink that I felt all over my body. But it was followed up by the familiar glare of the bride at the next table over.

I ordered blueberry pancakes because as soon as Amos mentioned them, it was all my stomach could think about eating. Amos regaled me with stories of flirting with Ellie's drunk frat boy friends, wondering if any of them could also be bisexual. He tried the flirting methods we used at Remix but to no avail. I let him know he didn't want anything to do with those guys. One of my ex-girlfriends junior year told me that Skeeter was known to be bad in bed among girls in her sorority.

After two cups of coffee, I had to piss like a racehorse. I went to the bathroom on the other side of the diner, away from our room. When I was done, I came out to find Ellie waiting for me.

Hands on hips.

"Hey. Congratulations!" I feigned cheerfulness to fight off the chill in her glare.

"Is there something going on with you and my dad?"

"What?" I tried laughing it off, but I didn't want to outright lie.

"You two have been...kind of flirty this weekend?" She had trouble finding the words, and I guess I didn't blame her because this was a horrifically awkward situation. "Other people have brought it up, asking if you two were together. And then last night, you danced with him. I...what is going on?"

"He asked me to dance because he didn't have anyone to dance with."

"He asked you? His straight bartender?" Her responses came rapid-fire, the lawyer in her showing.

"I'm actually kinda bi."

"Like bisexual?"

I nodded.

"Um, okay. Cool. But there were other people he could've danced with." She shook her head, seeming not to want to go down that path. "Is there something going on with you two?"

I was usually quick with an answer, but this time, I stammered. I didn't want to lie. I couldn't lie. My heart wouldn't let me shrug this off as much as I knew it was best.

"Yes," I said softly.

Her pupils went up in flames. I'd never witnessed blind shock and outrage form in someone so quickly.

"Are you for real?"

"Yes."

"What is going on?"

I managed a weak smile. "How much detail do you want?"

She clamped a hand over her mouth. "Oh, my God. Oh, my God. My dad and my ex-boyfriend?"

"I know how it seems."

She sat on a bench by a payphone, probably the first payphone I've seen in a decade at least. "People were whispering things yesterday, but I didn't believe them. That was outrageous, I thought. Oh, my God."

"Do you need a glass of water?"

She shot me a look. Water would not solve this problem.

"I know this is weird. It was weird for me, too. It's something that happened over the past couple of weeks."

"Weeks?"

I sat next to her to continue. "But if it's any consolation..." I twisted my hands in my pockets. "I like him." I exhaled a breath and prayed the truth would set me free. "I really like him."

Like clouds clearing up, the wall of shock slowly faded from her expression.

"I know it's crazy for lots of reasons. I'm still figuring shit out, but I like him, El."

"Holy shit." She put a comforting hand on mine as she continued to process. I could tell how hard she was working not to flip out. "Charlie, my dad is a good man. He's caring and loyal and thoughtful. He works really hard, and he doesn't mess around."

Her warm touch turned cold. "What are you saying?"

"I've wanted him to find someone for years. But he should be with someone more serious, someone more on his wavelength."

I took my hand back. "I think we get along well."

"You're fun. You're a lot of fun. But my dad isn't the type who messes around. He's built for a serious relationship."

"I can be..." Breath left my body.

"One of the benefits of this awkward situation is that I know what it's like to date you. It's fun, but it doesn't go beyond that. Things can only go so far. You're like a rocketship that just can't break through the earth's atmosphere into outer space."

I wish I hadn't dropped that astrophysics class sophomore year.

"My dad's been through a lot. It sounds like you care about him, but you have to know deep down that isn't what he needs." She patted my knee, and now I was the one with the cold look. She thought she was being helpful and diplomatic, but her words were a consistent kick in the nuts.

"Look, Charlie, my dad doesn't have many people in his life. I need to look out for him. I don't want him to get hurt when you decide to move on."

I opened my mouth to defend myself, but what if she was right? This was why I sucked at relationships. I couldn't be serious. I was destined to a life of little flings.

A firm, familiar hand clapped my shoulder and massaged the pain out.

"Ellie." Mitch's deep voice bellowed in this narrow hallway. "I don't need you to decide who I get to be with."

"Dad!" She froze like any adult child does when reprimanded by their parent. That feeling never went away.

"I know you're looking out for me, but you don't have to." Mitch gazed down at me, his lazy smile sending my rocketship into the stratosphere. "I know what I'm doing."

"Dad. This is weird," she said.

"I know, I know. It wasn't expected or planned, but I like him." He gave me a wink. "I really like him."

I stood up and interlocked our fingers.

"Things are serious between us. Whatever your experience was with Charlie in college, he's changed. He's mature and caring. And if he does decide to move on, I'll handle it. I'm not some piece of glass you need to protect."

"I'm not going to move on," I said.

"You seemed different this morning. Quieter. I didn't know if I did something wrong."

"I got scared. You said it yourself." I pointed at Ellie. "I was terrible at being a boyfriend. People only saw me as some fun-loving idiot. Soon that's how I saw myself, too. I figured all I was good for was being the court jester. I wasn't worthy of anything real." I tilted my head back to look up at the guy I had fallen for. "But you don't make me feel that way."

"Because you're not." His thumb smoothed over my cheek. "You are capable of so much more than you give yourself credit for. You're incredible."

A sniffle broke our gaze, and Ellie wiped tears forming in her eyes.

"I guess this is quite a shock," Mitch said. "I should've said something to you before I danced with Charlie in front of everyone. I didn't give it much thought beforehand."

"I can't believe this. This is–oh, my God. My dad and my ex-boyfriend. Oh, my God." Tears rolled down her cheeks. I didn't want to cause a rift between father and daughter.

"Ellie, I'm sorry," I said, then whipped my head to Mitch. "I mean, I'm not." Then back to Ellie. "But I am. You guys know what I mean, right?"

"Ellie Bear." Mitch massaged her shoulder, breaking through her icy protective shell. "What do you want most for me?"

"I want you to be happy," she said through tears.

"I am." His voice cracked with emotion. It was alarming to hear but also incredibly sweet how much he cared for me and Ellie and everyone else in his orbit.

"Dad, I wanted to make you proud so you knew your sacrifices were worth it. But I see this light coming out of you, this genuine light. It's so beautiful. That's all I ever wanted for you." Ellie squeezed Mitch's hand.

I reached for her hand, but she didn't take it. We weren't there yet, but I would work to get us there eventually. I was in this for the long haul.

"I'm going to be okay, Ellie." Mitch radiated pure love. I was getting misty-eyed, too.

"Thank you," she said, and I realized she was talking to me. "For making my dad happy."

We let out a laugh to ease the tension. Mitch kissed my hand.

"This is more than a little weird." She dabbed at her eyes.

"But we'll figure it out," Mitch said to his daughter.

"I love you." She threw her arms around him.

"I love you so much." He hugged her tight.

Once Ellie returned to her table, Mitch wrapped an arm around me. "Shall we go back to breakfast? I want to try those blueberry pancakes you got."

32

CHARLIE

Mitch decided it was best to end the unofficial rule about employees dating each other. That was the first thing Natasha asked when he told her about our relationship.

Not congratulations.

Not you're such a cute couple.

"Well, this means the fraternization rule goes away, right?" She crossed her arms and cocked an eyebrow.

Apparently, she and Penny were in a relationship. I asked for details, and all she said was she was over men. It seemed like Stone's Throw Tavern was the new Tinder. Mitch made us all promise no fraternization while at work. He looked me dead in the eye when he said that, but the flickers of doubt flew over his face. He was hoping we could keep our hands off each other.

I'd give it the old college try. Mitch was a slab of pure sexiness, and it didn't help that with the weather getting warm, he wore more T-shirts that showed off his large-and-in-charge chest and arms, the kind of muscles one got through living, not working out.

During one of the slower weeknight shifts, I happened to catch Mitch coming out of the supply room with a box slung over his shoulder. It demanded a whistle from me, but I played the part of the mature, responsible employee and kept it in my pants.

At the end of my shift, after Natasha and Penny (aka girl-friends!) left, I went upstairs to Mitch's office. He was still plugging away, as always. His dedication moved me. I sat on the couch across from him as he worked at his desk and just took in his hotness.

"What?" he asked without looking up.

"You."

"Me, what?"

"Just over there, doing your boss thing with the glasses and the computer and the whole jotting down notes. It's super hot."

"I'm not acting in a porn flick."

He might have thought that, but in my mind, I already heard the bow chicka bow wow. His thick-framed glasses gave him a Clark Kent quality with a raging hot Superman underneath.

I got comfortable on the couch and did the natural thing when in the same room as my sexy boyfriend with a heart of gold under his grizzled demeanor.

I stroked myself over my jeans. Didn't take much to get hard.

Mitch buried himself in paperwork, and I let out a moan to get his attention.

"Since the laws against fraternization were lifted per our earlier staff meeting, I take it this is okay?" I unzipped my fly and reached into my pants to touch myself over my under-wear. I flung my head back and groaned, imagining Mitch on top of me.

"That is very much not okay," he said sternly. "No sex in the workplace is a given."

"So I can't do this?" I pulled out my dick and stroked.

He shot me an ice-cold look that only caused me to get hotter. He waved me over with two fingers. Two fingers that I wanted inside me...

I ambled over, letting my pants fall to my ankles in the process.

"Yes, Boss?"

"Get on your knees," he growled.

When I did, Mitch rolled out from the desk, revealing his erection straining against his jeans. Want surged through my veins.

He waved me closer with those commanding two fingers. My mouth was on him the second he unzipped. I licked down his sweaty, salty cock, my tongue returning to swirl around his fat head.

"Charlie, this is so against the rules."

"That's true," I said between sucking.

"But I can't get enough of your mouth."

"Also true."

Fire glinted in his eyes. "Can we try something?"

I nodded heck yes.

He pushed me down until his cock hit the back of my throat. I choked and coughed. "Let's try that again."

He wiped my watery eyes.

Back down I went. The bitter taste of precome hit my tongue as his large cock filled my mouth. I inhaled a deep breath from my nose.

"Oh, yeah. That's it, fratboy. Take it all." His fingers threaded through my hair like they were puppet strings controlling me.

I moaned against his hardness, completely at his mercy.

He held me down for a few seconds until I gagged, then pulled me back up.

"Shit. That was hot," he said. "Are you okay?"

"Yeah," I breathed out, letting air refill my lungs. I loved the feeling of being completely taken over by Mitch. Who knew I had such bottom energy?

"We're going to do that again."

I nodded yes. I loved the new feeling of deep throating him, of wringing out more grunts of pleasure.

I licked my lips and disappeared his cock all the way down. He stretched my mouth as he had done to my ass. This time, he held me down and fucked my mouth.

"Yes, fratboy. Yes, keep taking it."

I coughed for air and looked up to find him smiling down at me. He pulled my head off him.

"I always wanted to try that," he said, almost apologetically.

"Me, too." However, I'd originally wanted to try it with girls. It was cool being on the other side of things. My lust for Mitch knew no bounds.

"Get up."

As I stood up, my cock unabashedly hard and pointing at Mitch, he opened his drawer and removed lube and condoms.

"What are you doing with those in the office?" I asked.

"I was planning to bring them home for the next time. I couldn't wait." His tone darkened for a moment, sending a jolt of want down my spine.

I loved me some impatience.

Mitch rolled on his rubber and slicked himself up. He had me turn around and slicked me up. His rough fingers found my opening. I shivered with need, desperate to experience what came next. After the all-time-greatest sex we'd had in the hotel room, I was so ready for round two.

He wrapped a strong arm around my stomach and pulled me on top of him. I sat on his lap as he maneuvered his hard cock inside my tight hole. I was completely enveloped by Mitch in every sense. I savored this bear hug from my bear. Mitch held me against him as he jutted his hips up and thrusted.

The warmth of his chest, of his lips kissing my neck, of his growly moans felt like home, like I was relaxing next to a crackling campfire. He turned us to face the mirror above the couch.

"Look at yourself," he whispered in my ear.

And there we were. I was like a ventriloquist dummy on his lap, only it wasn't his hand controlling me. My little self was cocooned in his large, strong arms. My cock flopped on my stomach as I watched his thickness slide inside me. I spiraled in pleasure. I'd never been controlled like this, not since my frat initiation (which looking back, I guess was kinda homoerotic).

Fuck. Mitch was fucking me. He curled a fist around my cock, sending me barreling toward the edge. A guttural moan ripped out of me. It wasn't going to take much. One pump and I would be a goner. Mitch tortured me by keeping his fist still like my dick was in a clamp.

He let go and pulled out of me, then played with my pink, wrecked ass, circling his thumb around the rim.

"Fuck. You are so goddamn hot. I lose all control with you."

"Same," I responded like I was shitfaced. I could barely form words right now. I just wanted him back inside me and to fuck me to completion.

Mitch smiled wide, his eyes crinkling as even aliens in space could see that I needed less talking and more fucking.

He shoved his cock inside me, restoring order to the universe. I moaned in ecstatic relief.

"Fuck me, Boss."

We picked up where we left off. Mitch, playing me like a violin, fist now jerking me off like a proper gentleman. And me, on the verge of coming and seeing stars.

He cuddled me against his hot, 1000% all manly body and jackhammered my hole like he was drilling for oil.

My balls drew up, and the outside world shut down as my body exploded with come in the most earth-shattering orgasm of my life. Jizz seeped over his large fist.

"I'm going to come inside you."

"Need it." My head lolled back on his shoulders.

With a few thrusts, he filled his condom with his hot load.

I blinked a few times to get my bearings. It was like being underwater. When I surfaced, I looked over my shoulder, and there he was with a tender glint that captured my heart.

"I hope you didn't mind that we went a little rough. I have decades of fantasies built up."

"Here for it." My legs wobbled as I found the floor.

The No Sex in the Workplace rule was going to be very hard to follow.

As I pulled my pants up, I noticed something on Mitch's desk that dulled my afterglow. As soon as he caught me, he shuffled papers to cover it up, but I'd read the most important words.

"You're selling the bar?"

33

MITCH

Dropping major news seconds after an orgasm was not my plan. I sighed and leaned back in my chair.

"Are you?" he asked again. "Selling the bar?"

"Most likely."

He stumbled back as if I'd stabbed him. "I need to sit down."

His frame flopped onto the couch where moments ago, he'd seduced me into, uh, fraternizing.

"I was planning to tell you and the staff. The deal is still in progress. It's still early."

"Not that early if you're already reviewing contracts. Do you have a lawyer? You should really have a lawyer review this for you."

I chuckled at his sincerity. Even flustered, he was looking out for me.

"Yes, I have a lawyer."

He opened and closed his mouth. A million starts and stops hung on his lips.

"I didn't mean to ambush you. Hannah's husband, Vince, is in real estate investing. He sees great potential with

Stone's Throw. He thinks he can build it into something spectacular."

"It already is spectacular." Charlie took a breath and tried to play the cool and collected boyfriend.

"He sees a lot of potential here."

"Thanks to you and the hard work you've already put in for the past hundred years."

"Thirty years."

"You know what I mean. He's going to profit off your hard work, your family's hard work."

"Trust me, I'm going to profit, too." Vince called me after the wedding, asking for the chance to at least make an offer. When he emailed over the offer, I nearly fell out of my chair. I'd never seen that many zeroes in my life. I really tried to keep my cool because, to him, it was just another business transaction.

"It was never about the money to you."

Ah, youth. I remembered when I was that innocent that I didn't care about money. Then I had a child to raise. "Charlie, we live in a capitalist society. It's always about the money."

His Adam's apple quivered in his throat. "Not everything."

"Why are you so upset? I still want to be with you. I'll have more time to spend with you. And you can get a job at another bar. I'll recommend and refer the hell out of you. You're a damned good bartender."

"I know I can get a job elsewhere. You don't think I've been approached by other establishments?"

Apparently, I hadn't. Even in the midst of angst, he found a way to be cocky.

"But I don't want to work someplace else. I want to work here. With you." His earnest, full eyes blazed into my soul, giving me serious pushback against my decision. "You gave me a chance when nobody else did."

He was breaking my heart.

"I'm tired. I've been at this for most of my life."

Charlie let out a dark chuckle. "You say that..."

"I mean it."

"You love it. You won't admit it, but you fucking love all of it."

I snorted a laugh. "Bullshit. It's a slog."

"The best things are. The things we love to do can suck at times. Do you think the players on the New York Rangers love playing hockey every day? It's probably a slog for them, too, but overall, there's no other place they'd rather be."

"They're also very well-compensated." I had to admire Charlie's passion.

"When the bar is busy, and you're zipping around putting out fires, checking on customers, and dealing with vendors, *you can't get enough*. It lights you up. I'm a bartender. I see everything." He flashed a smirk, proud of this newfound power that bartenders possessed. "Yeah, this wasn't the life you chose, but maybe it chose you for a reason. You could've sold the bar and gotten some nine-to-five desk job at any point in your life. But you didn't."

"It's more complicated than that," I said half-heartedly.

"Is it, though? Let me guess; you're going to use your typical excuse that you had a child to raise, so you couldn't leave. That story is bullshit. You didn't want to leave. You didn't want to give this up. And you've felt guilty about that ever since."

"How'd you get so perceptive?" I tried to manage a sliver of a smile, but Charlie was getting under my skin in a non-sexy way.

"I listen to a lot of people all day. It was a good thing I

minored in psych." Charlie paced around the tiny office quarters. "So what are you going to do when you sell? Retire on some beach? Read books in coffee shops? That's not you, Mitch. You'll be bored within your first day. You'll miss the rush and the hustle."

"The hell I will!" I burst out of my chair, my frustration hitting a fever pitch. "Managing this place has been a life-long, seven-day-a-week slog. There's never a break. Making sure I have staff to dealing with customer complaints and staying up to code, and having to scramble to make payroll and pay the bills. It's a never-ending struggle, and it's been time away from my friends and my family. Hustle and grit sound nice until you realize you can never take a break. Now finally, *finally*, there is a light at the end of the tunnel." My heart throbbed in my ears. The years and years of working my ass off rattled in my bones. "You've been working here for three months. Come back to me in twenty years, and we'll see if you're still singing the same tune."

"This has been your life's work, and you're just going to sell it to some dickhead in a suit who's going to turn it into some overpriced tourist trap?"

"If the price is right, he can do whatever he wants with it."

"You don't mean that."

I gathered my papers into a file and grabbed my jacket from the wobbly coat rack. "One day, you're going to realize just how idealistic you sound." I brushed past him, and as I walked down the spiral staircase I had descended a million times over the years, he called out to me:

"And one day, you're going to realize you're making a mistake."

A FEW DAYS LATER, Vince and his buyers came to Stone's Throw in the morning to do a walkthrough. They wanted to check out their investment in person.

Chad and Brett were two guys representing Alpha Bravo, a private equity firm based in San Francisco. They were younger than I expected, wearing Patagonia sweater vests and Bonobos pants. They had the confident stride and air of two men who believed in their own hype.

"This town is super cute," Chad said while popping his gum. "Sometimes, I get so tired of the Bay Area. It can be a scene, and I just need to get away to Napa or something."

Brett rolled his eyes. "Dude, even Napa's becoming too much of a scene."

"Sourwood's a great little town. It's one of the fastest-growing towns in the state," Vince said. "Lots of potential growth amid the prime demographic."

"So, uh, what is private equity?" I asked, and their reactions made me feel like a rube.

"We buy and invest in organizations and make them better," Chad said. "More efficient. More profitable."

I didn't love that the new owners of Stone's Throw would be across the country, but that was corporate life. I'd met chain restaurant owners whose management was based overseas. That was the way of the world.

"We have a small but loyal customer base," I added, and my comment fell on deaf, uninterested ears.

"Oh, we'll change that." Brett flashed me a cocky smile that, unlike Charlie's, made me recoil. "We're going to cast a much wider net beyond the town drunks. Kidding."

"I love this space," Chad said. "There's so much potential. You own all the land up to the falls?"

"We do. My parents had a chance to buy the property outright decades ago."

"Smart peeps." Chad popped his gum.

Peeps. I clenched my fist as I heard my parents rolling in their graves.

"Part of the appeal of Stone's Throw is the woodsy view against the falls," I said.

"We'll bring in a landscaping team to preserve that feeling," Brett said. "Vince, I'm thinking we would knock out this wall and expand closer to the bank. That would give us the space we need for the ball pit."

I stopped in my tracks. "Ball pit?"

"As part of the kids' playroom," Chad said.

"You want to bring kids into a bar?"

Chad, Vince, and Brett exchanged a look that made me feel like a thimble-sized moron.

"They're planning to go in a different direction," Vince said delicately. "They're thinking bigger."

Chad pivoted on his loafer. "Alpha Bravo wants to turn this place into the region's new family destination. Sourwood and the surrounding towns are seeing their biggest demographic growth among families with young kids. This area is older, and there aren't as many family-friendly options. We're going to fix that. There will be food and drinks, but also a kids' play area and a virtual reality arcade upstairs." He pointed up.

My office.

"That is primo space up there. I could see why you liked using it as your hideaway." Brett ribbed my side but quickly realized that was a bad move.

"I use it as my office. Lets me keep an eye on what's going on in my bar."

"Won't be your bar much longer." Brett laughed at his joke. His smile slid off his face when I did not reciprocate. "Relax, Mitch. Soon, none of this will be your problem anymore."

I shot Vince a glare, as he did not fill me in on their plans. He'd been curiously vague at the wedding, and now I understood why. "When are you starting renovations?"

"We're debating whether to renovate or start from scratch."

"Tear it down?" I asked.

"Rather than build on top of an older establishment, we can build something new, something more energy-efficient," Brett said. "Is this building even LEED certified?"

"No," I said flatly. "When my dad and grandfather built it with their bare hands, they didn't think much about energy efficiency."

He and Chad gave me exaggerated nods like they were placating a crazy old man.

"Times change," Chad said with a shrug as he took pictures of the space on his phone. He swatted Brett in the chest. "Dude, I'm thinking like blue and green racing stripes, maybe? Make it super colorful. Oh! And what if we installed a slide from the upstairs arcade down to the ball pit?"

"Dude! Yes!" Brett exclaimed. "That idea fully fucks."

Uh, was that a good thing?

Chad turned to me, all business again. He hopped up and sat on the bar, the same bar where my dad first taught me to pour drinks. The same bar where Charlie's lazy grins made me melt.

"Are any of your staff under contract, or are they all at will?" Chad asked.

Dread filled my stomach. I knew where he was going. "They're all at-will employees. They're loyal, hard-working people."

"They can all apply for jobs once we're operational."

"They have to apply for their same jobs?"

"Yeah," Brett said. "It's standard procedure."

I tried to picture Natasha happily serving helicopter parents and their screaming kids. It was a disaster in the making—a funny disaster, but a disaster all the same.

Brett and Chad clacked their loafers to the front doors. They shook my hand and thanked me for my time. It was all very pleasant with an ugly undercurrent.

"Did you have any questions on the contract?" Chad asked, his gum-chewing involving half his face.

"You should be excited, bro," Brett said. I hated being called bro. Charlie was the exception to that rule. "This new place is going to transform Sourwood."

"Did you get approval from the mayor's office for all these changes?"

Brett waved the question off. "We'll take care of that. We're not worried about some small-time mayor."

What kind of political tricks would they pull to get the green light from Leo? Builders like them were everything he fought against in this last mayoral campaign. Money wouldn't sway him. Would they resort to blackmail? To getting him booted from office to get their way? Maybe I was overreacting, but I felt an unnerving lack of control in this situation.

Once I sold, I would have no control. The thought made my throat go dry. Charlie was right.

"What do you say?" Chad held out his hand for a shake, a shake that would mean a yes to him. Yes to tearing down Stone's Throw. Yes to demolishing my legacy. Yes to a new chapter of my life, one that didn't involve coming here, didn't involve the round-the-clock care and constant headaches. But one that didn't involve bringing people together and putting something back into this community.

"C'mon, dude. Don't leave me hanging. Are you ready to be a rich man?" Chad asked.

Wasn't I? I tried to picture the new life an influx of cash would bring me. What did I want that I didn't already have?

I came up blank.

"You know, I've actually had a change of heart."

Chad and Brett looked like I stomped on their iPhones.

Vince cut in between us. "Mitch, I know this was a lot of information to take in today. They have big plans. Why don't you take the day to process?"

"I don't need another minute to process anything. I appreciate your time, gentlemen, but I'm not going to sell."

"What?" Chad blinked at me.

"I'm not going to let my family's work turn into Chuck E. Cheese."

"This isn't Chuck E. Cheese," Brett said. "We're disrupting the family experience."

"Well, find another place to do your disrupting." I pushed past Brett and Chad and ascended the spiral staircase to my rightful position.

34

CHARLIE

I t was impossible to hear drink orders, let alone my own thoughts, when a hundred people were scream-singing the lyrics to "Suddenly Seymour" from *Little Shop of Horrors* at the tippy-top of their lungs. The windows rattled with the vibrations of their voices.

At first, I didn't know the song well, but after multiple Musical Mondays with it on rotation, I was now able to mumble along by myself.

It was no "Don't Cry for Me Argentina" or "Seasons of Love," but it had its moments.

Amos pushed through the crowd at the bar as I finished pouring a line of tequila shots for a group of construction workers who had done a fantastic lip-synch and mimicked choreography to "The Schuyler Sisters" from *Hamilton*.

He slammed his empty glass down. "I'll take another Cell Block Tang."

I grabbed a fresh glass.

"These are good!" He glanced behind me at the chalk-board with the drink specials. "You made these up yourself?"

I nodded proudly. It was my first time creating new cock-tails, another idea I had to generate buzz and prove to Mitch that he made the right call by not selling. My drinks included: Cell Block Tang, Not Giving Away My Kamikaze Shot, Whiskey through a Window. I had been itching to learn more about mixology, and this presented the ideal opportunity. Lots of guests complimented me on their taste and their names, with one person suggesting I go into writing ad copy.

No thanks. I liked where I was.

I mixed the tang into the liquor for Amos's drink. It was so pretty. Such a shame it'd be downed in a minute for the sake of easing into flirting.

"Seems like you're having a good night." I cracked a knowing smile.

"With lumberjack guy? How'd you know about him?"

"I'm the bartender. I see everything." Including the burly man with whom Amos had been successfully flirting. Mitch had inspired a mini fashion trend among guests. He had all the tips down: the smile, the eye contact, the confi-dent puff of his chest. I was a proud teacher. "Is he a lumberjack?"

"He has muscles and is wearing a red-and-black check-ered shirt. It's good enough for me." Amos nabbed the Cell Block Tang and downed half of it.

"What about the guy from Remix a few weeks ago?"

He shrugged. Old news.

"Damn, you are quite the player. And I say that with no judgment." I held my hands up. "You are...what's the gay equivalent of ladies' man?"

"Cockhungry slut," he deadpanned.

"You do you. Just make sure to use protection."

"Speaking of, zucchinis are in season again. Maybe you

and Mitch can go to the farmers market and have a three-way."

"I'm three seconds from cutting you off."

Amos ran his finger around the rim of his glass. He wasn't leaving to return to lumberjack guy, and a contemplative look took over his sunny disposition.

"What's going on?" I asked. I had developed a bartender's intuition where I could tell when somebody wanted to spill their guts.

"Can I tell you something?"

"Of course." Other customers waited with thinning patience and raised their arms to get my attention, but I wanted to make sure Amos was all right.

"I'm not the whore you think I am."

"I never called you that."

"You've really helped me with my game. These guys that I go home with...we might fool around a little. Hands, mouth. But I don't have sex with them. They want to, and I want to, but something stops me."

"There's nothing wrong with waiting. Are you..." The virgin was implied and not something he'd want to have shouted in a bar.

"I've only been with one guy. And fuck, it's like he's ruined me for good."

"Hutch Hawkins?" I guessed.

He bowed his hand. A pain crushed my friend that I couldn't get rid of, no matter how many free drinks or flirting lessons I gave him.

"Pathetic, right? Closeted high school kid sleeps with the closeted popular jock and can't get over it ten years later." He downed the rest of his Cell Block Tang and slammed the glass on the bar. "But it wasn't just sex. It was more than that. We were in love." He nodded as if he were finally admitting something to himself. "And that's hard to get over."

I knew the feeling now that I was with Mitch and truly understood the power of love.

"It's not like I'll ever see him again." Amos pointed at his glass for a refill.

"You will move on. All it takes is the right guy." I made him meet my eyes. "Look at me, never thought I'd be into bros until I found the right one."

"You're right," he said half-heartedly. I would probably feel the same way if I slept with Mitch once, and then he wanted nothing to do with me. "Back to the apps."

Amos turned on a smile when Chase, Everett, and Julian joined us at the bar for another round. Conversation slipped into favorite musicals, and Everett regaled us with awkward school play moments among his students. We discussed plans for going to Remix next Friday, too. I loved hanging with these guys. So much better than my frat brothers. I had known those guys for years, but we were like strangers. They had changed, or maybe I had. They posted about wild adventures in New York and cool skiing trips they took. The evil beast of jealousy didn't flame up in me, though. That was their life, and while they probably looked at my life with pity, I loved every moment. Loved the bar, loved the town, loved my new friends.

Loved Mitch?

"We'll take a round of You Can't Stop the Beam. It has the highest amount of alcohol content and can conclusively get us drunk the fastest," Chase said. "You, too, Charlie."

"Yeah, you're an honorary teacher," Everett said.

"Actually, he's a real teacher." Julian pointed to the sign taped to the wall advertising my new bartending school. It was another revenue stream I thought of for Stone's Throw. I knew enough about bartending after doing it for months to teach beginners. It was a fantastic side hustle.

"Maybe I should sign up," Amos said.

"We're all full. Try the summer session." I smiled to myself and poured the line of colorful drinks.

Amos nodded, impressed. "Damn, you'll be running this place in no time."

Huh.

The guys raised their glasses and nudged me to join. Our glasses clinked in a tight circle.

"What should we toast to?" Everett asked.

"To right now," I said, my heart full from so many things.

———

THE BAR WAS at its messiest on Musical Mondays. What started with patrons singing along to Broadway songs turned into a full-tilt pride parade, with guests bringing streamers and props and glitter.

Most of which ended up on the floor.

We stayed until the wee hours cleaning up. Mitch pitched in, too. I didn't know how, but Natasha still had the energy to sing to herself. She said it was the only way she could stay awake. It was two in the morning when we finished. The balmy spring air made it comfortable outside as Mitch locked up.

"Good night, you guys." Natasha teased us with a smile as she walked backward to her car.

"See you on Wednesday," Mitch said, all business. It was an open not-at-all-secret that we were dating, but he was still determined to be clandestine about it. When other employees asked me for details, I stayed mum. It would kill

Mitch if anything personal got out, like how he loved to be cuddled.

Natasha drove off, and then there were two. Mitch rubbed my arms to keep me warm. His grin still took my breath away.

"Ready to go home?" Mitch asked.

"Hell yeah, Boss. I am dog tired."

Home.

Mitch's home. We drove the familiar blocks to his small house perched at the end of a street up against the woods. Lush green trees surrounded the home. Half of my nights were spent here. He gave me two drawers in his dresser and space on his sink for toiletries. It was cute watching him fumble with sharing his bedroom and bathroom at first. He'd lived by himself for years; he'd never shared his bed with someone since he was married. But he found a way to reshape his life to fit me in, and that meant the world to me.

I stripped down to boxers for bed. If I were cold, Mitch and his hairy chest would keep me warm. We got into the queen-sized bed. While we usually wound up with me as the little spoon, which I think I was built for by nature, first Mitch was the one who got cuddled.

Even big ole bears needed loving.

He rested his heavy head against my chest, his deep breathing humming on my skin. I crossed my hands over his broad chest; the thumbs could barely touch.

"When does your bartending school begin?" he asked me, already halfway to sleep.

"Thursday. We're full up. Depending on how it goes, I may expand to two classes in the summer."

"That's great. You're quite the businessman. All these ideas are keeping us afloat."

I had never thought of myself as a businessman. People

had told me I wasn't serious enough. I should take a job and keep my head down. There were so many times in my life when people thought they were being helpful with the truth when really they were making me feel small and stupid. Those past jobs and career paths weren't for me; at Stone's Throw, I unlocked a drive and a thirst to be my own boss. It was Mitch who believed in me, who showed me I could soar.

He peeked up at me with those warm, sleepy eyes. "What do you think about a promotion?"

"Oh." I sat up. It had been on my mind, but I hadn't broached the subject.

"Assistant manager."

"Really? Would I still work behind the bar?"

"No, you'd be entering the ranks of management. But you've shown that you have an aptitude for business."

"It helps I'm sleeping with the boss."

Mitch whipped his head around, his body tense. "Charlie, that is not why. Please don't think that. If nothing had happened between us, I would still be offering you the assistant manager role." He looked down at his half-naked self cuddled against my half-naked self. "Maybe not in this exact way."

"I'd hope not." I ran my hand across his beard for no reason other than I really wanted to.

He got serious. "You've proven yourself to be a vital asset to the bar. You work hard, are a great team member, and are full of passion and ideas. Trust me; this has been earned."

This wasn't a complete surprise, but my throat had still managed to get clogged with emotion. "This is my first promotion."

"It won't be your last."

"What about Natasha?"

"I'm still working out how to split your duties. I'd like to have one of you on each night." That meant I wouldn't get to see Natasha as much, but we would have to find time to hang out outside of work.

"Does this mean I get to interview for my replacement?"

"You can assist in the hiring process."

I rubbed my hands together. It was a full circle of life moment. Confidence and bravery swirled within me, making me ask: "What if we ran the bar together someday?"

Mitch's eyebrows jumped, but he didn't seem repulsed by the idea. "Someday."

"It is a family business." I pressed my lips shut. I was practically proposing marriage. "I can keep learning the business from you. And someday we could do this together, as equals."

"It won't happen anytime soon, but for the future, I like that idea."

How much of that idea did he like? Six months ago, I was into girls and not into relationships. Now I was thinking about having a guy put a ring on it. The world worked in mysterious ways.

"Any other ideas you want to discuss?"

Boldness had not subsided in me. With Mitch, I had an openness where I could be myself and say what I wanted. I circled my finger in his chest hair. "Actually, yes."

He let out a laugh. "I thought we were going to bed."

"It can wait until tomorrow." I turned to go to sleep, but he pulled me back to him, tightening his strong arms around me.

"What is it, Porterfield?"

"Well, as you know, I used to have sex with women."

"Will I like where this is going?" he asked. I ignored his comment.

"And so I have experience being on top."

He gave an exaggerated nod.

"I was wondering if we could try switching positions tomorrow morning." Because of our crazy hours, most of our sex was morning sex. It was a major benefit to waking up with morning wood, which only got harder when I felt his warm body against mine.

The thought of topping Mitch had been eating at me for weeks. He was so big and hot, and I wanted to feel my dick inside him. All of the incredible ways he made my body vibrate when he fucked me, well, I wanted to return the favor.

"Thoughts?" I asked.

"That sounds so fucking hot." He kissed my neck. "I want to feel you inside me."

"And I want to fuck you senseless." I wanted to watch his large body shake with orgasm. I sprouted wood at all times of day while thinking of having Mitch. It was a good thing a solid piece of wood separated me from my customers so they couldn't see the random tents I pitched.

Mitch pinched my nipple.

"But not tonight," I said. "I'm exhausted."

He breathed out a sigh of relief. "Me, too."

We went to sleep, and as I drifted off, I thought of the twists and turns that brought me to Sourwood, to Stone's Throw Tavern, and into Mitch's burly arms. Life was a helluva thing.

I was like a kid on Christmas Eve. I couldn't wait for morning.

35

MITCH

The next morning, I woke up to birds chirping, sun streaming in through the window, and my ass clenched.

Yeah, I was nervous.

I had never bottomed before, not in all my years of being out and proud. It wasn't like I'd had much sex. The whole raising a kid and running a business had sapped much of my energy. Jerking off was the more time-efficient means of getting off.

It wasn't something that had crossed my mind until Charlie brought it up last night. He looked so excited at the possibility that I instantly agreed without thinking about what it would entail.

My tail. Getting railed.

I wasn't against the idea. I wanted to give it a try. I was nervous.

But there was nobody else in this world with whom I wanted to try new things.

He turned to me with his sleepy grin that stole my heart each and every morning we woke up together. His eyes blazed with heat, and my dick jumped in response. That was the beauty of dating a twentysomething. They were always raring to go.

We kissed good morning, which quickly turned into tongues swashbuckling in the space between our mouths. His hands raked through my chest hair and up to my beard. He was obsessed with my beard. He was trying to grow one himself. The hair was patchy, but it would fill in. He'd also grown his hair out on his head—and downstairs. He was morphing into my little lion man; being around him meant having an erection for most of the day.

He pushed me back on the bed and ran his tongue down my neck, then kissed down my chest and belly until he slowly pulled down my boxers. My cock bounced out in the air, engorged and dotted with pre-come. He stroked me while tonguing my balls. I cried out in pleasure and willed myself not to shoot. He met my eyes and winked at me.

"Good morning," he said.

"Morning. Sleep well?"

"I had some very interesting dreams. And I'm ready to make them a reality."

He lifted my legs. Cool air hit my hole.

"Wait."

"What?"

I exhaled a deep breath. I wasn't exactly sure what I was nervous about. Pain? Not being in control? Could an old dog learn new tricks?

Charlie put a comforting hand on my chest. "Mitch, do you trust me?"

It was an unexpected question that threw me off. "Yeah, of course."

"I don't want to do this to check something off a list or

reclaim my quote-unquote manhood. I want to be closer to you. I love you."

"I love you, too."

He leaned over me, and our lips met in a sweet kiss. I threaded our fingers together over my chest and gazed into his warm chocolate eyes. I was sharing a new part of myself with Charlie. My heart surged with relief and confidence. This was going to be incredible.

"All right. Let's do this." He winked at me before moving back down south.

His tongue flicked on my hole. I gasped. He kept going, swirling around and unlocking new sensations within me.

I fisted the sheets as a guttural moan ripped out of me. His tongue fucked me up good, flitting in and out of my hole. Jolts of ecstasy hit my balls. His hands fluttered the hairs on the backside of my upper thighs.

He slipped a finger inside me, and I wondered why the hell I was so nervous in the first place. The feeling far exceeded the times I'd put my own finger down there.

"Fratboy, this feels so good." I writhed on the bed, my cock flopping against my thick legs straight in the air.

"Damn, you are tight, Boss."

Nowadays, he only called me Boss in bed. Because he knew how much it drove me wild.

"You going to stretch me out?"

"You bet your fucking ass. I may be short, but I'm big where it counts."

That he was. I'd gagged on his cock enough times to realize he was packing heat.

He alternated tongue and fingers inside me, pushing past my resistance and building up a dam of pleasure that was bound to explode soon. My muscles tensed with anticipation when he pulled the bottle of lube from the drawer.

The cool lube hit my hole. His sure fingers filled the space. Need devoured me from the inside out, making my balls clench and heart rate skyrocket.

"You okay, Boss?"

"I'm ready."

Charlie pressed his cock against my hole, giving me the same torture I'd given him during his first time. I shook with want and pleaded for him to fill me up. I wanted to know what this felt like. I wanted to feel the pleasure he had felt that night.

His fat cockhead breached my opening, hitting new sensations and nerves I didn't know I had. It was like I'd made it to a secret level of a video game. Grand Theft Anal.

Charlie's eyes rolled into the back of his head as he sunk inside my opening. His compact, smooth body hovered above me, David overtaking Goliath.

"Oh, fuck. This is..." He bit his lip. "Damn," he uttered in complete bliss.

My body acclimated to the new feelings of his dick. He thrust inside me balls deep. I arched up my lower back to meet his cock.

"How does this feel?" he asked.

"Good."

"Can I go faster?"

I nodded yes. Fire burned in his eyes. "Boss, if it's all right with you, I want to fuck you hard and wreck your hole."

God, that was hot. I couldn't answer in English. I could only moan in agreement.

His chest and arms glistened with sweat. His hair fell into his eyes, making him seem sweet with a dark side. I wanted that dark side.

Charlie pounded into me. Skin slapped on skin. His

breath hitched with each thrust. He grabbed my ankles tighter, pummeling me and sending heat barreling into my core.

My balls tightened as my ass clenched around his dick. I was losing control, the orgasm taking ownership of me as heat built up in my chest. When he grabbed my rock-hard dick and began to stroke, pre-come leaking over his fist, I was unable to hold on any longer.

"Gonna come," Charlie muttered.

He took the words out of my mouth. I came hard, fucking into his fist and hitting my stomach with my release. His body quaked, and his eyes went into a daze as he emptied himself into my hole.

We'd stopped using condoms a few weeks ago once we realized we weren't sleeping with anyone else.

I was already on the bed, but still, I felt myself collapse. Eventually, breath and rational thought returned to my being. Charlie rested his head on my chest, my breathing lifting and lowering him.

"How was that?" He looked at me with vulnerable, curious eyes.

"In-fucking-credible." I raked a hand through this messy, sweaty hair. "Amazing."

He smiled to himself.

"What's so funny?"

"You were technically a forty-year-old virgin."

"I suppose you really can teach an old dog new tricks."

"You're not that old."

Right now, I felt alive and strong, a type of youth that wasn't measured by years on this earth.

36

MITCH

Two weeks later, I felt a familiar type of being old—the sore back.

"Lift with your legs, Mitch!" Cal yelled at me as we lifted his massive audio soundboard. I managed to release one hand from the grip to flip him the bird.

"Hire a moving company!" I put down the piece of furniture, and Cal had no choice but to do the same. I rubbed my tight lower back.

"You gotta protect yourself." Cal started massaging my back, kneading the muscles like he was stretching bread.

"What are you doing?" I pushed him away.

"Trying to help."

"This is how you can help." Leo approached us with a lamp in one hand and shaking a bottle of aspirin in the other. I swiped the bottle and tossed two pills down my throat. "Drugs."

"Medication," I said.

"Remember to lift with your knees." Cal demonstrated by doing squats, which would've annoyed me had I not been impressed by his flexibility, something you don't regularly see with a chubby guy like him.

Cal had a recording studio setup in his basement. The basement and the bedrooms were the only rooms that weren't staged with fake furniture since Cal and Josh still needed to live here.

"Mitch is right, though. Why didn't you hire a moving company?" Leo asked. He wore a faded South Rockland High School basketball t-shirt from when he was on the team for a brief season. A V of sweat trickled down the middle. "Russ can afford it."

"Russ isn't my sugar daddy. And excuse me for being sentimental, for wanting my closest friends to help me pack up my childhood home. Our childhood home."

Growing up, the Hogan basement had been home base for after school hanging out. Cal's mom usually had snacks at the ready for us. Even though he made it his own, there was plenty that reminded me of the old days. The funky wallpaper in the bathroom, the scratch on the wall from when I threw my Nintendo controller.

Nostalgia hit my chest. Another marker of the passage of time, and I could tell the guys felt it, too.

"We had a lot of good times in this house." Leo craned his head around the room.

"You're welcome to come to Russ's house now."

"It's your house, too." I pressed a finger into Cal's chest, making him squirm.

"Wild." Cal shook his head in disbelief. "I'm moving in with my boyfriend."

"Is Josh excited?" Leo asked.

"He's already picked out his room and is there Quentin, playing some kind of VR thing Russ got him. My kid is going to be so spoiled." Cal said it ominously, but deep down, I knew it warmed his heart. After years of struggling financially and always worrying about not being able to provide for Josh, he had found love with a man who would make that go away. Not that Cal was going to be some kept man. But now, he could focus on pursuing his voiceover career full-time.

He could breathe.

"Russ is a great guy," Leo said proudly. "You did well."

"I came back to Sourwood as a last chance." Cal's voice went wobbly with emotion.

"Let's save the teary moments for after we're done hauling shit," I said.

"You're right." Cal wiped at his eyes. "Let's try this again." Cal slapped the soundboard. "This time, squat and lift with your legs."

My legs were sore from going doggy style with Charlie this morning. Not a detail I needed to share with my friends.

On the count of three, we lifted the soundboard, which was dense and heavy. My quads throbbed in pain, but that was better than my back. Leo directed us up the stairs and through the living room. We were slower than paid movers, but we managed to get it outside without scratching the walls or the equipment.

That was the toughest piece to move. Most of the other big furniture items had been sold or donated. Russ was particular about the furniture coming into his (their) house, making sure everything went together. He loved his vintage-meets-Pottery Barn aesthetic. Russ was a great guy who treated Cal wonderfully, but man, there was no way I'd ever want to be with him. I'd go nuts.

We picked up odds and ends and filled up the van. Eventually, the Hogan house was empty. As I walked around checking for any remaining items, the gravity of the moment hit me. This was my home, too, in a way. Infinite memories were made here. That was one of the downsides to getting older—there were more endings than beginnings. But Charlie would be at my house waiting for me, and that was a beginning that filled my heart.

The three of us gathered in the bare living room.

"I think that's all she wrote," Leo said.

"I'm not gonna cry," Cal said. "I'm too tired."

Russ knocked on the open front door. Cal's face lit up in the sweetest way.

"Need any help?" he asked.

"Not anymore," I said.

"Cal said he wanted to do this with you two." Russ stepped inside and strolled around the house. "Great job."

"You are giving me a massage when we get home," Cal demanded.

"You got it!" Russ's voice echoed in the hall.

"So, how's loverboy?" Leo leaned against the banister. Even after a day of hard labor, he still had the energy to be a son of a bitch.

"Loverboy's working his shift," I said. "And he has a name."

"Charlie Porterfield. Do you doodle it in your notebook?"

"I'm three seconds away from putting you in a head-lock." I fake lunged at him, and Leo jumped back, hitting the banister.

"Don't be an asshole, Leo. We don't want to scare Mitch away. I mean, the fact he is in a healthy, loving relationship with a human man being is a big deal."

"Why are you talking about me like I'm not here?" My friends were pinheads. The best friends a guy could ask for, but still...pinheads.

"We're still processing," Leo said. "I never thought I'd see the day when you would be blushing over a guy."

I felt my face. Was I blushing? Fuck.

"We're happy for you," Cal said, a serious look taking over his face. "We didn't want you to be alone."

"I'm happy for both of you. When we were in high school, did you ever think we'd all wind up with serious boyfriends?" I asked them.

"We were still thinking of girlfriends," Leo said.

"Speak for yourself," Cal snapped back.

The footsteps of Russ echoed in the room as he returned, hands on hips. "Cal, you forgot a box."

"I did?" Cal looked at us. "We searched the house when we finished, and we didn't find anything."

"You didn't search thoroughly, I suppose." Russ crossed his arms.

"Is it a big box?"

"It's decent sized."

"Couldn't you bring it then?"

Russ nodded for us to follow him. He walked into the kitchen. When we joined him, Cal immediately gasped.

In the center of the tiled kitchen floor was one ring-sized box.

I turned to Leo in shock, but he already had his phone out filming. Did he know about this?

Russ gingerly waltzed to the box. He got on one knee to pick it up. He opened the box, presenting a silver band.

"Holy fucking shitballs," Cal said.

Russ squirmed at the profanity, but the sweetness in his

eyes never left. "Cal Hogan, against all odds, I love you. You're opinionated, and you don't know how to use a vacuum properly. And I want to spend the rest of my life with you. Will you marry me?"

Cal held up a finger. "Y'know, mess is a sign of genius."

"Cal," I grumbled, emotion clogging my throat.

"Yes! I will absolutely marry you." Cal ran over and sat on his knee. Russ slid the ring onto his finger.

Their kiss was soft but powerful, and despite my sore back, I was grateful I got to be here for this moment.

———

A FEW WEEKS LATER, the entire Single Dads Club met up at Stone's Throw to premiere the first short film of Leo's daughter, Lucy. The stage had a projection screen set up, and Natasha had put out fake Oscar centerpieces she found online. Soon, friends and interested locals would be showing up to watch the film. Lucy had convinced all of us to take small parts.

Leo's son, Ari, played life-sized Jenga with Josh and Quentin. Russ and Cal watched from the sidelines while being their own brand of schmoopy. Lucy, looking chic in a rolled-up blazer and jeans, worked with Natasha to do checks on the sound and picture quality.

The Single Dads Club had expanded. Our little found family kept growing. More kids, more significant others.

And by the bar, Charlie chatted with Leo and Dusty. The new bartender, Allison, refilled their drinks. He kept glancing over and giving me secret smiles, which tickled my soul like butterfly kisses. Damn, being in love had made me all sappy. Good thing I still had my fearsome beard.

I sidled over and joined the conversation, wrapping my

arm around my boyfriend—and assistant manager—for the whole world to see.

"What are we talking about?" I asked.

"Our acting debut," Leo said with a full cringe.

Dusty ribbed him in the side. "We're all going to be great. Leo, since when are you scared of getting people's attention?"

"Since I had to perform a speech I didn't write or approve."

"Your poor ego," Dusty shot back.

"I can't believe my daughter roped me into doing this. I'm going to look like such an idiot." Leo palmed his face. "You know when politicians are running for election, and there's this video dug up from their past that completely derails their campaign?"

"Kind of like how a leaked Milkman profile almost derailed your mayoral re-election?" Dusty studied his boyfriend with a knowing grin.

"Touché." Leo narrowed his eyes at his best friend turned boyfriend.

"This can only have positive ramifications. People will love that you agreed to act in your daughter's film. And if you're bad, it'll be in an embarrassing-dad kind of way. Not the wearing-blackface-at-a-college-party way."

"Have I told you how sexy you are when you talk political strategy?" Leo growled.

"Many times." Dusty flashed him a smile filled with promises of foreplay.

"We have a rule at Stone's Throw," Charlie said. "No public sex."

"What do people do at Musical Mondays then?" Dusty asked.

We all burst out laughing.

"I can't wait to see Mitch on screen," Charlie said. "You were the angriest extra on set."

"I'm not an actor."

"You only have one facial expression." Charlie impersonated me and my stone-faced glare. "Which I guess is why Lucy cast you as a man fighting off a zombie invasion."

"Wouldn't you be grumpy if zombies destroyed your party?" I asked my boyfriend.

"Probably." He shrugged his shoulders.

"Mitch, would you like anything to drink?" Allison asked me. She was a great hire so far. I had entrusted Charlie to lead the hiring process and bring me his recommendations. He certainly had an eye for talent. She was polite but could draw a hard line like the best bartenders.

"I'll have water."

Other guests filtered in—friends of Lucy, friends of Leo. They circled about and eventually took their seats. Ellie and Tim rushed in before the movie went on. They took the seats on the other side of me.

"You almost missed it," I whispered to them as the lights went down. "My acting debut."

"I wouldn't miss this for the world," she said. Ellie gave Charlie a polite nod. Things weren't the same between them, but we were all getting there slowly. I understood. I knew this was a lot to handle, Charlie and me together. But I was determined to smooth out this bump and have the two people I cared about most care about each other.

The screen went black, then "A Film by Lucy McCaslin" popped on. I cheered along with everyone in the room.

"Dad," Ellie whispered into my ear. "I have to tell you something."

"Can it wait until after the movie?"

She leaned in closer. "I'm pregnant."

Just then, I appeared on screen. My stone-faced expression captured for all to see. But in real life? I was a smiling fool.

I started laughing. I had to put my hand over my mouth to shut myself up, but I couldn't stop. I was so damn happy.

37

CHARLIE

SIX MONTHS LATER

It was a huge relief to attend a wedding where I didn't have to work. For their nuptials, Cal and Russ decided to keep it lowkey and hold a backyard wedding. Chairs were set out leading to an altar made of wood and rope, created by their Falcon troop, trellised with wisteria. The weather had delivered a freak warm day, likely the last one before fall transitioned to early winter.

Mitch and I took our seats in the front row. We were family, basically. Leo stood under the altar; he was an ordained minister, apparently. I had the feeling he just liked being in the middle of things.

I turned to Mitch. "Have you looked over our latest revenue report from September?"

Mitch arched a suspicious eyebrow my way.

"What?" I asked.

"You're wanting to talk shop at a party?"

"The party hasn't begun yet." I gestured around at the big nothing happening around us. People were still finding their seats and schmoozing. The band had not started. "We had a great summer, and it looks like we're going to have a strong holiday season. Musical Mondays and the other themed nights have increased foot traffic and drinks purchased per customer."

Man, I needed a pair of thick-framed glasses and a pocket protector with all the math I'd been doing as assistant manager. My background in finance finally bore fruit as I found myself diving into numbers and data. Mitch had run Stone's Throw Tavern on feeling, but backing up those feelings with analytics helped to surface certain insights about what our customers liked. By doubling down on what was working, we were able to grow profit without sacrificing the charm of what made the bar special.

"Have you given any more thought to hiring a second bartender?" I asked.

He see-sawed his head. "It's a tight space behind there, as you remember."

"We could try it out. As we're getting busier, it could help with serving people faster. When people have to wait forever for a drink, that's when they get annoyed and leave."

He nodded as he listened, his lips pouting as he inhaled all the information. Mitch was a sexy thinker, like that Atlas guy.

"And..." I leaned in, snaking my arm around his shoulders, putting on my boyfriend hat for a second. "I've been thinking..."

"Yes?" Mitch turned to me, those dark eyes penetrating me with their natural bolt of hotness.

"Have you thought about expansion?"

It was not the question he thought I was going to ask. Did he miss my past fun fratboy self?

"There's an empty space over in Hudsonville."

"A second Stone's Throw?"

I brought my shoulders to my ears. Was it the craziest idea in the world?

"I don't want to turn my bar into McDonald's."

"Opening a second location isn't turning us into McDonald's. We're doing really well. We could strike while the iron is hot. This could be a great opportunity. After a hundred million years of running the same bar, maybe it's time to shake things up."

He rolled his eyes at my joke, but I could tell the wheels were already turning in his head. I didn't want to diminish the appeal of Stone's Throw. It had small-town charm; Mitch had built it into something special. We would maintain that spirit. That beautiful spirit of Stone's Throw could spread to other towns, bringing joy to others.

Kicking ass in my job—finally finding something I was passionate about and doing it with the man I loved—had poured gasoline on my fire of ambition. With Mitch behind me, I realized I was capable of incredible things, and that was the most powerful feeling in the world.

"I don't need an answer now. Think about it."

"We'll talk about it later," he said.

"Okay."

"Because we're at a wedding."

"I'm aware."

That wasn't a no. Hopefully, he saw my excitement. It was practically seeping out of my pores. I turned back to face the altar.

"Where in Hudsonville is this space?" Mitch asked me moments later. "Is it in their downtown or off the highway?"

My lips perked into a smile. Success.

Before I could answer, another couple joined our row with a toddler in tow. The dad holding the baby had a shaved head and tattoos creeping out of his collar up his neck, while the other dad seemed more straightlaced. They made a sexy couple.

And that toddler was a cutie pie.

"You made it." Mitch jumped up and wrapped the non-baby-holding father in a tight hug. "We didn't know if you were coming."

"We caught the red-eye, which was not easy with a two-year-old. But we weren't going to miss this."

"You remember my boyfriend, Charlie?"

"It's so great to see you guys again." I gave all of them hugs as if we'd known each other for years. Mitch's friends felt like my family. "How's married life?"

"Not much different," Shane admitted. He and Buzz had gotten married over the summer, right after Mitch and I had officially gotten together. Buzz had insisted on keeping it simple. We flew out to Seattle, and Buzz and Shane had rented out a small bistro for the ceremony. My heart swelled watching them say their vows and kiss. I found myself getting mushy at all weddings now, maybe because I wondered if there'd be one in my future.

"Apologies in advance if Anne acts up. She's officially in her terrible twos." Buzz motioned for Shane to move down, and they sat at the end of the aisle.

Mr. Tatted Hunk and Mr. Clean Cut. It worked, though. They gazed at each other and their daughter, bursting with love. And I supposed people looked at Mitch and me as an odd couple, but to me, it made the most perfect sense.

"Forgive us if we yawn during the ceremony," Buzz said. "We had a long day of flying."

"We know we're those fuckers who brought a baby to a wedding, but we couldn't find a sitter," Shane said. I had a feeling I was going to like him the more I got to know him.

"How are things going in Seattle?" Mitch asked his friend.

"Wonderful. Joining Burnham Cosmetics has allowed me to put in place the kind of work/life balance I wasn't able to enjoy at my evil old company. We have on-site daycare, flexible time off, and half-day Fridays. I get to spend more time with this little lady, and it hasn't impacted revenue one bit." Buzz pretended to take a bite out of Anne's pudgy arm. She giggled in delight.

"We're in the process of adding to our brood, too," Shane said. "Anne's going to have a brother she can boss around."

"Congratulations." A new feeling took hold of me, a wistfulness about what it would be like to be a dad. Mitch wasn't too old to do the parenting thing all over again, was he? This time, he would have a co-pilot. Perhaps in a few years. Our baby for the moment was Stone's Throw.

"Buzzy a dad, who would've thought..." Mitch smiled at Anne.

Buzz looked at Mitch, then me, a knowing smile crossing his lips. "People can surprise you."

Anne was the best toddler in the world. She didn't cry one peep during the ceremony. Quentin and Josh walked down the aisle as co-ring bearers. Then Cal and Russ walked down arm-in-arm. Cal had made it clear that he didn't want anyone giving him or Russ away. They were grown-ass adults.

Leo shocked everyone with his sweet service. He gave a speech, something he loved to do, but it was meaningful. He talked about love, about finding that one special person. Like a typical politician, he hit the familiar beats, but he said it in a way to make it hit home. It hit me square in the gut. Mitch, too, as evidenced by him squeezing my hand tight in parts.

When Cal and Russ were announced husbands squared, their scout troop all ran up and gave a bird call salute.

Caroline's catered for the reception. Tables and chairs were set up in the back yard and inside the house for those who were cold. Kids ran around and played frisbee. It was a super laid-back vibe, like a house party that just happened to involve two people getting married. I thought back to where I was last winter—aimless, jobless, friendless, homeless. Now I was surrounded by a new kind of family.

Life was funny that way.

Mitch shot the shit with his friends at a table next to the altar. He was laughing up a storm; his loud chuckle could be heard from where I was on the deck.

Ellie waddled over, resting her plate of food on her very pregnant belly.

"You're ready to burst," I said. I took her plate as she sat down, which was a complex effort. "Where's Tim?"

"He's tying knots with the scouts. He was a Falcon years ago, so he's bonding with his people."

Sure enough, Tim sat in a circle with Quentin, Josh, and their troop demonstrating with rope. He was a dork. A completely lovable dork.

"Listen, Charlie, I want to apologize for what happened months ago when I confronted you about my dad." She moved her fork around her plate, glazing over the pile of food.

"We already had it out. We're all good." But since then, Ellie had been acting supportive, but I could tell she wasn't fully there yet. I knew to give her space.

"It's been taking me a little while to get used to the whole thing. Not just that it's you dating him, but that my dad is dating someone, period."

People were still getting adjusted to seeing Mitch in love

and happy. He had played the grump for so long, it's a wonder his face wasn't frozen that way.

"You make him really happy, Charlie."

"He makes me happy."

"I'm glad you two found each other." She patted my hand, and I squeezed hers back.

"Technically, it wouldn't have happened without you."

She cringed at the statement. "We don't need to bring that up."

"Fair. Does this mean you won't call me your stepdad?"

She shoved my shoulder playfully. Her stomach protruded like a hot air balloon shoved under her dress. She was about to burst. And that meant Mitch would be a grandfather.

Who knew grandpas could be sexy?

Grandpa I'd Like to Fuck—and do, regularly.

"What are you thinking?" she asked. "You're smiling."

"Oh, nothing."

————

THERE WASN'T any kind of formality to this reception. At some point, Lucy plugged in her phone to play Spotify through the speakers. People created a small dance space in the backyard where Cal and Russ were cajoled into their first dance. Then other couples joined in. The whole afternoon was purely delightful. It was how I wanted my wedding to be.

If we ever decided to cross that bridge. I was turning into one of those people who thought about my wedding when at other weddings. Love, future, it all blended together.

Mitch and I joined in on a slow dance. My heart melted at the way he looked at me.

"Do you ever see us getting married?" I asked him. It was a subject we hadn't broached. We were so busy with the bar and other physical activity that til-death-do-us-part never came up. It seemed more implied.

At least, for me.

Mitch hadn't answered my question yet. He considered it as if I asked him about the meaning of life.

"It's crossed my mind here and there."

"Oh." What kind of crossing were we talking about? Like a fleeting thought?

"You?" he asked.

"Yeah. I mean, I...well, yeah. I don't see myself wanting to be with anyone else. I have a hunch you may feel the same."

"That's true." He was back to his stoneface. It drove me crazy, not in the sexy way this time.

"We make a good team."

"That we do."

"With the bar and with other things."

He nodded, his face indecipherable. Maybe he thought I was crazy or clingy, or he just wanted me to shut up. After all, the man had been married before and hated it. He didn't want to go through that rigamarole again.

"So maybe it's worth thinking about?" My confidence faded with each second I clocked his stoic response.

Mitch stopped dancing. He reached up his arm and flagged someone down on the deck. Someone who would cart me away probably. Me and my big mouth.

Leo came over, fixed his tie and his hair. "What's up?"

"Will you marry us?"

I could feel my eyes bulge out of my skull. Like, pain shot through my sockets.

"What?" Leo looked between us, most likely noticing the shock bleaching my face white. "For real?"

"Yeah. Is that allowed?" Mitch craned his neck to Cal and Russ. "Hey, is it cool if Charlie and I get married right now?"

The newlyweds shrugged at each other. "Sure," Cal said.

He turned to me. "Is that cool with you?"

"Is that cool with me?" I repeated the words slowly, trying to process the fuckery of the current moment. "Are you asking me to marry you?"

Mitch nodded yes. "You said you could see yourself marrying me. I could see myself marrying you. I love you, and I want to spend the rest of my life with you. We have an ordained minister. So why wait?"

I...the man's logic was tough to crack. I did love him. I did want to spend the rest of my life with him. I didn't need a huge ceremony to codify that statement. I just needed Mitch. The spontaneity took hold of me.

"Let's do it!"

Right there, on the mock dance floor, Leo pulled out his script. The music stopped, and soon everyone crowded around us. I got hold of my parents via FaceTime, and Russ held up the phone so they could watch. Ellie put Amos on FaceTime, too. She caught him mid-burrito at Chipotle. The whole thing was the most wonderful kind of insanity.

"Do you, Mitchell Dekker, take Charles Porterfield to be your lawfully wedded husband?"

"I do."

I inhaled a deep breath. Tears welled in Mitch's eyes, his once stone face alive with feeling. Just because this was spontaneous didn't mean he took it lightly. My throat clogged with emotion. I had never felt so loved.

"And do you, Charles Porterfield, take Mitchell Dekker to be your lawfully wedded husband?"

"I do."

"Then, by the power vested in me by the state of New York, I pronounce you married. You may now kiss."

And kiss we did. It was restrained and classy but still managed to give me a religious experience.

"What are you thinking?" he whispered into my ear during our first dance as a married couple.

"Well..." I leaned into his ear. "I'm jacked. According to multiple sources, I'm packing heat. I've got a hot-as-fuck husband and the most primo job in the world. I have to say, I'm the man."

Mitch studied my face as he massaged my cheek. "You're *my* man."

"And you're mine."

———

Thanks for reading!

The Single Dads Club continues with *The Fireman and the Flirt*. What happens when Cary's old crush, Cal's mysterious older brother Derek, returns to Sourwood and needs help house hunting?

Amos and his teacher friends have their own spinoff series called South Rock High. They're teachers giving out A's, getting some D, and holding out for the big L. The complete series is available, starting with Amos and Hutch's story, Ancient History.

To read about how Buzz and Shane got together, join my mailing list *The Outsiders* and receive the free story, *Three Nights with the Manny*. It's filled with humor, heat, heart, and creative uses for baby oil. https://www.ajtruman.com/outsiders/

Please consider leaving a review on the book's Amazon page or on Goodreads. Reviews are crucial in helping other readers find new books.

Join the party in my Facebook Group and Instagram. Follow me at Bookbub to be alerted to new releases.

And then there's email. I love hearing from readers! Send me a note anytime at info@ajtruman.com. I always respond.

ALSO BY A.J. TRUMAN

South Rock High

Ancient History

Drama!

Romance Languages

Advanced Chemistry

Single Dads Club

The Falcon and the Foe

The Mayor and the Mystery Man

The Barkeep and the Bro

The Fireman and the Flirt

Browerton University Series

Out in the Open

Out on a Limb

Out of My Mind

Out for the Night

Out of This World

Outside Looking In

Out of Bounds

Seasonal Novellas

Fall for You

You Got Scrooged

Hot Mall Santa

Only One Coffin

ABOUT THE AUTHOR

A.J. Truman is a gay man living in Indiana with his husband, son, and fur-babies. He writes books with **humor, heart, and hot guys.** What else does a story need? He loves spending time with his family and occasionally sneaking off for an afternoon movie.

www.ajtruman.com
info@ajtruman.com
The Outsiders - Facebook Group